THE BLUE ALLEY

A NOVEL

P C CUBITT

THE BLUE ALLEY

http://pccubitt.com

Cover Design by Jem Butcher

ISBN-13: 978-1-7398897-2-2 (Ebook Edition)

ISBN-13: 978-1-7398897-3-9 (Paperback Edition)

ISBN-13: 978-1-7398897-4-6 (Hardback Edition)

❀ Created with Vellum

For all the unknown Kaidis, Billys and Marias.

PROLOGUE

The girl waits beside the priest, observant of the bold yellow line she must not cross until the moment they are called to step forward.

The man is calm. No hint of nervousness in his expression. His cassock is buttoned neatly to his chin, its white collar stark against the black clerical robes. A crucifix hangs low against his chest and an attaché case rocks to and fro in one hand. The other hand is clamped around her wrist.

He is slender and handsome – thick black hair set firmly in a parting to one side, his olive skin smooth and closely shaven. Brown eyes, frigid and remote. Beneath his robes his shoes poke out – vigorously polished and neatly laced. To the observer, he is every inch the missionary man.

But the girl eyes him knowingly. For sure, he's not a missionary man. He was not dressed in clerical robes the day she first met him in the squalid holding place behind the barracks. No. Then, he had been someone else entirely. But as they stand and wait behind the painted yellow line, his air of priestly confidence gives nothing away.

The girl looks sideways at the queues that wait beside

them. The place is hot and busy. Noisy too. Announcements from loudspeakers overhead. Shrills from mobile phones and squeals from trolley wheels echo against the tall steel structure of the building. People stand in the heat, stupefied, unaware of what takes place beside them. A fake priest, waiting with his mal-intent.

The girl stands passive. There is no sign of the churning going on inside her chest but anxiety clutches at her. The T-shirt she is wearing was a gift from her father. Across the front a map of the world is printed in bold colours – but never did he imagine she would explore the world like this.

The line beside them shuffles forward. People edge along, dragging their bags, the intense heat bearing down and rolling affectionately over them. The rainy season has arrived and rain like spears hammers on the vehicles that draw up at the terminal. The automatic doors jerk open and closed – people rushing in, shaking droplets from their attire. The girl observes them keenly, considers she could run – across the hall, out of the building and into the storm. And her heart quickens at the thought. Because once across the yellow line, there will be no more opportunity before they board the flight to Europe.

Indecision pulls at her.

She looks at the boy who travels with them, a dim and spontaneous lad, eyeing the doors for himself. If she goes he will follow and spoil her plan. She looks down at her trainers which abut the yellow line.

Not now.

The girl shrugs the rucksack up her shoulders. It's not heavy. Her belongings are few, and the packets the priest sewed into the strap add little to her burden. The rucksack reassures her, warm against her back. On the outside a red and white logo reads 'Ghostbusters!' and hidden inside there are secrets of her own.

The official calls them forward and she is yanked across the line. The priest opens the attaché case, removes documents and slides them under the glass with cool audacity.

'No sir. I can no do that!'

The official is unimpressed and slaps the desk, edging off his seat and out of the booth, waving the forged papers to emphasise his point. The priest stands calm and unaffected, but his grip around the girl intensifies. She flinches but is resigned to the outcome of this exchange. If they are sent back or allowed through, something bad will happen either way.

The other lines edge forward. People are now watching and the girl slides her eyes away, ashamed.

On the other side, a woman is staring with the green-eyed intensity of one who has caught you stealing their maize. The girl feels uncomfortable and shifts under her gaze. For a moment they appraise each other, the girl spying out under her lids. The woman is tall and lean with the distinctive ghostly appearance of the pale European, her thick dark curls tied up with a lemon scarf – the kind you can buy at the Big Makit, a bazaar in town that is popular with tourists. Her expression is of concern, and her unflinching stare is drawn towards the priest.

Like she knows.

The official stands his ground beside their group – upright and affronted, his jacket too tight for his body. With practised sleight of hand, the priest retrieves an item from his cassock and hands it over.

'No sir!' the official says in a voice deliberately loud. 'I see something I don't like, it is my democratic right to report it.' His chest is puffed and he narrows his eyes. 'I am telling the authorities.'

The priest is unconcerned. He dips for a second time into his pocket and withdraws a more substantial bribe, which satisfies the man who pockets the wad. With quick, short strides he returns to his booth and waves their party through, the priest dragging the girl behind.

She looks back. The woman in the lemon headscarf is pointing a phone camera their way. She lowers her arm and slips it back into her pocket.

ONE

KAREN

The West Noord police station overlooked the green expanse of Rembrandtpark next to a busy highway carrying traffic in and out of Amsterdam. The insignia of the Dutch police – a yellow flame emerging from a book of law – was sprawled across its red-brick façade. On a pole jutting out of the wall, the Netherlands flag rippled and snapped in the wind, and on the pavement below, rows of squad cars were neatly angle-parked.

I strode through the entrance marked National Police Intelligence Service, Special Investigations Unit and asked at the desk for Inspecteur Lucas Bliek.

'Yes, Inspecteur Bliek,' said the officer, a smiling woman with blonde streaked hair tied up in a bun. 'Please, who it is would like to see him?'

'Tell him it's Karen Hamm.'

I passed her my card and explained that I had spoken to the inspector several times on the phone and that he was expecting me. I didn't add that I had travelled to Amsterdam from the UK because I had tired of the phone calls and figured it would be harder for him to fob me off if we were sitting face to face.

It had been a week since I had reported seeing the children abducted from West Africa on a KLM flight bound for Schiphol. At first, the inspector had been polite and responsive, acknowledging the problem of trafficking through the Netherlands, but soon he had become platitudinous and had prevaricated for seven whole days, promising to get back to me with news. By now, the children could be anywhere and a seed of panic had lodged in my chest.

The lift opened and Inspecteur Lucas Bliek walked across the lobby with a rolling stride – a young man of medium height and athletic build with thin hair that was greying prematurely.

'Ms Hamm – you have come all this way to see us.' His hand was outstretched, a hint of sarcasm in his tone. I recognised his voice from the phone calls, a lightly accented monotone which was slow and intentional.

'Thanks for seeing me,' I said. 'You know why I'm here?'

'Of course. The English lady searching for the children.'

He indicated that we should sit in two uncomfortable-looking angle-backed chairs arranged to each side of a window. Between the chairs, a low table was set with a box of tissues and an arrangement of pink plastic flowers. He leant back into the strange angle of the chair and brushed a speck from his trousers. His hair was slick with gel, an attempt to control the straggling grey.

'How was your journey, Miss Hamm?' But he didn't look at all interested in my journey to Amsterdam.

'Straightforward, thank you.'

'So, how can I help you?' His question was insincere.

'What progress have you made on Hendrikus Broek-mann?' I said. 'Have your computer systems come up with anything yet?'

'For sure, we have made progress on the details you supplied.' He was being deliberately misleading. 'And we have found no record of this man you say is smuggling children into our country.'

His pale eyes stared expressionless through rimless spectacles to a spot along my hairline. On the sleeve of his dark blue uniform the rank of inspecteur was displayed – a single gold crown and a gold stud.

'No record?' I said. 'Were you able to check the national database as well as police files, like you said?'

'That is so.' He cleared his throat and pushed the glasses up his nose with his middle finger.

'Did you run his photo through as well?'

'Of course.'

'And there's no match?'

'No match.'

How odd.

'You're telling me the software didn't recognise his photo?' I was trying to lean forward but the angle of the chair did not allow it.

'It is not a foolproof system,' he admitted. 'But even if we had a match for this man, there is no evidence for us to make an arrest. After all, you did not see him …' He looked blank for a moment, pretending to search his memory for the name. 'Yes, Hendrikus Broekmann, isn't it? You did not see him with the children?'

'Not exactly, but …'

It was not a random name. I had been working in West Africa for several months, only recently returned. Hendrikus Broekmann, a Dutch national, was a name synonymous with crimes in the region, in particular the supply of slave labour to the palm oil plantations. It was true, I had not seen Broekmann with the children at the airport, but he was a professional criminal who let others do the soldiering, such as the man who was dressed up as a priest to smuggle children out of the country.

'OK,' I said. 'But what about footage from Schiphol?

You've got the flight number. There must be CCTV of the children with the priest after they landed. Did you get any ID on *him* – the priest?'

'No … there is no ID on this priest you speak of.'

'Any footage?'

'No footage.' He shifted in his chair, brushing his trousers in a search for further specks.

'But he must have been on the passenger list.'

'As I say …' Bliek shrugged, looking helpless. He was restless, like he was about to get up and leave.

Visitors to the station were coming and going behind his back, a continuous stream in and out of the glass doors – an officer with a young lad in handcuffs, citizens waiting at the desk, an elderly woman with an arthritic dog wandering about as though lost. There was a ruckus and the handcuffed lad started shouting, wrenching his shoulders. Backup arrived and got him under control, the lad stretching out his tattooed neck to seek an exit. Soon he was inert and being pulled by the officers down a corridor towards the cells.

I wondered why Bliek was lying. The anxiety that had been building as I considered losing the trail on the children was now very close to full expression.

'We are short on resources at this time,' he was saying. 'The increased terror threat is taking up much manpower.' He offered more excuses, droning on about all the reasons he wasn't going to help me.

Then I said recklessly, 'I have a photo. Of the priest.' And immediately I had his full attention.

'You have a photo?'

'Yes. I took it when they were waiting at passport control. Maybe you can run *that* through your systems.'

The words were out.

'They? Where is this photo? May I have it?' He leant in and I felt uncomfortable under the new display of scrutiny.

'I don't have it with me.' I crossed my legs and moved my

bag to the other side of my body defensively. 'But I can send it to you if you think it might help.'

The photos were on the phone in my pocket.

Bliek took a card from his shirt pocket, slid it across the table and muttered under his breath, 'Here are my contacts. Send the photo to this email address. It will help us find the children.'

He pushed his glasses up his nose again. His attitude had changed completely now he wanted something from me, and I felt the power. An unpleasant sensation crept across my skin, a feeling that I recognised from before.

'Thank you. I'll do that.' I tried to sound enthusiastic. 'Will your team keep looking for CCTV … of the priest at Schiphol?'

'Yes. No doubt, we will keep searching. Something will come up.'

I left the building, apprehension fluttering in my chest.

I STOOD outside the address shown on Hendrikus Broekmann's passport. The elegance of the house surprised me. I had expected an overindulgent home – an ostentatious display of all things crass and disagreeable to match the man himself.

Instead, I was staring at a traditional house of perfect proportions constructed in sandy-pink brickwork with white trellised balconies and striped awnings at the windows. Half a dozen chimney pots rose from the roof and elaborate Dutch gablets emerged at either end. In the garden red-brick beds were planted with box, standard trees and small palms. Elegant terracotta pots stood in shady corners and low shrubs of lavender and rosemary lined a short brick path that led to an elaborately carved door overhung with wisteria.

From where I stood, it was a short distance to the door. There were no gates across the footpath separating the property from the road, but security cameras were fixed on every corner of the building – the opaque all-seeing eye. I wondered if I could be observed where I was standing in the road. And whether anyone was watching.

The ground-floor shutters were locked and blinds had been drawn at upper floor windows. The place looked deserted, as though someone had disappeared for a six-month holiday. To West Africa, perhaps. But it didn't look the sort of place criminals would stash their goods. Was it really likely that Broekmann would bring trafficked children to his home? The idea seemed absurd on this genteel avenue of plane trees in the quiet and exclusive neighbourhood of Amsterdam-Zuid.

I returned down the shady path and crossed over the bridge at Lyceumbrug, and soon I was standing on the opposite bank of the Amstelkanaal, looking back at the house. The rear of the property was shuttered like the front. Terraced borders ran down to the water; a mooring place under the willows lay vacant.

An inspection of the local land registry had revealed the property had been bought ten years earlier for a sum of four million euros. There were no details of the purchaser's name on the register, but the property's address was shown on the passport of Hendrikus Broekmann and on his check-in papers at the Kangari Hotel in Freetown where we had both been staying. It was in a downtown bar called Frank's that I had observed him with the man at the airport who had dressed up as a priest. That was how I knew they were connected.

My local contact in Freetown, Dorothy Turay, already suspected Broekmann was involved in trafficking young children to work on the plantations. Her sister, Songola, had been investigating rumours about child slavery when she was killed in a road accident. It seemed implausible that the connection between Broekmann, the fake priest, Songola's death and child slavery was a coincidence. So I had sent

Dorothy photos of the airport kids to see if they had been reported missing. But so far she had drawn a blank.

It was hard articulating my suspicions in the cold European light when everything felt so out of context. But I knew Broekmann was bad, and I had to find those children.

ONLY A WEEK earlier I had returned home from work in Freetown and the adrenalin was still flowing. I had pulled off an exposé of a UK minister while on research for a PhD and should have been pleased just to get home safely given all the powerful people I'd upset, but I had seen the children at the airport and knew the priest was fake. The kids were being abducted and I wanted to help them. But first I had to tell my anxious partner, Graham.

We had been labouring in the garden at our home, Owl Cottage, appearing like normal people doing normal things: Graham meticulously measuring the exact position, diameter, depth and breadth of every boulder planned for the new rockery, and me harbouring thoughts about where the priest had taken the children and how I was going to rescue them.

Our relationship had never been ordinary. Graham and I were an unorthodox couple, odd and indecipherable, neither of us able to conform. Our personal circumstances were comfortable – a beautiful home and plenty of cash – due in part to an inheritance from my diplomat father, but mainly thanks to Graham, an expert in the development of computer software. Like so many on the spectrum he could be socially and emotionally dysfunctional but, in other respects, Graham was quite brilliant and his skills and tenacity had made him a successful entrepreneur.

It had been years before I recognised there was something different about him – that the characteristics I found so attractive were, in many people's eyes, deficiencies. All through the years, I had never considered his behaviour in any way unusual, or identified it as 'other'. On the contrary, I had always seen his qualities as superior.

During our fifteen years together I had been his dependable facilitator, putting my own ambitions second, until the frustration had become too much. We had wanted a family but, after years of miscarriages, we decided to give up. So I returned to education and became something of an expert in African politics. Study had dulled my own yearning, but I had no idea how the yearning for fatherhood had really affected Graham. We never talked about it, padlocking our feelings in safe places – me, not daring to express them, and him not knowing what they were. But despite all we had been through, we had stuck together and consolidated the good bits. It was testament to the deep affection we still had for one another. Graham knew my vulnerabilities just as I knew his and, even after my affair in Freetown, we knew we could find a way to stick together.

At the end of that day, he had set a coffee pot on the iron table at the edge of his clipped lawn and we sat together, sipping from porcelain cups delicately painted with boxing hares. So very English. But the atmosphere hummed with tension, the words hanging on delicate threads. Graham stared out at cushions of cloud floating unhurried over the round of Milk Hill. The heat of the afternoon had dissipated and a gentle breeze was teasing at wisps of his sandy hair. I could scent his anxiety.

'It's taking too long,' I said carefully. 'I've got a bad feeling about the children, Gray.'

He got up from his chair, the ironwork scraping on the stones, and pulled a weed from a crack in the paving. Brushing the soil from his hands, he sat down again and examined his nails. Eventually, he said, 'And you think these kids are your responsibility?' He was leaning back in his chair, speaking directly to the wizened hawthorn that grew at the corner of the meadow beyond the wall.

'If I can find them, they may be able to identify Broek-mann. You know ... as the one who trafficked them.' I was leaning on the table, trying to catch his eye.

'So?'

'Someone killed Songola, Gray. It was no accident.'

'But not necessarily him.' His voice was tight.

'He's connected though, isn't he? Songola was getting too close to finding out about the kids he was trafficking to the plantation.'

Graham looked around the garden at everything but me, a telltale nerve throbbing along his jaw. I refilled his cup. Strong and black. Decaf to reduce his anxiety.

'Why do you think you're responsible for Songola's death?'

There was no logical answer.

'Because you are not responsible, Karen.'

'But someone has to pay.' My voice was a little high, my chest swollen with emotion. Displays like this were unlike me. I had learnt to keep control after so many years with Graham and there was no point having an illogical conversation.

'And you are determined to avenge her yourself.' He took a slow slurp from his cup.

'It doesn't make sense, Gray, does it?'

'Which bit?'

'Why can't the Dutch police find Hendrikus Broekmann on their system?'

'It's probably not his name.'

This was true. I had made a deep internet search and come up with no trace of the man myself. But, while I had been waiting for news from Inspecteur Lucas Bliek, I had done some digging on the Dutch police themselves and found plenty of reports about infiltration by organised crime gangs, and several officers had been suspended for corruption.

When I first reported my suspicions to Inspecteur Bliek,

the conversation had quickly degenerated into a dialogue about Broekmann and how I knew his name, why I thought he was trafficking children and what it had to do with me, and for the past couple of days all contact had dried up.

As we sat in the sunshine, an excitable flock of long-tailed tits landed in the hawthorn, their chatter the only sound. The sun was starting to dip behind Milk Hill and Graham stared past me, his pale skin flushed with the effort of the day's work, his nose peeling slightly from the sun.

'It might not be his real name, but it's somewhere to start,' I said.

The calmness in my voice had nudged the chimes in his head and his pupils had dilated – a sign of stress from within. He sat tense beside me. I knew that inside him the conflict was raging between the pull of his own needs and the desire for me to find my way.

'Is your bag packed?' he asked, but he wouldn't look at me.

'I have to go,' I said. 'Find out for myself …'

'And how do you intend to do that?' The nerve was pulsing strongly in his jaw.

'I don't know, but I'll work it out when I get there.' I reached out and took his hand, slipping my fingers through his. 'Can you trust me again, Gray?'

He squeezed gently before pulling away, moving his hand to trace the outline of the boxing hares on his cup, the grey paint raised against the porcelain.

The long-tailed tits swooped in undulating flight and landed on the feeders near the house. They gorged on the seeds, their pale pink bellies warm in the sunshine.

TWO
KAREN

My accommodation in Amsterdam was a narrow canal-side boarding house called the Absalom, so named after the proprietor's favourite tulip. It was squashed between others that leant together in a colourful row, all with ornate gabled structures attached to their roofs. From my room on the fourth floor, I could look across the canal to a similar row of confectionery-style houses, steep pitched roofs at differing heights, shutters flung wide, the slanting sun pouring into drawing rooms of residents unknown. In a melancholy mood, I stared at the view from a sloping table positioned by a low sash window to make the most of the light. It had been an unsatisfactory day.

A large shot of whisky was warming in my hands and I took a swallow, feeling the burn, reminding myself I had no qualifications for this job. No police background or spook status. I wasn't even an investigative journalist. I was just an ordinary woman with a stalled PhD and grand ideas of doing good for my beloved Africa. It was so clichéd. So chaotic and impulsive.

Much of my childhood had been spent with my diplomat father in Africa and the place and its people were part of my identity. I harboured a deep yearning for it, and the irrational belief I could make a difference was strong – a deep sense of something yet to do.

My phone lit up and it was Graham.

'Hi.' I pushed away the whisky glass in one smooth stroke.

Our habit as a couple was never to feel we should speak every day, even when travelling – he on business, me on my 'missions', racing around the world trying to find a point to life. We were not like other couples – messaging, calling, catching up with the minutiae of life in a daily dose of trivia. Graham wasn't the trivia kind of guy. He was straight to the point with no preamble, and I'd grown to appreciate this minimalist approach because, lately, it had been most useful in situations of high drama. So it was a surprise that he was calling so soon after I'd left for Amsterdam.

'Got there OK?'

'Yes, no problems.'

'And Bliek?'

'He's lying for some reason, so I'll have to find out why.' And immediately I cursed myself for voicing it aloud.

Graham was saying something about whether I had to get involved.

'I'm already involved,' I said. 'How can we stand back when we see children in danger?' I knew very well he felt the same. 'I won't take chances, Gray. And I'll keep you posted.'

The simplicity of the lie fell flat so I waffled on a bit about my accommodation, the sloping floor, the ornate woodwork, the beauty of Amsterdam.

He butted in. 'Is he corrupt?'

'Bliek?'

'Yes … is he bent, do you think?'

'Possibly,' I said. 'Why else would he be lying?'

'You seem very sure he's lying.'

'Well, he's telling me there's no footage of the priest at

Schiphol. I mean, it's Europe's biggest hub. Cameras every-where. And you're telling me someone dressed as a Jesuit priest with two African children hasn't been caught on CCTV.'

'That's unlikely,' he agreed.

'Quite.'

'Maybe Bliek hasn't checked the CCTV yet.'

'Ok, so maybe he hasn't checked. But he said he had, so he's lying about that.'

'Are you sure you know what you're getting yourself into, Karen?' His voice was a little high now. 'If Bliek's got some-thing to hide then he's dangerous. You must know that.'

There was tension in his tone and it would only make things worse if I came out with more platitudes. He was right about the risk, and I regretted mentioning the photos to Bliek. If he was corrupt and working with criminal gangs, then identifying the children could only endanger them. And me.

'I'll call you again tomorrow,' I said, pulling the glass of whisky closer towards me. 'I need to think about what to do next.'

Through my window, I watched the smooth flow of the canal moving beneath the elms. Angry clouds had assembled teasingly overhead and cyclists were gathering speed on the cobbles, rattling between the pedestrians.

It was seven days since I had seen the children board the flight to Amsterdam and there was every chance they were no longer in the city. I imagined them in a little boat, drifting in the current away from me, the rope of security slipping through my hands as their little faces moved further and further downstream.

I had recognised the 'priest' straight away – the thick black hair, the severe side parting – but I didn't know his name or anything else about him other than, for sure, he wasn't a man of the cloth but an associate of Broekmann.

It was the girl who had first drawn my attention, spurring

me to slip the phone from my pocket and take the photos. About twelve years old, the boy a little older. She held such a resemblance to Songola, and maybe that was what first made me notice her – the slight build and very pretty face, the purple ribbons woven in tight cornrows across her head. The same heart-shaped face, the same midnight complexion.

The same look of foreboding.

It was as though Songola's ghost was reaching out to me, demanding my attention, reminding me not to forget her – the young activist in Freetown who had helped me and paid the final price. The memory of her death chilled my blood.

Now the screen on my phone lit up with a message from Lucas Bliek.

Have you the photo? Please send through so I can help find the children.

And a second message, sent as an afterthought.

No more news about HB. We still search for video of the priest.

I clicked the off button and laid the phone face down on the table.

Something about the airport scene didn't make sense. I suspected Broekmann was trafficking children around West Africa, moving them to work as slaves on the plantations and in the mines, in domestic service, and God knows what else. It was a relatively low-risk and cheap enterprise in a country where children were seen as economic assets. Even from the age of six they could be absorbed into family labour pools and the traffickers tapped into this, taking advantage of poor families' desire to place their kids outside their immediate community where opportunities could be more rewarding.

So why would Broekmann go to all the trouble, risk and expense of trafficking two children into Europe?

I fired up the laptop. It was time to ditch official channels and go directly to the experts. I opened the browser:

'The recruitment, transportation, transfer, harbouring or receipt of people through force, fraud or deception, with the aim of

exploiting them for profit.' United Nations definition on human trafficking.

I searched for 'NGOs and human trafficking in the Netherlands'; immediately one organisation stood out, and its office was in Amsterdam. Campagne Tegen Menselhandel, or CTM, roughly translated as the Campaign Against Human Trafficking, a non-governmental organisation set up to identify the extent of modern slavery in the Netherlands and to defend the rights of people who found themselves its victims.

Their headline:

Open your eyes! It is happening right under your nose! See it, report it, stop it!

They could have been calling to me.

THE NEXT MORNING, I was sitting in the small hectic office of Eva Taal, director of CTM. Over the phone, I had explained the reason for my visit to Amsterdam and she had booked me in the same morning.

I boarded a tram and rode to the CTM office, which was situated in a modern block of chrome and glass in a quiet neighbourhood close to the end-of-the-line terminal at Amsterdam-Zuid. The smooth elevator transported me quickly to the top and I stepped into a wide lobby where a wall of glass gave out over a panoramic view of the suburbs and eastern docks.

It was an impressive location, but Eva Taal's operations took place in a set of windowless rooms situated to the rear of the building and sandwiched between more salubrious suites – lawyers on one side, financial services on the other. I was to learn that CTM operated rent-free courtesy of the lawyers next door who had a philanthropic interest in the welfare of trafficked persons. The place was brightly decorated; a large fish tank ran along one wall where peaceful neon-coloured guppies and pearly iridescent danios wove their leisurely way through fronds of waving foliage.

Eva Taal was a diminutive woman with cropped blonde hair sticking out at angles. Her dark-framed spectacles looked too big for her pretty face where pale blue eyes shone through. Around thirty, she seemed young to be heading up an organisation such as this and I deduced her qualities must be exceptional. She collaborated with the Dutch government and its Ministry of Social Affairs and was an expert on a national problem that had reached epidemic proportions. She spoke perfect English and was a calm and professional woman with little time for pleasantries but plenty of time for the problem at hand. I liked her immediately.

'Actually, Amsterdam is a *hub* for the transit of THBs,' she said, her eyes magnified to huge proportions behind her glasses. 'That is how we refer to trafficked human beings … THBs. Yes, we have Schiphol airport, excellent road networks, and of course ports. But increasingly, I am sorry to say, the Netherlands is itself the country of origin for trafficking gangs.'

She waved a bottle of water at me, then filled a paper cup for me to drink quickly before it disintegrated.

'People are mostly young and vulnerable,' she continued. 'They are moved around the country for cheap labour, prostitution and sometimes slavery. But our city is welcoming to traffickers from all over the world and thousands are trafficked in, often for onward transit.'

She was smiling pleasantly as though talking about the weather. 'We encourage the public to report anything suspicious they have witnessed themselves,' she said. 'I thank you for coming to us.'

As we talked, Eva had one eye on her phone sitting on the desk in front of her.

'Please excuse me,' she said politely. 'I am waiting for a message.'

I wanted to know how big the problem was in West Africa and whether she had experience dealing with people trafficked from that region, especially children.

'Hundreds of thousands of children are trafficked within and without West Africa,' she said. 'Every year, actually.'

'What are they trafficked for? Farming and domestic work?' There was hope in my tone, but I knew it was naïve.

'Yes, that,' she said. 'And fishing, begging, soldiering, prostitution, and many other criminal activities.'

The little seed of panic was growing in my chest.

'Please let me get you some coffee,' she said kindly.

Striding out in clumpy trainers from behind her desk, she dipped her blonde head out of the door and spoke in Dutch to the young man at the desk.

'What intrigues me, Ms Taal …' I said as she returned to her spot.

'Eva.'

'Eva, what intrigues me is the cost of flying children to Amsterdam. What extra value might they have that the trouble and expense will have its payback for the traffickers?'

'I like your question,' she said. 'Children from Africa, girls in particular, they can net the trafficker between ten thousand and twenty thousand euros perhaps.'

I stared.

'Yes,' she continued. 'Girls bought for prostitution at private parties in exclusive penthouse suites are very valuable for the buyer. And therefore for the seller. Innocent girls in particular demand a very high price.'

I felt nauseous.

'So let's do the math,' she said. 'Traffickers may pay one to five hundred dollars for a child. That is life-changing for some families who receive it. Then there are costs for documentation, flights, bribes, etcetera, which may add up to two thousand. An African child sold in the US might bring as much as fifteen thousand dollars. So the trafficker makes a profit of nearly thirteen thousand. So you can see it is worth the trouble.'

'Excuse me,' I said, putting down my coffee cup and leaving in search of the bathroom.

When I returned, she was on her phone, but indicated for me to stay and sit with her.

The call soon ended and she looked at me kindly.

'I am sorry,' she said solidly. 'But it is good you know the facts.'

'I'm grateful to you,' I said.

Over the phone I had given Eva the details of Hendrikus Broekmann and she'd said she would search her database for me.

Pulling up the files on her computer, she said, 'Yes, we know him. You have the right address, but he is rarely in residence.'

'You know him?' I felt a rush of adrenalin and vindication, my head light with confusion and excitement.

'He has been on our radar for some time,' she was saying. 'We suspect he is trafficking but as yet we have no evidence. His operation may be small scale – at least compared to the Russians and Serbs who traffic large numbers of mostly young women from Eastern Europe.' She looked at her screen through her spectacles, squinting a little.

'If your organisation is aware of him,' I said, 'then the police must know?'

'Yes,' she said, 'that is so. But, as I said, there is no evidence. We think he is a small player and our police don't have the resources to follow up every suspect, although we ourselves try to compensate where we can.'

Bliek had lied about Broekmann and my suspicions were now confirmed.

'I've already approached the national police,' I said tentatively, wondering what her reaction would be. 'They told me they did not know Hendrikus Broekmann. That he isn't on their system.'

Eva looked unperturbed. 'Well, that's pretty bad from whoever you spoke to. They do know about Broekmann but, as I say, he is not an important target for them. There is no current investigation.'

She was jotting down notes from her computer screen and printed off a copy of all they had on him, which wasn't much more than I knew myself. Except for one thing.

'He has a nightclub,' she said.

'A nightclub?'

'It's just off De Wallen. It seems we have been watching some of the activities there, but nothing solid so far.'

'Have you been investigating him?' I asked.

'We haven't put in much resource.' She was still reading what was on the screen. 'If you are willing to ask a few questions yourself that would be helpful. We are tied up with the Serbs right now. We have informers in a gang bringing girls from Albania, Romania and Moldova. It's not just the prostitution, but also drugs and organs.'

'Organs? You mean for transplants?'

'Yes. It's big business because it's so lucrative.'

I was getting to the point where I could process no more horrific implications for those children.

'These people are very violent,' Eva was saying. 'They like to protect their investments and gangland killings are not uncommon. This means we work with homicide too. The gangsters have no boundaries. Often you find the drug cartels are also trafficking humans as a way to move the drugs around. People are ruthless. Only last week a man's severed head was left outside a shisha lounge.' She smiled benevolently at my expression. 'Yes. Right here in Amsterdam. We think it was the work of the Moroccan Mafia. Maybe they were sending a message to their competitors.'

Moroccan Mafia. It sounded like a joke.

'I'm sorry,' she said, noticing my expression. 'But these are the realities and it's best that you know.'

I fell quiet for a while. It was so much to process. But her expression was understanding.

She said, 'May I ask … if it's ok, Karen … why you did not alert the authorities before the priest got on the plane with those children?'

From an outsider's point of view, if I had been convinced of what was happening at passport control, why didn't I speak out? Why did I allow the priest to board the children on that flight?

'Well, things were a little complicated,' I said, the memory making my skin prick and my muscles contract with tension.

Eva nodded encouragement. 'Was it something to do with the exposé of your government minister?'

'Yes, it was. Nigel Hurt.' I was choosing my words carefully although there was no reason to do so. On the phone, I had given Eva the background on my work in Freetown, but she knew little detail, and the only person I had to protect was Dorothy Turay who had leaked the crucial evidence against Nigel Hurt at my request from an anonymous shack in the settlement. For myself, I had nothing left to lose.

'At the airport,' I said. 'When I recognised the priest … well, essentially I was doing a runner. You know, out of the country, and I couldn't risk drawing attention to myself. You never know who may or may not be sympathetic. After all, the customs official himself was taking a bribe.'

Eva was bobbing her spiked blonde head and smiling more encouragement.

'Unpleasant people were on my tail,' I went on. 'I couldn't risk a delay at the airport, it would have ruined everything if they had caught up with me.' And Dorothy was poised to release all the evidence I had gathered on Nigel Hurt the moment I touched down in Gatwick. But I kept that information to myself.

'Of course,' Eva was saying. 'That makes perfect sense.'

Just then, her cell phone rang with a tune from *Tubular Bells.* She picked up and spoke in Dutch. *Wait for me before you go in.*

Something was pressing that she needed to attend to. She stood up and took a denim jacket from the back of her chair.

Nodding at the printout in my hand, she said, 'Good luck. Let me know how you get on.'

I HIRED a bicycle close to the offices of CTM and cycled back from the quiet business district towards the pretty square of Rembrandtplein on the edge of the medieval quarter that contained the notorious De Wallen. The bike was hard to master with its reverse pedal braking system, and I felt vulnerable crossing the multitude of tramlines that criss-crossed the main routes. The city, bounded by the huge arc of the Singel Canal, Amstel River and Oude Schans Canal, was fiendishly difficult to navigate. The layout of concentric canals dissected by straight roads and a tangle of medieval streets meant it was hours before I found Rembrandtplein and Club VG sandwiched between two busy cafés on the western side of the square.

It stood innocuous, two solid black doors behind a group of hoardings that displayed the tram timetables. A window board announced the club's opening hour of 10.30 p.m.

Then I cycled down a road that ran alongside one of the cafés and dismounted to wheel the bike along a narrow alley that appeared to give access to the back of the building. About fifty metres down near a row of industrial-sized wheelie bins there was a pair of black doors, similarly anony-mous to those at the front. They were padlocked, with a fire exit sign fixed to the paintwork. There was a strong stench of weed and I noticed someone propped against the bins drawing on a reefer. She was stoned, pale skin visible through her torn jeans, her short black hair clinging to her head where she'd slept. I searched in my pocket and gave her twenty euros. She grabbed it and thanked me.

'Do you speak English,' I asked.

She looked blank for a moment, then replied, 'Of course!'

She grinned. A stud gleamed in her front tooth.

'Do you know if this is the entrance to Club VG?'

'Sure,' she said, not trying to get up. 'One time I work here … now, I come to piss on their door.'

'You used to work at Club VG?'

She put her finger to her lips, making a shushing sound. Her eyes were glazed and sad.

'What's your name?' I asked.

'No name,' she said, pulling on the reefer that had now reached her fingertips and was disintegrating. She dragged herself up and started moving in a steady weave towards the street, pulling her jacket around her thin shoulders though the temperature was warm.

'Do you need help?' I asked, concerned for her.

I moved to take her arm but she struck out limply.

'Piss off,' she said.

I grabbed the bike and wheeled it alongside her, but she was lost in a world more pleasant than her own.

She broke into a cough, dragging her feet.

'Can I help you?'

'Fuck off,' she said, so I left her and cycled north across Rembrandtplein in the direction of the Absalom Guest House. It was going to be a difficult night and I needed to get some sleep.

THREE
KAREN

I woke up suddenly, sweat coating my body, struggling to breathe like something heavy was pressing on my chest. The weight had sharp edges, like iron. Sounds of scraping metal and squealing brakes echoed through my head and claustrophobia squeezed at my body. An uncontrollable sense of panic.

I sat up to search the room, dragging in gulps of air, but there was no one there, just the leaves of a plane tree rustling against the window frame. I reached for the water bottle and took a long draught, my heart racing, then I moved to stare out at the canal, waiting for the feelings to pass.

The dream wasn't new – flashbacks to an accident I had never witnessed, only imagined. In the local press, there had been a photo of Songola's pretty face printed beside a snap of the twisted motorbike. Of course, she had known the risks. But she never imagined those people would actually kill her.

The images flickered on and off in my imagination, in my dreams and conscious wakefulness, and the idea I was accountable for her death ran through my veins like a toxin. It kept me going. The possibility I might find a way to atone.

And now here I was in Amsterdam. Searching for redemption.

I SHOWERED and dressed and looked at myself in the mirror, wondering whether Hendrikus Broekmann would recognise me if I met him at his club and deciding it was a real possibility. We had conversed only once, briefly, at Frank's bar in Freetown when I had been drunk and trying to seduce him into giving away his secrets. Straight away he had made plain his uninterest. He had been waiting to meet his conspirators and left me the moment they walked in – the besuited 'priest' and his muscled henchman.

When I thought back to that encounter, shame spread like heat inside my body. How irritated I had been that he was so indifferent to my charms. I wasn't familiar with cursory dismissals. To be sure, the meeting had lasted only minutes and the whole time Broekmann's attention had been fixed upon the door, preoccupied with the arrival of his accomplices and the deals they would be brokering. He had barely registered me.

But I couldn't be sure.

Behind the till in a quiet boutique off Keizersgracht, a relaxed girl with coppery red hair chewed gum as she flicked through a magazine. I ventured in, looking for something transformative among the vast array of sparkly gear in which the shop seemed to specialise. She eyed me from her spot as I rummaged through the rails and after a while, she asked, 'You looking for professional clothes?'

She clacked the gum loudly as she spoke, running her sharp eyes over me.

'Professional? Oh, no … thanks.'

'Ok,' she said, looking doubtful.

I thought I owed her a little more and said, 'I'm not looking for *professional* clothes, but I don't want to look like, um, you know …' I searched for the right word and came up with, 'myself.'

She checked me up and down, blowing a bubble and assessing the job at hand.

'Something for a club,' I added hopefully.

She nodded and came out from behind the till, walking the rails and fingering the stock with an expert eye. She held up a few items, which I looked at blankly, then she ushered me into a booth.

After a short time, I chose some discounted Victoria Beckham leather trousers, skin tight with a split front, and a silver sparkly top, cut low. Observing my cleavage sympathetically, the girl disappeared to find a padded bra.

'You need shoes,' she said, moving towards a different part of the shop and returning with a frightening pair of red stilettos. I eventually chose strappy silver heels, still too high, and teetered in the booth for approval.

She sat on one hip analysing her work as I fiddled with my hair, trying to make it do something different.

'You wait,' she said, and disappeared once again to return this time with a wig – a blonde heavy-fringed bob, the opposite of my dark curls.

I stepped out into the shop and checked my reflection in the mirror to find with satisfaction that I barely even recognised myself.

IT WAS ALMOST midnight when I arrived at Club VG and the dance floor was crammed with happy clubbers gyrating to the beats. Electro house music thumped from huge speakers on the stage, and a DJ bent over his decks, headphones askew on his tattooed pate, pumping his shoulders to the pulse of the beat. Walls of light panned the crowd illuminating jerky silhouettes, euphoric dancers throbbing to the sounds, arms overhead, their bodies close and intimate.

I moved around the space, elbowing my way to the bar which was stacked three deep. When I landed on a stool I bought an alcohol-free beer from a barman skilled at lip-reading.

The club was arranged over three floors and from the central bar I could see all the way to the roof – a glass atrium with strobe lights pulsing, flashes of purple and pink illuminating the walls and the dancers below. Cool air blasted across the space but people were slick with sweat; the floor beneath our feet throbbed as they stomped.

I scanned the room and wondered what I had been expecting – Hendrikus Broekmann standing behind the bar waiting to serve me a drink? I watched the dancers for a while and sipped at the cold and refreshing beer, my heart rate steady, my nerves sparking like electrical wires.

Around the central drop, the first and second floors were set like a gallery above so I finished my beer and made my way to the first level where the steel bannisters were elaborately welded in the shape of fornicating couples. Along the shiny black walls, reproduction Van Goghs hung at intervals illuminated by miniature spotlights jutting out from the wall. I guessed the paintings gave Club VG its name. In between two masterpieces – *The Pink Orchard* and *The Olive Grove* – a pair of heavy curtains draped across the carpet, held in place by breast-shaped ironwork. It was an entrance to a different part of the club and I passed through into what must have been the adjacent building. It was a strip club; girls in tiny thongs astride steel poles artfully undulated to the throb of 'Pour Some Sugar on Me'.

It was a dimly lit space with customers seated at circular tables around a raised platform. I skirted the edges until I found an upholstered bench to sit and watch the show. A waiter approached, young and bow-tied, a sleeveless gilet showing off his muscled arms and smooth black skin that shone in the glow of the lamps.

'Good evening,' he said in English.

I strained to hear above the music.

'Can I find you a table, ma'am?' His voice was heavily accented, but his native tongue was not Dutch. The inflection in his pronunciation was familiar to me – English-speaking, West Africa.

He led me to a spot close to the rippling girls where I ordered alcohol-free wine. It arrived promptly with a small gilt bowl filled with Chinese crackers. There were groups of 'stags' as well as lone men, couples, and groups of middle-aged friends. The demographic made me feel comfortable and, as I watched the show, I wondered about the histories of the girls performing, some of whom were gyrating their way towards the punters, lap dancing for extra tips.

According to Eva Taal, a good proportion of these girls were likely to have been trafficked. They were young and beautiful and skilled at their trade. Hand-picked by someone. I wondered how many were willing and how many had been tricked by the traffickers and were now performing to pay off an invented 'debt'.

A girl dancing close to me – a dark-haired beauty with fragile features, her pale skin almost translucent, the thong like a thread across her body – stepped down off the platform. She slunk determinedly in my direction and the wine glass froze at my lips. Recognising my panic, she diverted to a nearby group of lads who were beckoning with wads of euros.

The waiter returned with an offer to replenish my drink.

'Can I help refresh your glass, ma'am?'

His English was good but his accent was thick. West African for sure.

'Yes, please,' I said happily. 'What's your name?'

'My name Billy, ma'am.'

I didn't think Billy was his name. He was about nineteen years old, with a beautiful face that had a small dagger-shaped scar above one eye. I asked him where he was from, but he didn't answer, just backed away politely to fetch another drink.

Billy.

Could he be paying off a 'debt' to his traffickers? A young West African man working as a waiter in a strip club. Nothing unusual about that, I supposed. He could be here legitimately if I stretched my imagination. A student, perhaps? But maybe he was trafficked to Amsterdam just like the boy I saw at the airport, and I wondered what Billy had been promised and how old he might have been when he first walked through the doors to work at Club VG. I held the panic down with a slug of wine.

After a while and no sign of Broekmann, I returned through the heavy curtains that were embroidered with the outline of Van Gogh's cherry blossom, then back into the main atrium above the nightclub. The dancers were jumping as one now, low fog spreading out across the dance floor, lasers crossing the space creating images of the Club VG logo.

I moved around the space to another staircase which led to the second floor. Club VG was vast behind its modest front façade. The steps were deeply carpeted and ornate handrails rose on either side like the entrance to a Renaissance palace. I hesitated as my sparkly heel touched the pile. The top of the staircase was obscured so I couldn't determine where it led, but there was something obviously exclusive about it. Tentatively, I ascended, my pulse quickening.

The level of noise from the club below diminished the further I ascended. On a half landing a bronze sculpture of two naked women *en amour* was set on an inlaid table. My feet kept climbing, disconnected to my brain as fear crept in, and grew. It was a feeling I recognised from before – the feeling someone knew I was coming.

At the top of the stairs a small vestibule was lined with purple flock wallpaper and hung with giant reproductions of

Van Gogh's *Sunflowers*. Another brocade curtain was draped seductively to one side and behind it, a heavy mahogany door with elaborate Dutch-style carvings. A thickset man with shaved head and earpiece stood beside it and immediately I realised my mistake.

He looked at me expectantly and I half smiled, my nerves building sweat beneath the wig.

'Good evening,' he said. 'Do you have your membership please, madam?'

But he knew I wasn't a member and his beady eyes roved over me appraisingly, a cynical smile on his lips.

When I hesitated, he asked helpfully, 'Do you have an invitation?' But his tone was sly.

I straightened up for a charm offensive despite the situation being futile.

'I'm sorry,' I said in a girlish fluster and rummaged in my bag. 'I've forgotten to bring the invitation. My fault.' A high titter emerged unexpectedly from my lips.

'Who is the invitation from?' he asked, pleased at my discomfort.

In a timely fashion, the door opened and a lavishly dressed woman in her sixties stepped out with a younger man. They brushed past me and down the stairs, but before the door swung shut I caught a glimpse of the band and heard the soft brushing of a snare drum.

'It's alright,' I said to the security guard. 'I'll go. I think I've made a mistake.'

The man nodded, pushing at his earpiece, listening to something.

The door opened again, wedged open by the expensive brogue of a man who had paused to speak to someone inside. It looked like a private club, all wood panelling and chandeliers and seating lit by dim red glows from small table lamps. Recklessly, I stepped forward to scan the room, but the security guard stretched out his arm, one hand still pushing the earpiece. So I turned to leave and made my way down the carpeted staircase, the adrenalin flooding my veins.

Someone hurried past me. It was the man who had been holding the door – handsome and wearing a sharp Italian suit, a severe parting in his thick black hair. He trotted down the lush pile and disappeared into the club below.

I STOOD in the dark near the line of black wheelie bins now overflowing with rubbish, cardboard boxes piled up around them. The wig was now in a bag across my body, and my hair pushed up under a cap. The night was warm, the stink from decomposing refuse wafting in the air. I had been lurking in the shadows for two hours, my feet now numb with the pitch of the sparkly heels. Only a few had passed me: a group of drunken lads smoking dope, reeking of ganja that crept into my lungs; a cyclist taking a shortcut home; kitchen staff emerging from the club to empty food into the bins. My nerves were like an overstrung Stradivarius, so tense I could pluck them, the effort of keeping calm draining my reserves and making me feel light-headed. A screech of laughter made me jump – a group of revellers passing the end of the alley. Their voices died away and I was left alone in the silence.

An hour later it was long after closing time at Club VG and groups of jaded girls had already emerged and walked unknowingly past me, making their way towards the end of the alley and turning in the direction of Rembrandtplein. The doors opened again and a middle-aged woman hurried past, followed by a lean staff member with a cigarette hanging and a crate of bottles to pitch into the wheelie. The crash of breaking glass echoed along the concrete walls.

No sign of Billy.

I hadn't seen him leave the club and was beginning to consider there may be another exit when the doors opened quietly and he slipped out, his bow tie and waistcoat now discarded in favour of a yellow T-shirt and dark pants. He headed down the alley in my direction.

'Hello, Billy,' I said in a low voice, stepping out beside him.

He drew up, startled for a moment. Then hurried on head down.

'You don't know me,' I said, trying to keep up with his long strides, 'but it's important I speak to you if you can give me a few minutes of your time.'

'No,' he said and kept walking.

'I was in the club earlier,' I said. 'A blonde wig.'

He slowed to look at me properly, checking out the stiletto heels and split-front pants, but he picked up speed again, not wanting to engage.

'You're from Salone, aren't you?' I said.

His body tensed at the mention of his motherland. I'd used the local vernacular and his reaction assured me that my guess was correct.

His pace slowed a little so he could listen to me.

'A week ago I was in your country,' I said. 'Please, can I talk to you?'

He didn't answer, but I knew he was listening. I stopped to yank off the heels then hurried to catch up with him. We had crossed Rembrandtplein and were now moving in the direction of Amstelstraat and the Amstel river that fed the city's Canal Ring. He reduced his speed so I could draw level.

'When I was at the airport waiting for my flight I saw a priest with two children,' I said. 'I think he was smuggling them out of your country and into Amsterdam.'

He stopped abruptly, looking left and right, and I could sense his nerves.

'Who are you?' he demanded, but his voice was hushed.

'My name is Karen Hamm,' I said. 'I am investigating child trafficking from your country and there are children in Amsterdam who need help.'

He started walking again, headed towards the Blauwbrug – the blue bridge over the wide Amstel river close to the National Theatre.

'Please,' I pressed on. 'I need your help.'

He stopped on the bridge and turned aggressively, his body towering over me.

'What do you want?' he hissed, looking over my shoulder to see if anyone was coming.

I backed up a little; the water running underneath the arches was deep at this point, black and slick, like oil. A monumental stone street lamp stood behind Billy, its ornate twin lanterns emitting a glow that illuminated the top of his head and cast dark shadows around his face. I sensed his anger and his fear.

Taking a gamble, I said, 'You were smuggled here too, weren't you, Billy?'

Silence.

'You can help me find the children,' I continued. 'At the club, I saw the man who dresses himself as a priest. You know who I mean, don't you?'

'I can't speak to you,' he said forcefully, but I saw he wanted to engage.

We started walking again, his pace quickening as we passed a group of drunken lads singing some football song. It was difficult to keep up with his almost jogging pace, and when we came to the junction of Valkenburg, he stopped.

'Go away,' he said. 'You must leave now.'

I wondered if we might be close to the place where he lived and that he didn't want me to follow him there.

'I need your help,' I said, breathless. 'Please.'

'Don't follow me,' he said, panic in his eyes. 'Is not safe.'

'Not safe?'

'They will kill me if I speak to you.' His eyes darted about, not looking directly at me, the fear in his expression almost hysterical. 'I have seen their weapons.'

'Weapons?'

'Go away.'

'I understand,' I said, digging in my pocket for my contact card.

'Karen Hamm.' He said the words slowly, reading from the card. It was my university ID and that seemed to reassure him.

'Please call me,' I said. 'If you can talk. Any time. Please call me.'

I tried to keep the desperation from my voice.

He turned and I let him disappear into the night.

BY THE END of the next day, Billy hadn't called me. Eva Taal promised to get some resource to the club when I told her I had seen the priest, but I didn't have time to wait, so that night I returned to the alley hoping to catch Billy again and build the pressure.

I walked in the dim lamplight along the cobbled street of Herengracht, under the elms and around the half-moon-shaped Canal Ring, a triumph of Dutch engineering, and past the elegant Renaissance façades of seventeenth- and eigh-teenth-century merchant houses. It was late and people were emerging from the old quarter of De Wallen and pouring themselves into the few canal-side bars that were still open. Moonlight glinted on the water where abandoned tourist vessels were moored up for the night alongside pretty painted houseboats, cosy lamps illuminating their interiors. Bicycles in their scores lay abandoned on the pavements.

When I turned into the alley behind the club something was wrong. I checked my pace and ducked into the shadows, my pulse quickening. Up ahead, an altercation was taking place between a group of men – two thickset types raining blows on someone on the ground. I slipped out of sight among the bins, sinking deeper into the shadows with my back against the wall, fearful for the victim, a young man with blond hair, emaciated in a way that made you think a kick would kill him. I peered out. A third man wearing a dark suit was standing by, watching the action distractedly. He checked his big chunky watch that reflected the light of the street lamp. His cigarette glowed red as he took a drag.

One of the attackers lifted the youth by the back of his shirt and smacked his head against the wall, pinning his face against the concrete. Threats were issued in Dutch, and then a couple of punches to the kidneys and the lad fell heavily. There was silence. The man exhaled and smoke floated like gossamer towards the slash of black sky. A nod towards his men and they were gone through the doors into the club, their victim slumped, a nasty gash on his head where blood seeped through.

The man turned and moved in my direction and I flattened myself against the wall, trying to slow my heart and hoping the dark would hide me. He passed, the bright glow of his phone illuminating his face, the familiar severe parting in his thick black hair.

I waited a few seconds before exiting the alley. He was striding quickly across Rembrandtplein and I followed him in the direction of the Blauwbrug Bridge then over the canal and into the Botanical Gardens. It was cool and fragrant under the trees, and my trainers were silent on the footpath behind him.

After a while we emerged from the gardens and headed out towards the ugly footbridge of Entrepotdok, a crossing that led into the eastern docklands. The bridge's yellow iron canopy loomed eerily in the dark above and I hung back until he was clear of the bridge then scuttled after him just as he turned into an area of old warehouses converted into offices and flats. Then a shortcut down a narrow street and onto the Nieuwe Vaart footbridge where we emerged onto the island of Wittenburg. The man walked quickly. He was tapping on his phone, making calls, sending messages. He never looked back. My heart pounded against my ribs, my breath short and shallow; I did not want to make a sound. Where was he leading me?

Soon we were in a less salubrious part of town where utilitarian-style buildings lined the street, cheap apartment blocks, shops and office accommodation. At the entrance to a five-storey building the man stopped abruptly and tapped a code into the keypad. The buzzer sounded and he disappeared within.

The address above the door read – Lang Huis, Wittenburg.

FOUR
THE GIRL

The engine droned on, grinding through the miles, the steel floor vibrating beneath the travellers hunched in the back, belongings stacked on their knees, bodies tipping against each other with every brake and turn. Too much intimacy for strangers.

There were no windows. No lights, no seats, no blankets, only a worn, stained carpet too small to cover the space. Vents in the roof allowed a weak flow of air in an atmosphere thick with the stench of stale sweat. A single jerry can lay on its side half filled with water.

It was hours since they had pulled up in some woods, the doors flung wide, and the group ordered out by one of the drivers – the tall, bearded one whose name was Valon. Weary and anxious, they were grateful for the sharp surge of oxygen and a chance to relieve their bladders. They had hurried to the bushes knowing they would not be stopping long, Valon stood watchfully by, the tiny steel crucifix quivering on a chain attached to his ear, his attention fixated on the girl. He was a slow-witted man, but he was violent and spontaneous, and he carried a weapon to stop her running. She was trouble, the girl.

The travellers had returned quickly to the van but the girl took her time, using the opportunity to scan the woods behind the bushes and get her bearings, deduce their location, and plan her escape. She had brought the rucksack with her. It never left her side just in case there was an opportunity to run.

Valon came looking for her. 'Fuck. Get in van.' He waved the pistol, menacingly.

She had looked contemptuously at him so he tucked the weapon in the belt of his jeans and grabbed her by the rucksack, marching her back to the vehicle and cursing under his breath.

Now she sat cramped on the floor again – no space to stretch her legs, lie down or go to sleep, the stink of sweat and stale tobacco filling her lungs. Exhaustion flooded her body and confusion clouded her mind, but her spirit was not diminished. They would be stopping again soon. She sat close to the doors, her rucksack on her knees. If she tipped her head against it she could close her eyes and rest a while. Biding her time.

The level of water in the jerry can was running low, and it slopped to and fro with the motion of the van. They were still travelling at speed, the elevated noise of the engine echoing against the vehicle's thin steel walls. Much of the journey had been like this. Swift, smooth and speedy, like they were travelling on the highways, with the occasional roar of juggernauts.

The men were bad drivers, swerving, braking and then accelerating unexpectedly so that people in the back were thrown against each other, getting close to people they did not know. Like the couple from South America, a short, wiry man of middle age who was travelling with his larger proportioned wife, who had journeyed to Amsterdam hidden inside a shipping container. The couple were poor and looking for work but the wife had been compassionate, sharing biscuits and other scant rations with the girl. Rare acts of kindness in this hostile world.

Then there were the two young women from Côte d'Ivoire, beauties who clung together like sisters and conversed in whispering French. And the boy, Foday, who had travelled with the girl all the way from Freetown on the KLM flight to Amsterdam. A lad of fourteen years snatched by the traffickers while begging outside the courts of justice.

THE GIRL SLEPT LIGHTLY in her hunched position and dreamt she was back in her village in the home of her mother and father, and that they weren't dead. It was a pleasant but strange dream.

She had been in her mother's garden and they were planting carrots in straight drills beside the yam, the tall stems of cassava leaves standing to attention in rows up and down. A man arrived and stood by. He was somewhat familiar, so her mother offered a friendly greeting and engaged in conversation, but the girl could not recall his name. The man's smile was broad but insincere, and as he spoke his gaze passed over the woman's shoulder to the girl who was kneeling with carrot seeds in her hands.

She woke up abruptly, her head banging against the side of the van as it swerved round a corner. The character of the road they were travelling had changed. The engine pitch had deepened and they were climbing, swinging in arcs around tight bends.

Recalling the dream, the girl realised now who the man had been – he was the cousin of her aunt. The one who collaborated with criminals, stole kids from the villages and sent them far away from their families. Yes. That was the man in her dream. He had bought her for one hundred US dollars. A good sum for a village child, but that was because a premium was attached to such as she – educated and clever and speaking good English. But the girl had spoken not a word since the day she had been sold. A defiant gesture. Her symbol of resistance.

The day she had been sold, the girl was transported with four other girls and two boys in the back of a rusting pickup whose backdraught drew choking fumes into their lungs. They had travelled rough roads through bush and mountain landscapes, over the Kabala Hills, and past settlements where villagers stood gawking, knowing what business they saw.

The girl knew something of the business herself. Kids abducted from the villages ended up in bad places, stealing or begging, or working as domestic or plantation slaves. Even taken to gold or diamond mines to dig underground. But in the rural areas of her country, uneducated people were easily tricked with false promises of better lives for their children, or even an education which people could not afford to buy themselves. Opportunities like that could drag whole families out of poverty. These were simple people.

But the girl's family had been anything but simple.

It had been the rainy season when they took her, and the rusting pickup had slid and swerved along muddy tracks through swamped vegetation, sheets of rain lashing on the kids in the back. At this time of year, roads became impassable, vehicles sticking in the mud. Rivers and their tributaries flooded and had to be navigated around or waded through or floated over.

And this had presented the girl with her first opportunity to escape.

The pickup had stopped at a flooded tributary of the great Rokel River where a makeshift ferry had been set up with a rope fixed to either side, a sturdy raft in between. Two men with glistening muscles operated the ferry, and village lads stood by in the hope of earning tips. An argument ensued as the price was negotiated, then the pickup edged slowly onto the raft, the driver's tongue hanging as he checked from side to side, ensuring the wheels locked in position. Distracted.

The girl clung to the side peering down into the muddy waters. Then, stealthily, she gathered her rucksack and edged towards the tailgate.

The ferry moved away from the shore and she dropped to the ground and slithered across the mud, everyone looking the other way. The area was churned up, the ground saturated with the deep cloying earth. Her trainers slid as she worked to gain traction, to pick up speed, her heart racing as her legs laboured hard and her feet slipped beneath her, impossible to find purchase on the thick red clay.

She heard the rush of water moving further upstream. If she could just make it to the forest. She edged into some elephant grass, picked herself up and ran. Then a shout from behind. Someone had seen, and two lads set off in pursuit. She turned and looked straight ahead, focused on the periphery of the bush, higher land, longer grass, the edge of the forest. Gaining speed, she moved away from the pickup towards thicker vegetation where there was cover.

The lads were faster.

She struggled on, the rucksack bouncing on her shoulders, her breathing quick and heavy, the rain, lighter now, cooling her face as she moved towards the forest.

Hands grabbed her from behind and she was down. Flat on her face on the rain-soaked earth, the red soil warm in her mouth. The lads turned her. Uselessly she kicked and punched. Pinning her arms and legs, they carried her like a fallen tree all the way back to the pickup, throwing her in and tying her hands. Then her feet. Then a blow sending her down against the grit of the vehicle's floor.

The ferry edged its way across the river and the village lads pocketed their tips.

. . .

NOW, in the back of the van, she was planning her next attempt. There was no way of knowing where they were, or where they were headed, or what the gang had planned for her. The day before, she and Foday had been taken from the apartment in Amsterdam to meet up with the rest of the travellers outside the city at some farm, although it didn't look like a farm to her. No animals, nothing growing, nobody working in the fields. Then they'd been shoved into the back of the van with a group of strangers, their backpacks and trolley cases.

The girl had slept badly the first night. She knew it was night because others were snoring and she could see darkness through the air vents and the occasional lamplight as they passed through towns. Now there was a trickle of daylight through the vents but she couldn't see the angle of the sun – otherwise she would be able to work out exactly which way they were headed. She knew that north of Amsterdam were the Scandinavian countries. She had paid attention in geography because her friend Aminata's uncle lived in Finland. He was a lecturer at the University of Helsinki. He was multilingual and clever, just like the her own father.

But she didn't think the van was on its way to Scandinavia.

The terrain they were travelling had changed. The van was now labouring up steep inclines, its engine making a growling sound. Then they were hurtling down hills at a frightening speed.

Eventually, the van slowed and turned off the road, veering left and right on uneven ground before stopping. The front doors slammed as the men got out, then the rear doors opened and sunlight poured in, the exhausted cargo instantly illuminated, blinded by the startling intensity of the light.

'Out!' ordered Valon. 'Go piss.'

His weapon was waving in one hand indicating the way, his mood dark and threatening. He grabbed one of the beauties from Côte d'Ivoire and dragged her out, the second girl falling out behind her, startled by the crisp white light and unable to see the step.

'Get up, get up!' he shouted, and the two stumbled off towards the shrubs. Others followed.

They had stopped down a track on a mountain pass.

As the girl alighted, her rucksack firmly on her back, she saw for the first time the wonder of snow, the tops of the mountains tall and close, threatening and embracing. The silence was frightening in its magnitude. Her fingers moved to check the fastening of the rucksack, but it was securely bound around her waist.

A rush of mountain air filled her lungs, the pristine sensation making her dizzy. Snow, cold air and soaring mountains. She had never imagined a place so beautiful. She pulled her jacket closer round her body and zipped up, then moved with the women through the shrubbery, Valon with his anger and his weapon close by.

Mountain pines and their citrus scent surrounded the small lay-by where they'd stopped. The peaks soared behind, their white tips blinding against a clear blue sky. Through the pines a steep drop led to a meadow that spread down towards a road curling in hairpin bends.

Where was this place? The mountains in Europe were the famous Alps. Perhaps they had arrived in Switzerland. The girl tried to recall the map of Europe, a bit fuzzy in her mind, and concluded they must have travelled east if they were now in Switzerland. But the winding road below was headed south, not towards the sun, which was rising behind a different range of mountains.

The women in the group had risen from their squats and were zipping up discreetly. Valon was urinating against a tree, his back turned, the weapon tucked loosely in his belt.

The girl searched for the second driver, Gëzim, who had returned to the vehicle and was speaking into his phone.

A vast lump, maybe her heart, stuck in her throat. She looked down towards the road. A truck chugged slowly down the mountain, manoeuvring carefully round the bends. She could hear the low moan of its engine as the driver changed gears.

She was sure of foot, nimble, young and quick and sped through the pines. It wasn't much distance to the road, and the men were too stupid and slow to catch her. If she could make it there she would be safe. She would stop a vehicle travelling down the mountain. Someone would help her. It would not be like her first escape when no one wanted to help her. Switzerland was a friendly country, and welcoming. What else would a girl like her be doing alone in a snowy mountain landscape if she didn't need help? She would throw herself on the road and someone would stop to help her.

Swift and agile under the stately pines, she ran through a carpet of fallen needles, her feet rustling softly against the springy ground. Nimbly picking her way across an irregular patch of boulders, knees up, her trainers barely touching the ground, she emerged onto the steep grassy slope of a meadow, the cold air piercing her lungs. There was a shout from behind but she didn't look back. She must get to that road before the next vehicle passed.

Out in the open now, the grass was wet with dew. The road below was very close. The girl's heart thumped in her ears, her breathing quick and shallow, the running easy. More shouts from behind in a language she didn't understand, but now she could hear the sound of a vehicle coming round the bends, making its way down the pass. She would step out and halt it.

Almost there. Keep running, and don't look back.

The vehicle's engine was getting louder. Unknown help moving down the road, braking at the hairpins with dull screeching sounds. She leapt from the grass down a short vertical drop and landed on the tarmac, then ran easily back up hill in the direction of her rescuers. Help was moments away. The sweat was running down her neck, the jacket heavy and hot, the rucksack still firm across her shoulders.

Hands grabbed it. Hard breathing entered her ears, the familiar stale breath reaching her nostrils, and she came down hard, her cheek pressed against the tarmac.

Valon wrenched her arms and dragged her to her feet, cursing in his own language. She struggled pointlessly and spat in his face, spittle attaching to the tip of his beard. Then something struck her head and a high-pitched jingling filled her ears and when she opened her eyes, the mountains were upside down, the pine trees blurry, swaying in wide arcs. Immense pressure was cramping her stomach as the hardness of his shoulder dug in, his arm wrapped tightly around her legs.

The vehicle was close now. It wasn't too late.

But the noise of the engine sounded familiar.

It stopped and the driver got out, leaving the door ajar.

'What the fuck!'

Then the metal doors slammed shut behind her, the familiar odour of perspiration, blackness as she drifted off into an unnatural sleep.

FIVE

KAREN

'Lang Huis. Wittenburg. That's the address.'

I was back in Eva Taal's office explaining that I had followed the 'priest' from Club VG to an apartment block in the eastern docklands.

'It was definitely him,' I emphasised. 'I'd know him anywhere. He was in the club. I saw him. It's him.'

I'd barged in unannounced. There was no time for formalities. A link between Broekmann's club and the man who had abducted the children was now established and I wanted to know about the apartments in Wittenburg.

Eva came out from behind the metal cabinet where she'd been filing buff-coloured folders.

'You followed him to the docklands?' she asked, looking at me with a different expression. 'That was bold of you.'

She was dressed in wide-legged trousers, cropped at the ankle, and chunky trainers that made her feet look too big for her body. She indicated that we should sit and ordered coffee over the intercom.

'Yes,' I confirmed. 'From the back of the club in the early hours.'

'And you think the kids are in those flats?'

'They could be in the flats, yes. I have a strong feeling about it.' I sat heavily in the chair. 'Why would he go to a place like that in the middle of the night?'

'The middle of the night is when criminals do their work,' she said obviously. 'But what do you mean by "a place like that"?'

'It's a rundown neighbourhood.'

'There could be any number of reasons for him going there,' she said logically.

But I was convinced it was the hiding place. 'That man brought children into your country with false papers. I saw him. He must be hiding them somewhere. If he's linked to Broekmann and they're trafficking others, then they must have some sort of holding space.'

'Of course,' she agreed. 'That would make sense.'

I knew she wanted to help, but there was only so much she could do.

'Can you check?' I asked. 'I mean, find out whether Broek-mann has other properties in Amsterdam. Like in the docklands.'

She was already reaching for her mouse. 'Yes, I can do that, but I think we already checked.'

She started typing into her keyboard. 'I want to help you,' she said. 'You took quite a risk in Freetown.'

Eva Taal had done her homework. I would expect no less, and now I could detect new respect in her voice. My reports on corruption were accessible online. My exposure of UK minister Nigel Hurt had been hard won but worth the risks I had taken to bring him down.

'No,' she said, still scrolling. 'There is nothing else in his name, but let me check the company register.'

'You mean Club VG?'

'Yes. The company itself may have assets. Many do.'

The wait was excruciating as she trawled through the lists of data on her computer, murmuring in Dutch as she did so, eyes flicking across the screen behind her huge glasses.

'Ah.'

'You've found something?' I moved around the desk to join her.

'Club VG owns three apartments in Wittenburg. They are on Derde Wittenburgerdwarsstraat.'

'Wait.' I searched through the notes on my phone where I had recorded the name so I would remember it.

'Yes. That's it. That's the place.'

'And a farmhouse,' she added.

'A farmhouse? Where's this farmhouse?'

'In West Friesland.' She indicated the entry on her screen. 'It's a farming region north of Amsterdam. Forty-five minutes by car.'

My heart was racing. This was progress. Maybe the children were at the farm.

'I doubt the children are at the farm,' she said, reading my thoughts. 'They will need to move them on quickly. More risk involved with minors.'

'So you agree perhaps the children are at the flats?'

'Maybe they have been there. You saw your man go from the club to the flats. This is the same man you saw with the children. It makes sense.'

Eva's voice was slightly raised, maybe in hope or excitement.

'With child trafficking,' she went on, 'the crime is more serious than with adults so gangs are less likely to sell them or move them on in this country, unless it is the domestic sector.'

'The domestic sector in Amsterdam?'

'Yes. Much goes under the radar in that way. Domestic slaves are usually children, and once they're settled inside a home they are invisible.'

That didn't fit with our discussion about the cost of

airfreighting children from Freetown. Domestic service would not bring a high enough return.

'My guess is the kids have been moved out straight away,' said Eva. 'Overland, maybe, or another flight for the right customer.'

Panic was building as the realisation dawned that the children may already be on their way to another country. There was no time to lose. I should have been here days ago.

Eva set her printer to work and passed me the information.

Flats 17, 30 and 55, Lang Huis, Wittenburg.

'See what you can find,' she said. 'If you bring me any kind of evidence it's possible we can get a police raid organised. But we have to have something substantial if we don't want to break the law ourselves.'

'Right,' I said. What did she expect me to do?

'You have the address.' Eva looked at me as though wondering what I was waiting for. Like I was leading the investigation myself. Which, in effect, I was.

'Got it,' I said, perplexed.

'I have to concentrate on the Serbs right now,' she said by way of an apology, and I was sorry Eva felt she had to explain herself. 'We are close. Their operations are huge, bringing girls from across Europe into De Wallen.'

'Of course,' I replied, feeling like a sideshow to the main event.

'They feed these girls all kinds of lies,' she explained. 'Take their passports and papers so they have undocumented status and therefore no rights, subject them to violence and withhold even food so they comply with all demands. They wipe all contacts from their phones. Sometimes the girls are freighted out of Rotterdam to the US in shipping containers specially designed with vents built in the roof.'

'Do you know who's responsible?' I asked.

'Yes, we know him. He has a chain of casinos across the

Netherlands – a front for laundering the money. His organisation is brutal. We have found girls in the canal.'

This was the point of Eva Taal's organisation – to encourage girls and boys, women and men, to escape from slavery and come to CTM for support and protection.

'They can be deeply traumatised when they get here,' she said. 'Girls think they can make their fortune when trafficked into a prosperous country. It's so sad for them. Some don't want the shame of repatriation so we help them find work and accommodation in the Netherlands and sort their papers for them. But they live in fear of this man. He has such a psychological hold – it's hard to convince them to talk.'

I thought of Billy, the waiter at the club, and realised what he might be risking by talking to me. I had not mentioned my conversation with Billy to Eva because I was sure she would warn me off speaking to a vulnerable person, someone who was probably trafficked himself.

There was a knock on the door and a young woman stepped in – dark haired and petite like Eva – the same woman in the photograph on Eva's desk. The photo showed the pair of them in running shorts, holding up some kind of medal. She smiled at me and nodded a greeting. This was Mimi, Eva's girlfriend.

'Please excuse,' Mimi said, then spoke to Eva in Dutch.

Eva rose quickly from her chair. 'You will have to excuse me now.'

'I understand,' I said, seeing how distracted she was, and added recklessly, 'I will get you what you need on Broekmann.'

I left the building and cycled back towards the Absalom Guest House planning the next move, wondering about Eva's thoughts – that the children could be long gone, already moved out of the flats and on their way to a different destination, possibly even to another country. Anxiety clawed at my chest, like the feeling you need to hurry but have nowhere to go. How could I get into those flats?

I STOOD on the footbridge over Oosterdok looking down into the water where a group of swimmers was moving along with regulated strokes, colourful caps gliding, goggles dipping in and out, each trailing an orange buoy to alert boats they were in the water. A stiff westerly breeze was up, cumulus sprinting across the dark blue clouds advancing close behind. Tall elms stood along the water's edge, their slate-ribbed bark mottled with lichen, their leaves rustling boisterously in the wide canopy above.

Not far away, Lang Huis rose in a hard-edged block, an unattractive building with pebble-rendered concrete where flowering plants trailed over balconies breaking up the grey, and washing hung on plastic lines. Bold graffiti was spread across the stuccoed walls and the miserable foliage of dusty weeds grew through cracks in the paving.

From where I stood, I had an unrestricted view of the entrance to the block. Residents had been coming and going all morning. I unlocked my phone and studied the photos of the children so I would know straight away if I saw them in the flats. One photo stood out because the girl was staring at the camera. She carried a rucksack with the eighties-style logo of Ghostbusters! I wondered if she had seen me taking her photo. It had been her resemblance to Songola that made me zoom in on her and, as I looked more closely at her expression, a new emotion pulled at me – one I didn't recognise – but for a moment it drowned out the fear.

I tucked away the phone and lowered my cap to shield my eyes from the drops of rain starting to splat against the pavement. Across the canal, De Wallen beckoned. It wouldn't be long before activities began behind the velvet curtains of the red-lit windows that lined the sleazy alleys.

Then I saw her, walking back to the bridge towards me. A short, middle-aged woman in a faded pink tracksuit and turquoise trainers, a laden carrier bag in each hand, her hair dyed black and drawn back in a tight rubber band. She had left Lang Huis about two hours ago.

Discreetly, I slipped in behind her, keeping a few paces distant. The bottles in her carrier bags clunked as she moved along with quickening steps as the rain fell more heavily. She stopped at the door, placing one bag on the ground while she punched the code into the keypad. The buzzer sounded and she picked up the bag, turning to shoulder the door. I stepped in and put my arm above her, pushing it wide so she could enter.

'Bedankt,' she said, her head down. Thank you.

She headed to the staircase and moved down to the lower floor.

I ascended silently to the fifth level and made my way to the door marked 55. I stared at the spy hole in a heightened state, my nerves taut with fear, indecision confusing my brain. I couldn't guess what I would find behind the door or how I would react when I saw it and if I hesitated a moment longer, I would run.

I pressed the buzzer, my head lowered, so the spy hole would reveal only the top of the cap.

There were no sounds from within. No voices, no music, no noise from a TV.

I pressed again. Someone emerged from a flat three doors down, but they didn't look my way, and after a few minutes, I concluded that flat 55 was either empty or the people inside wanted it to look that way. Relief flooded in and I retraced my steps down the stairs to level three, wondering what I would do if all the flats were the same.

There were voices coming from inside flat 30, an argument taking place in a language I didn't recognise, but when I rang the buzzer, all went quiet. Imaginary footsteps approached the door; maybe someone was peering through the spy, assessing my identity. I waited several minutes, but no one opened the door. My finger hovered over the buzzer, fear making it tremble. When I rang a second time the silence deepened.

The last apartment owned by Club VG was on the first floor and I wondered if I should change my strategy. Perhaps just wait around until someone came out, so I stood there, wavering, trying to make a decision, when suddenly it was made for me and the door opened.

A man of around thirty wearing ripped jeans and a U2 T-shirt looked at me in surprise. His head was shaven and three gold studs pierced his ear.

'Who are you?' he asked aggressively.

I had my answer ready.

Behind him a slow-moving girl with sunken eyes crossed from one room to another in her underwear. She slunk a look my way. Two younger girls sat on the stairs, arm in arm. The place stank of weed. Strident voices were having a forceful conversation somewhere within and the language was East European.

'I'm looking for Dominique Strasse,' I said to the man, trying to make my voice sound different to the one inside me. 'She lives here.'

'She no live here,' the man said. 'Who told you come?'

'She gave me this address.' I pulled out a scrap of paper with the address of the flat in my handwriting. 'She said she lives here,' I said, showing him the note.

'She's not here.' He stared at me, his body arranged in a threatening stance.

'Maybe I have the wrong floor,' I said, trying to see past his shoulder.

'Yes. Wrong floor. Piss off.'

He shut the door and stood outside waiting for me to go. I

moved hastily to the stairwell feeling the heat of his eyes, my heart like a piston. But I had got what I wanted.

THE FIREARMS UNITS took their place, out of sight, waiting for the command from their senior officer. The entrance doors to Lang Huis were wedged open and residents had been moved to safety behind the tapes. I waited with Eva Taal, grateful she respected me enough to believe my story and invite me along to witness the police raid on the apartments. Her trust meant a lot. It was lonely in the risky world I now inhabited and it felt good to be part of a team alongside someone like Eva.

The Special Security Missions Brigade had encircled the whole building. The unit was trained to combat organised crime and terrorism, its main job to neutralise armed offenders. Three teams were poised ready to go, the plan being to assault each flat simultaneously.

On the signal, the special forces teams made their move, running with bent knees, armed with Glock pistols and semi-automatic weapons. They were dressed in thick protective gear, balaclavas and helmets. It felt surreal, like I was in the movies.

We hung back with officers from immigration waiting for the signal that the threat was neutralised and it was safe to follow the the teams into the flats. Eva would go with them to support the THBs living in the apartments. Tensions were high, even among experienced professionals with heavy weaponry, and I feared for the women and children who might get caught in the crossfire.

Screamed warnings echoed through the building, then the splintering of wood, heavily armed officers appearing briefly on the balconies to check the outdoor spaces then retreating inside. But there was no resonance of gunfire.

Eva took a call and then left with the immigration officers to enter the apartments.

I stood waiting behind the tapes, something unpleasant gnawing at me, an impression of defeat implanted in my mind. The children could still be here, they could already have moved on, or they could never have been here at all.

First out of the building was immigration, then Eva, and they stood talking for some time outside the doors. I knew then that something was wrong. Where were the girls I had seen in flat 17?

Behind the tapes, a small crowd had gathered to watch the drama, and I stood with them, my spirits sinking. Before long, the special forces teams reappeared, their weapons secured, and they headed for the vans. Only the police stayed inside, waiting for forensics.

Eva walked towards the tapes and beckoned to me.

'They were tipped off,' she said, matter of fact.

'No!'

'It's not unusual.' She was calmness itself. 'We're hoping that forensics will find something useful. We find the gangs are good at covering their tracks but occasionally they miss something important. A fingerprint. Traces of drugs, or gunshot residue. Sometimes sim cards are left behind, even.'

'Who tipped them off?' I demanded.

'Of course, we do not know that. There will be an investigation. We have a few bad apples, but mostly we are all on the same side.' Eva placed a hand on my arm. 'Don't give up,' she said. 'You've done good work here.'

'Who tipped them off?' I repeated, disillusionment swamping me, anger and mistrust.

'We don't know that yet.'

'Someone must know,' I said with a fluttering in my chest, anxiety building.

'Karen, please don't distress yourself.' Her arm was round my shoulder now.

'I'm not distressed,' I said, shrugging her off, wondering if I could trust Eva herself, and cursing myself at the thought.

'Karen …' Her voice was soft, like she was talking to one of her rescued THBs. 'Can I ask … what are these children to you?'

I couldn't answer her.

It was another dead end. I was no closer to finding those children or trapping Broekmann than I had been when I'd stepped off the plane at Schiphol.

The police tapes were being wound back, the crowd beginning to disperse, and officers were emerging from the building and among them a familiar face in his inspector's uniform. He stood alone, talking into his cell phone and directing his gaze straight at me, making sure I had seen him. Lucas Bliek, sending an unambiguous warning for me to back off.

SIX

KAREN

I sat in my room at the Absalom Guest House watching the shadows grow long against the houses opposite. Laughter was coming from a bar on the corner of Keizersgracht and Brouwersgracht where a single-arch stone bridge linked the two cobbled streets. Small tables had been set under the elms and drinkers were enjoying the evening sunshine. Along the street, cyclists wove in a steady flow in and out of the pedestrians: elegant riders with flowing hair and billowing scarves; lads with heads down and elbows up, tuned in to their oversized headsets; businessmen in suits; elderly ladies with wicker baskets attached to their handles.

A high-pitched shriek followed by laughter, then the clanking of a tram headed east to Central Station.

I stared at the scene below.

Bliek had tipped off the gang holding the girls in the flats and now the trail on the kids had gone cold. The police had found no evidence in the apartments even though I knew the girls had been there only hours before the raid. Nothing had been found at the farmhouse in West Friesland, either. The traffickers were professionals, exiting their crime scenes cleanly, leaving nothing behind for forensics. Or maybe forensics were corrupt themselves.

Lucas Bliek had made sure I'd seen him. He had warned me off and now I was considering how much I had to fear from him.

Earlier I'd rung Eva, though I knew there was nothing more she could do.

'Don't worry. It happens.' She was calm and pragmatic.

'They were there, Eva. Young girls. Foreign. My guess would be Eastern European. And their minder was aggressive when he thought I'd seen them.'

'Don't worry,' she said again. 'I do believe you, but there's nothing I can do when the police find no evidence. All we have are three empty apartments owned by Club VG and, of course, the company denies all knowledge.'

'Have you interrogated them?'

'They say the flats are empty awaiting improvements,' she said. 'New bathrooms, they say. What can we do?'

I could think of no answer.

There was an awkward silence. I liked Eva. I didn't want to think this was the end of the road and the end of our relationship. But if it had to be, then I would continue alone.

'What about Lucas Bliek?' I asked. 'My guess is he's the one who tipped them off.'

A hint of a sigh.

'I will pass on your concerns,' she said, but she had more pressing matters. She worked closely with the police and had to trust them. It would be foolish to jeopardise that relationship.

Eventually we hung up.

THE SUN HAD DIPPED and its rays had completely disappeared from the group of friends drinking at the corner café. It was getting dark and there was only one thing left I could think of to do.

An hour later, the tram dropped me at the Dam, clanking as it moved slowly off, warning cyclists of its approach into Damrak with its obelisk monument, the Royal Palace and wide-open plaza. It was the closest stop to De Wallen and I would have to walk from here.

The air was warm and thick with the odour of weed as I headed east in the direction of the red-light area. It was some distance away but I sensed the energy as I moved closer along the cobbles. I strode down the adjacent canal behind a group of Japanese tourists whose excitement was tangible. I couldn't see it yet, or hear it, but I could feel it – the thrill and anxiety approaching a seedy underworld.

Sex shops, tattoo parlours and waxing establishments became more obvious and, down the next alley, I caught a glimpse of a red strip light above a shop window and followed it.

The shop was a tiny booth, dimly lit, with red curtains pulled to either side. At first, I didn't see the girl, but then I realised she was sitting right there, looking out, positioned like a mannequin, her expression blank. Dark hair, dark skin, heavy make-up and scant red lingerie. She stared back and I moved on. I knew what I was looking for, and it wasn't her.

Through a cloud of marijuana, I emerged onto the infamous Oudezijds Achterburgwal, a canal lined with elms, the cobbled streets on either side jammed with pedestrians, red strip lights reflecting garishly off the canal. Music pumped out of clubs' open doors. Rows of booths nestled between the sex shops, strip shows and brothels, their windows opening straight onto the cobbles … punters tapping on the glass, the glass opening a little, a price negotiated, the glass opening further, the punter stepping inside, and the red curtains drawing behind.

I trawled the streets searching the booths, pushing

through immense throngs that packed each side of the canal. Most of the girls were dark-haired and dark-skinned beauties. South American, I guessed. Very few were pale or blonde; a diverse assortment of women, young and old, fat and thin, but most were striking-looking with enhanced bodies, surgically altered faces and uber-confident attitudes, dressed in lingerie that was hardly even there.

Others looked like 'the girl next door'.

One such had ash-brown hair tied back and wore studded leather gear with many buckles. A group of lads tapped on her window and she opened up, speaking with an accent that was East European. She smiled and tittered. With no glass partition between her and the wave of testosterone on the street, she seemed vulnerable. A man stepped in and the curtains closed behind him.

The whole place was alive. People buzzing with good-humoured expectation, groups of men, couples, tour groups, women. Punters moving up and down the cobbles staring into booths, falling out of noisy bars and strip clubs and sex shows. Unexpectedly, I felt safe.

I moved across an under-lit bridge to explore the other side where girls stood brazen in their windows. Others were on their phones, doing their make-up, arranging their hair, filing nails. It was discomfiting looking at the women, trying not to judge them as commodities.

De Wallen was a seedy place, but alluring, and I wandered fearlessly through the alleys towards Oude Kerk, Amsterdam's oldest building, a beautiful church on the periphery of the red-light district, where I decided to return to the girl with the studs and buckles. A man walked into me and apologised, smiling. Tall, attractive, Middle Eastern. He asked if I wanted to go for a beer, and I wondered how long he'd been following me.

The girl with the buckles seemed different from the rest. Young, fresh, out of place among the heavily tarted pros in the neighbouring booths. She was doing her hair when I approached her booth and when I stopped she looked out at me. Did she know how many times I'd passed her window?

I took a step in and knocked on the glass. She stood and opened the window.

'Hi. You want business?' she asked.

'Yes,' I replied in a voice that wasn't my own.

'Fifty euros. Nothing kinky,' she warned.

'Ok,' I said. She opened the window wider and I stepped in, my whole body shaking. She drew the curtains.

'What I can do for you?' she asked, unfastening her long, silky hair.

'What's your name,' I asked.

'Maria,' she said, moving towards me and making to undo her bra.

'No, I don't want sex.'

'No sex?'

'I just want to talk to you.'

She looked suspicious. 'Talk dirty?' she asked.

'No.' A strange little laugh escaped from me, and she stepped back. 'No,' I went on, trying to settle. 'I'm looking for someone. Maybe you can help me.'

'What I can do?' She looked puzzled.

I took fifty euros from my bag and handed it to her. She took it quickly and put it in her bra. Then I showed her the photo of the priest and the children.

'Why you show me this?' Maria asked.

'These children,' I said. 'They have been trafficked from Africa to Amsterdam. Have you seen them?'

'Trafficked?'

She looked at me part confused, part alarmed.

'You police?' she asked.

'No,' I said, trying to reassure her. 'Not police. My name is Karen Hamm.' I showed her my university card but I didn't expect it to mean anything to her. 'I'm a researcher from England. Please don't be afraid.'

'What you research?' she asked angrily.

I sensed she was undocumented and illegally in the country. Prostitution was regulated in the Netherlands and girls were protected by the state, but undocumented workers had much to fear from the police.

'Don't be afraid,' I repeated quickly. 'I'm just looking for these children. Do you know them, have you seen them?' I pressed the photo on her again. 'Perhaps you know the man with them.'

She wasn't convinced but took the phone from me and studied the photo.

She shook her head. 'Why I know them?'

I wanted to say *because I think you've been trafficked like them*, but there were many gangs who could be working this girl and I didn't want to frighten her any more.

'Could this girl be working here ... in De Wallen?' I asked.

Maria looked again at the photo. 'Too much young,' she said. 'Too much young for working here.'

But not much younger than Maria, I thought and I wondered if she knew where she was headed when she left her country, what lies the gang had told her.

'Are you sure,' I asked again, pressing the phone back in her hand.

'Yes, I sure.'

'Ok.' I decided to try something else. 'Maria, can you tell me where you're from? Where is your home?'

'Why you ask?' she said defensively.

'I'm working with an organisation called CTM. They can help you.'

I pulled out Eva's card and gave it to her.

This time there was vague recognition when she saw the CTM logo.

'They help people who have been trafficked to Amsterdam,' I went on. 'People who are being forced maybe to do what they don't want to do. Maybe they have to give their money to the men.'

She studied Eva's card.

'Do you need help?' I asked.

'No,' she said unconvincingly, and for a moment she wavered, her vulnerability bare, and I searched through my phone for the photo of Hendrick Broekmann, deciding it was time to take the risk.

'Maria, do you know this man?' I asked carefully.

She panicked when she saw him. 'You get me killed,' she said, looking round, her voice a whisper. 'Get out.'

I followed her gaze towards the panic button on the wall … who knew what minder lurked unseen. But I knew she wouldn't press it.

'You know him, don't you?' I said.

'No. I not know this man.'

She drew back the curtains and opened the booth to let me out onto the cobbles.

But I'd found another connection to Broekmann.

THE ABSALOM GUEST HOUSE was deserted when I returned in the early hours. I headed to the bar and took down a bottle of Glenlivet from a glass shelf behind the counter, left a note for the staff, then climbed the steep stairs to my room on the fourth floor, ducking under the bulkheads. The girl in De Wallen knew Broekmann. She'd reacted when she'd seen his photo. Recoiled even. Had she met him personally? Maybe Maria had met Broekmann at Club VG. Perhaps she had started off there in the strip club and then moved on to the more serious business of De Wallen.

I sat at the desk and studied the bottle of Scotch, but only for a moment. Then I removed the foil and withdrew the cork, the squeak of the twist a comforting sound; the palatal click as the cork left the bottle was reassuring, and I breathed in the scent of Speyside as the golden liquid slid into the glass – woody and grassy, spicy and sweet. The first glug hit the roof of my mouth, the familiar sting lingering there.

The heat of the day was rising from the floors below and it was stifling in my room. I flung the windows wider to allow in cooler air and try to think. I pulled out my phone and noticed that I'd missed a call from an unknown number and considered it might be Bliek using some sort of burner phone to threaten me, ensure I back off. If he was in the pocket of Broekmann, who knew to what lengths he would go in order to stop me searching for the children.

But the missed call might have been from Billy.

I stared out at the night and the rippled reflection of the street lamps on the canal. What options had I now? The girl in De Wallen – Maria, if that was her real name – might help me, but at what risk to herself, and how much would she know? Would she keep the card with the information about CTM and be brave enough to seek help, and then be bold enough to give away Broekmann's gang? But when I considered what Eva had told me about girls ending up in the canal I shivered with guilt and foreboding.

Next to the whisky my phone vibrated and this time I picked up straight away.

'Hello?'

Silence at the other end. It was an unknown number like before.

'Hello? Who's calling, please?'

Whoever it was didn't want to say, so I knew it was important.

'This is Karen Hamm,' I said. 'Can I help you?'

Another slight pause and then, 'Is Billy, ma.'

He'd found the courage to ring.

'Billy. Are you ok?'

'I know about the kids from Salone,' he said rapidly, his voice low.

My heart rate quickened. He was taking a risk. How much could I get out of him before he hung up?

'What d'you know, Billy? What can you tell me about the kids?'

'The boy and the girl, from Salone.'

'Yes. Have you seen them? Can you tell me where they are?'

'No.'

'What is it you know, Billy? Why have you called me?'

'They not in Amsterdam.'

This was my fear – they had already left.

'They leave Holland,' he continued.

'Do you know where they've gone?'

There was a much longer pause and I feared he would hang up.

'Billy, are you still there? What is it you know?' I tried to keep the desperation out of my voice.

'They go in van with Albanians,' he said. 'They bad men.' Billy's voice was a bare whisper now and I imagined him hunched up somewhere, fearful of being overheard.

'Who are these Albanians? How do you know them?'

I had too many questions but this might be my only chance. It was three o'clock in the morning. What risk was he taking to get away from the club and make the call? And I wondered where he was, whether he was safe himself.

'Billy,' I soothed. 'Thanks for calling me. I'm so grateful. Can you say any more about the Albanians or where they might have taken the kids in the van?'

'They say they go Spain. They go last night.' His voice was quickening. 'They go with others in van to Spain.' Then the line went dead.

It was time to tell Eva about Billy.

． ． ．

A FEW HOURS later I called Eva. It was still early.

'We have to meet. Something's come up and I can't discuss it on the phone.'

'I'm not working today,' Eva replied. It was Sunday. 'We are running the Mizuno but come to the houseboat for ten o'clock. We don't have to leave until twelve.'

It took me twenty minutes to cycle south-west from Keizersgracht to the smart little neighbourhood of Schinkelbuurt where Eva lived with Mimi on a houseboat. I dumped the bike on a patch of grass and secured the wheel to the frame with a fiendishly difficult cable lock. Residents had landscaped the canal bank with colourful flowers and seating areas, and walkways linked their homes to the canal side. Most resembled regular houses, modern angular floating structures, but Eva's home was a traditional Dutch barge, the wheelhouse standing proud of the deck, two bicycles resting together in a floating garden overflowing with vegetables.

'Karen, come in.' Eva stood on deck in the sunshine dressed in lemon Lycra, a cup of tea in her hand. I boarded and she embraced me with one arm, inviting me into her water-bound home through the wheelhouse, which was overrun with red and white geraniums. I ducked my head and descended into the handcrafted galley with its granite worktops, polished wooden units, and shelves stacked with delftware. The living space beyond was spacious and light and furnished in soft upholstery. An attractive man sat on the couch drinking from a sky-blue mug, his eyes soft and warm over its rim. I eyed him suspiciously.

'Can I offer you some tea?' Eva asked.

Mimi was approaching in turquoise Lycra bearing a teapot and a mug with the 'Mizuno 2016' blue and red logo.

'What's the Mizuno?' I asked as she poured the tea, but really I was wondering about the man and when he would be leaving.

'It's a half marathon that we run here in Amsterdam,'

Mimi replied. 'We participate every year, raising money for the centre. We run through the city and finish at the Olympic Stadium just like real champions!' Mimi smiled broadly, tiny even teeth and deep dimples.

I eyed the man, probably in his thirties, light beard, dark brown hair flopping over his forehead, the same cobalt eyes as Mimi.

'Karen, let me introduce you to my brother, Finn der Weese,' said Mimi happily. I smiled and offered a greeting, but I was annoyed that Eva and I were not alone to discuss the important developments on the kids.

Maybe he read my mind because Finn der Weese rose from his spreadeagle. 'Actually, I'm just going,' he said with a smile. 'These ladies are tired of me, for sure.'

His voice had a deep timbre with a light Dutch accent, and when he stood up he stooped so his head wouldn't hit the skylight. Mimi muttered something in Dutch and kissed her brother on both cheeks. He extended a hand towards me, strong and warm.

'Good luck with your work,' he said, and I wondered what Eva and Mimi had been saying about me.

'Thanks,' I replied, thinking I should apologise for disturbing time with his sister, but it would not have been the truth. His long legs disappeared up the steps.

It was a stunning home, a steel vessel lined with polished wood, natural light pouring in from windows looking over the canal and roof lights that flooded the space with sunshine. Peruvian artefacts adorned the space: an alpaca poncho hung on the wall, colourful striped rugs were scattered on the floor, an Inca warrior statue carved from quartz and a number of brightly painted gourds displayed on shelves.

Eva sat me down among the vastness of the upholstery still warm from the weight of Finn der Weese.

'What's new?' she asked, sitting cross-legged on a

beanbag holding her cup in both hands and looking even tinier than her CTM self, her blonde hair stuck out wildly.

'There've been developments,' I said. 'I couldn't talk on the phone.'

'You've done the right thing,' she said. 'Let me have it.'

I decided to start with Maria and explained to Eva that I'd visited De Wallen and found a girl that I believed to have been trafficked by Broekmann.

'What do you mean, you believe she was trafficked by him?'

'She didn't say so directly, and of course she was frightened, but she recognised his photo.'

'And?'

'I gave her your details. Information about CTM. How you might help her.'

'Good. Did she say she needed help?'

'Not exactly.'

'Of course we can help,' she said patiently. 'But people need to come to us themselves. We can't go knocking on windows trying to rescue people. It's too dangerous for them. And, of course, some are OK with their situation. But if Maria comes to us we can protect her.'

'I hope she gets in touch ... but, Eva, last night I heard from Billy.'

'Billy? Remind me, please.'

But this was the first time I had mentioned Billy.

'Billy is a young man who works at Club VG, he is a waiter at the strip club. I met him when I was there and then I waited for him at closing time, but he wouldn't talk to me.'

Eva's usual neutral expression evaporated, and she looked at me with a fixed stare that suggested she knew what was coming. 'Why did you think this waiter would want to talk to you?'

'Because he is from Salone himself.'

Eva's eyebrows raised slightly. 'And you think, because of this, he knows where the children are?'

When she said it out loud, it did sound fanciful. Like something I only wished to be true. 'I gave him my card,' I continued. 'And I'd all but given up but then he called me last night.'

'And what has he told you?'

'That the kids are on their way to Spain in a van with other people, driven by some Albanians.'

Eva and Mimi exchanged glances.

'Karen, why didn't you tell me about Billy?' Eva asked.

'Because I knew you wouldn't want me to approach him,' I said. 'Not while he was working in such a difficult environment.'

'You would be correct in that assumption.'

But it was hard to reproach myself. I had been right about Billy. He could help me find the kids.

Mimi had been following our conversation. 'Male vulnerability to trafficking is not commonly appreciated,' she said seriously. 'But they are also at risk. People consider men to be perpetrators of trafficking rather than its victims, but more and more we find they suffer terribly at the hands of the gangs.' She glanced at Eva, and went on. 'Men and boys rarely self-identify as trafficked for obvious cultural reasons, especially if they have been sexually exploited. There is huge stigma around same-sex conduct in some cultures.'

Mimi's words exposed my prejudices. Perhaps I felt more empathy towards female victims of this horrible crime. Perhaps I believed men had more agency. Perhaps I was wrong.

'It was brave of Billy to call me,' I said. 'I don't know his exact situation at the club.'

'You can be sure it is not a happy one,' Eva replied pointedly.

'If he took the risk of calling me, he must be sure of his

facts. What's going on? Where in Spain could they be taking the children? Do you have intelligence on this route?'

Eva looked at Mimi who was nodding.

'Yes, we have,' she said. 'There are several known trafficking and smuggling routes to Spain from Amsterdam. Usually, the transfer of Europeans to southern Spain is for agricultural work at this time of year. Many nationalities work those greenhouses. People are brought from South America, North and West Africa also. The most frequent destination from here is to Almería and the polytunnels.'

'Polytunnels? What are these polytunnels?' I asked.

'Fruit and vegetable farms that operate under plastic on a peninsular near Almería. It's in southern Spain. Many of the workers are undocumented migrants and exploited by the gangs who have trafficked them there.'

'Do you think the children could have been taken there to work?'

'Well, no, I don't think so. This is Spain we're talking about, not West Africa. People don't get away with exploiting children right out in the open. That's too obvious. But if this van you talk about was also carrying others … you say this Billy saw others in the van? Then that would make more sense.'

'But why put the kids in the same van?'

'That, I can't answer you. Maybe they have domestic situations lined up for the kids. They could take them on from Almería or have even dropped them off somewhere on the way. And, of course, we don't know they have gone to Almería. There are plenty of other farms on the Costa del Sol that use migrant workers, official and unofficial.'

My heart was quickening. It was all guesswork, but at least now I had some kind of trail to follow. If only Billy had given me some details of the van.

As if she was reading my mind, Mimi asked, 'What do we know about the van?'

'Nothing,' I said. 'Billy hung up before I could ask any questions about it.'

'They could be moving drugs,' Mimi suggested, looking at Eva.

'I was thinking the same,' agreed Eva. 'It's likely Broekmann has drugs in his portfolio.'

'Could the children be involved in moving drugs?' I asked.

'It is possible,' she said. 'The Netherlands is an established entry point for drugs coming in from South America – cocaine, cannabis, and also ketamine from Lithuania – which goes for distribution around Europe. Kids are sometimes used as mules, but I have to say that something doesn't fit in this scenario.'

The three of us sat there thinking. So many questions, and no answers.

After a while, I said, 'All we know is that two days ago the kids were loaded into a van with other people, possibly migrant workers trafficked by the same gang. Broekmann's gang. For some reason, Billy knows this van is going to Spain. He was very clear about that. And you're telling me the most likely place in Spain is the polytunnels at Almería.'

The two women looked at me expectantly. Like there was only one way to find out.

SEVEN
THE GIRL

Twelve months earlier the girl had been living with her father Jacob and her mother Mariame in their remote village in the north-west region of Sierra Leone. They were well known in their community; Jacob was the medical doctor, and Mariame the head teacher of the district girls' high school. Their only child, a clever daughter, was destined for similar standing in the village.

The family lived together in a comfortable brick-built bungalow in Sumbufari, a community that lay thirty miles east of Kambia Town, the district capital, which was situated on the Great Scarcies River. The medical clinic was the only facility for miles around and Doctor Jacob ran the place with two newly qualified nurses. It was a single-storey building with a wrap-around veranda and a deep overhang that provided shade for patients who waited in the heat. People would travel vast distances with their sick family members strapped to their backs or slumped undignified in strong wooden barrows. The queue often looped right around the building and down the dusty track to the cluster of dura palms that grew at the gate.

Dr Jacob was always busy. The country had the lowest density of medical doctors in West Africa. Officially, his patients numbered forty thousand – if they were to be counted in a systematic fashion, which they were not because records got lost or were never filed, or people entitled to services did not register themselves but turned up on the veranda in an emergency when their traditional healers had failed them. So the number of patients in Jacob's charge was much higher than the official forty thousand.

He was a handsome man, kind and patient, a generous and effective practitioner who gave his patients comfort. They put their trust in him, even willing to endure the outcry when traditional healers discovered their ancient remedies had been spurned in favour of the modern doctor.

Jacob was married to Mariame, who had fallen in love with him when they met at a political rally in the provincial capital, Port Loko. Mariame was from the neighbouring French-speaking country of Guinea, but after the death of her father, her family had moved across the border so that her mother could marry again – a rich rice farmer in the bolilands of Sierra Leone. Mariame was a clever child who did well at school and university, progressing quickly, and becoming head teacher of the Kambia High School for the Education of Girls where her own daughter would join the ranks of the privileged few who were clever enough and rich enough to go there.

Life was good.

But that was before the sickness began.

Quicker than anyone expected, the Ebola virus crept its way across the border from Guinea, sliding its tentacles across the countryside, eventually devouring the whole nation. The virus raged for three years and thousands died a harrowing death before eventually the sickness started to burn itself out, the numbers of new infections dropping rapidly, deaths reducing every day.

For three years, Jacob had struggled to convince his patients, and had battled with traditional healers about how to treat the disease. He spent much of his time trying to persuade people to change the way they mourned their dead and conducted traditional burial rites. Bodies infected with Ebola were highly contagious and the community's historic rituals were incompatible with the safe procedures of the official Ebola teams that moved through the countryside in their white hooded coveralls and respiratory masks.

One day, after the death of a pregnant woman, overexcited mourners came to claim the body, determined to remove the foetus before the burial to save the woman from eternal wanderings, and from disturbing the natural cycles of the world. These were common beliefs and very powerful among rural folk, so Jacob had to find a solution. If the mourners proceeded with the burial, many more would be infected and die, so he set about finding a 'reparations ritual' – a way for the community to atone if the traditional burial could not be performed.

He asked around the villages and surrounding communities and eventually found an elderly gentleman who knew of such a reparation. It would require twelve yards of white tissue paper, salt and oil and rice, and the sacrificing of a goat, which the villagers were willing to accept as a solution to the problem. So, with her foetus still in her womb, their deceased relative was buried by unknown sweltering workers dressed in sealed Tyvek suits.

This was the nature of Doctor Jacob. Close to the people.

It was just a matter of time before he caught the disease himself.

The fever started suddenly in the early hours and he knew straight away what it was, ordering Mariame from their bed, demanding he be isolated without delay. But it was only six days later that he died, and not long after that Mariame herself succumbed to the disease, leaving their only child an orphan.

IN THE CRAMPED interior of the van, the girl awoke to find the boy staring at her over a hunched shoulder. He was sitting under the vents, the weak slanting light illuminating his features, his body swaying as the vehicle moved steadily towards their unknown destination. The girl was drowsy, her head ached with a painful hum, and she was desperate for water, her body weak with dehydration.

She found she was slumped against someone and when she shifted her position realised that her hands had been tied. The woman mumbled something in her own language and tried to help by propping the girl into a seated position where she could rest against the side of the van. A water bottle was pressed against her lips and she gulped greedily, spluttering as it hit the back of her throat.

She lowered her gaze, not wanting to look at the foolish boy, Foday, who stared at her through the gloom.

'Stupid girl,' he hissed. 'Why you cause trouble?'

But she didn't answer.

Her attempt to escape in the mountains had not been well considered, she had to admit that herself. But how could she plan when she had no idea when her next opportunity might come? Foday himself was an expert in failed attempts and he had his own disasters to dwell on.

Before they left Freetown, they had been held in the same dilapidated house downtown and close to the barracks where the stench from open drains made them retch. The place had no furniture, no electricity and no water, and everyone slept together on dirty mats spread out on the concrete floor. For three days, they were stashed in the crumbling building, none of them sure where they were going, with whom and what for. But the girl was sure they were in for nasty surprises.

During the days they had spent waiting, one by one the other girls and women had been taken out by the guard, and when they returned they were crying, their clothes in disarray. But the man never came to take her, and the girl wondered why that might be. Every time the door opened, she feared she would be next, but she never was.

Foday tried to escape several times, on each occasion succeeding for only a few hours before he was rounded up, beaten, and returned to the house limping. The girl admired his spirit, but not his brains. His escapes were never planned. He just ran.

Foday had been picked up by the gang on the streets of Freetown where he had been begging for a different group who had abducted him weeks before from his village near Port Loko. His cousin, who was working for the first gang, had visited Foday's parents and convinced them to send the boy to the town for education and for work so that plenty of *leones* could flow back into their pockets and boost the family income. This was called *menpikin*: a way for their son to fulfil his obligations to his family. But really he was headed to a life of crime on the dangerous streets of Freetown.

When Foday was picked up by the second gang outside the courts of justice, the first gang started searching for him, convinced he had run away, while the second gang were intent on foiling his escapes. By staying awake all night and earwigging their conversations, Foday had learnt that he was to be a 'mule', travelling to Europe where someone would be waiting to receive the goods – diamonds – and once the merchandise was safely delivered, the boss would then decide what next to do with him. There were several possibilities for a strong and good-looking boy in Amsterdam, but in the end they had sent him in the van with the girl.

· · ·

THE TWO SAT BROODING, planning their next escape, each knowing that together they may fare better but pretending they were strong enough alone.

The van slowed and turned sharply, then came to a stop on rough ground. Doors slammed as the drivers got out, then they were speaking to others in a strange lispy language the girl did not recognise. Time passed. Voices raised, then lowered. When the doors opened, blinding light surged in and the travellers edged out, eager to stretch their limbs and discover what awaited them, hoping this would be their final destination.

The girl shuffled her haunches across the floor and followed the group into the blistering light and dusty heat where a bewildering scene awaited her. Spread out across the landscape a vast sea of silvery mirrors reflected the sun in a blinding glare – a bright mirage extending across endless fields, a low flat plain, and seeping up the valleys of the sparse and rocky hills.

Exhausted and diminished, they all stood gawking at the spectacle before them, dazzling in its brilliance. The man and wife from South America pressed together, clutching hands, uncertainty rising among the group like the early morning mist across the valleys. Valon elbowed among them, untying the girl's hands, then handing round bottles of water and packs of sandwiches while the second driver, Gëzim, stood a little way apart still negotiating a deal with the farmers.

The girl drank thirstily, taking stock of her surroundings. The silver-topped greenhouses were full of foliage and dark-skinned workers harvesting vegetables and loading them into low carts. From this she surmised she would be slaving in the plastic tunnels for those who had trafficked her here. But she could see no children working in the tunnels, only adults, nobody labouring who was as young as she.

Gëzim broke away from the farmers, an impassive expression upon his pasty face, his weak pencil moustache glistening with sweat. He ordered the travellers to retrieve their things from the van. The girl stayed put, her rucksack still set firmly on her shoulders, she wasn't getting back in that van. She hitched the bag protectively, grateful the journey had ended.

Everyone except the children and the two women from Côte d'Ivoire was ordered by Valon to follow the farmers to a nearby makeshift settlement that resembled a refugee camp. A twirl of acrid smoke snaked through the air above it.

Something was wrong.

A black Honda car parked near the van revved into life. Behind the wheel a man in a baseball cap was smoking a cigarette, his arm hanging loose out of the window. The girl eyed him warily and Foday started shifting foot to foot, seeming to sense trouble, his nerves on edge, seeking an opportunity to run. And this time, the girl would run with him.

Valon approached, slugging the dregs from a can of Coke. He opened the rear door of the Honda and gestured for the boy to get in. Foday hesitated, and Valon brought the weapon from his pocket.

'Get in car,' he snarled, waving the gun in a covert manner.

The boy moved hesitantly towards the car. His eyes were fixed on Valon's handgun. Would he be crazy enough to run when a weapon was aimed in his direction? The girl felt his indecisiveness, but she sensed that Valon would not use the gun. But it was too late and the boy was shoved onto the back seat, his bag thrown in after him, the door slammed shut.

Foday tugged at the handle, panic on his face. He struck the window, staring out at the girl who stared back. But the vehicle was already reversing, and the boy's anguished features soon disappeared in a cloud of dust rising behind the car.

Valon strode over to the three left standing.

'Get in van,' he said, grabbing the girl and hauling her across the dust after the women. She kicked out, fear rushing through her, forgetting the pain of this man's fist.

'Get in!' he repeated, tipping her over his shoulder then into the van like a rolled-up carpet. The doors banged closed behind her.

EIGHT
KAREN

I took the afternoon flight to Malaga, the closest airport to the industrial-sized farming project that was Almería. According to Billy, the van had left Amsterdam two days earlier and the distance by road was 1,500 miles, which I figured was twenty-two hours of continuous driving. If the children had been taken directly to Almería they could have arrived only hours before I landed at Malaga. This prospect spurred me on.

I hired a Fiat Punto at the airport and headed east towards Murcia along the busy A7, the ancient Mediterranean highway that ran down the Costa del Sol. Crumbling stone watchtowers marked the route, defences that had stood on the sands for millennia. On my right, the azure of the Mediterranean sea and to my left, the hills of the Sierra Nevada. Down the central reservation of the highway, pink oleander flowered vibrantly, lifting my spirits as I drove steadily east towards Almería.

After two hours, small islands of plastic started to appear in the arid scrubland on one side of the road marking the spot of isolated farms, but soon the white carpet grew to cover either side of the highway – regimented rows of polytunnels on the rocky, arid landscape.

Turning off at a signpost to Almerimar, I was soon among the maze of tracks that criss-crossed the low acres of white plastic, miles after miles of it, broken up by the occasional patch of wasteland or small copse of palms.

Once in the maze it was hard to get a sense of scale, except that every turn presented a similar vista. Polytunnel after shimmering polytunnel, interspersed with bland concrete buildings graffitied with the words *plastico* or *rights for workers*, and patches of dry, rocky scrubland that marked the boundaries of individual farms.

I switched off the AC and wound down the windows, slowing my pace so I could better understand the landscape, breathing in the hot dry air of southern Spain. In the polytunnels, where the plastic was stretched over vast metal frames, I could see workers labouring in lush lines of foliage, women in hijabs were bent low harvesting the fruit and vegetables, placing them carefully in red plastic crates balanced on green trolleys.

Beyond the polytunnels the barren, parched ground was littered with shanty-style migrant camps: *chabolas*. People were milling around the camps so I parked the Fiat under a spindly pine and went in search of someone who might speak English.

A group of men stood smoking by a sloping telegraph pole, but they ignored my attempts to communicate, chatting only among themselves. I ventured to the camp behind them, but no one there spoke English. At the second camp, a middle-aged man told me he was from Guatemala. When I said I was looking for two African children he directed me to a bunch of lads seated on crates beside a black cooking pot set on rocks over a fire. They were from Ghana.

'I'm searching for a boy and a girl from Sierra Leone,' I started. 'They may have arrived today. Do you know of any children in the camp or working on the farms?'

A man in a striped shirt smoking a pipe said, 'No kids work on the farms. Why asking?'

I showed him the photo of the children. 'These are the children I'm looking for. Have you seen them?'

'The kids in this camp are with their parents,' he said. 'They don't work in tunnels.'

As if on cue, a woman walked past with babe in arms.

The man looked at the photo, but I could tell he wasn't interested. He shrugged his shoulders and passed it to the others.

'Kids don't work in tunnels,' he repeated. 'Is illegal here.'

The other men shook their heads and returned the phone to me.

I pressed on. 'They travelled in a van with others. Men and women coming to work on the farms here in Almería.'

'Try another camp,' the man with the pipe suggested, then turned his back to chat to his friends.

I got back in the car and moved north again, away from the coast and back through the lanes of polytunnels towards the A7 where there was a greater concentration of camps and perhaps people more willing to talk. But three hours later, the story was still the same. Nobody brought kids to work on the farms, and nobody had seen the children I was seeking.

The people I found living in the shanties were undocumented migrants whose papers had been confiscated by the gangs trafficking them to Almería. They were caught in the same trap as the girls in Amsterdam, owing criminal gangs for the cost of their transportation and therefore bound by debt, working to pay off a random sum that never seemed to get any smaller. Without documents, they couldn't rent proper homes, but the wages were so low, and the gangs took such a cut, they couldn't afford decent homes anyway. So they had to make do living like refugees.

. . .

IT WAS GETTING dark so I checked myself into the Maribel Hotel in Roquetas de Mar, a small town squeezed between the plastic farms and the Mediterranean Sea. The hotel was located down a cobbled alley that opened onto a small square dominated by an eighteenth-century church. The Maribel Hotel was a tatty building with dirty striped awnings jutting out above the windows and a neon-lit café bar where elderly men drank coffee and played cards at a table on the street. I woke the sleepy man behind the bar and he jotted down my details and handed me a key.

Despondent after hours of hopeless searching, I threw my belongings on the bed and lay down next to them. I would try again the following day. There were plenty of migrant camps to explore and I wasn't going to stop until I had visited every one of them. What else could I do?

I slept badly and at four in the morning decided to phone Graham, a chronic insomniac, who I knew would be awake and thinking I was still in Amsterdam.

'It's me.'

'Aren't you sleeping?' His voice was tight. 'Are you ok?'

I could hear the soulful trumpet of Miles Davies in the background.

'Yes, I'm ok,' I said. 'Just thought I'd let you know I've moved from Amsterdam and am now in southern Spain.'

'You're following the kids?'

Since our last call so much had happened. If Graham knew how hopeless the situation had become after the raid on Lang Huis, and the threat from Lucas Bliek, he would want to know why I wasn't making my way straight back home. He had a clear and analytical mind, unencumbered by emotions, and, in the past, it had been good to share work challenges. But he worried incessantly, often unnecessarily, and I had to consider carefully just how much information I could give him. This time I had my own anxiety to manage.

'Yes, I'm following the kids,' I replied. 'I think Broekmann's gang has moved them to Spain, possibly to the farms in Almería.'

'How do you know that?'

I explained about Eva Taal and her organisation, CTM, that they specialised in support of trafficked people and that I was working closely with her, a truth I knew would reassure him. But there was plenty I didn't want to share. Like how I'd met Billy at Club VG and how I'd met Maria in De Wallen. So I summarised the situation, making a big thing of Eva so that he wouldn't worry I was working alone.

'The information about the transfer of the kids to Spain has come from Eva,' I lied. 'In fact, the route from Amsterdam to Almería is known to them.'

'What about this guy at the Dutch police?' Graham asked. 'Bliek.'

'Yes, I think he's corrupt,' I said, thinking I could mention Lang Huis in a vague third-party kind of way.

'Have you new evidence?'

'Well, CTM organised a raid on some flats they'd been watching which they thought were being used as holding spaces for trafficked people. It was all set up … the raid. But when the special forces teams arrived, the flats had been emptied and everyone was gone.'

'What's that got to do with Bliek?'

'It was too much of a coincidence,' I explained. 'He was there, at the flats, supervising the raid. I think it's possible he tipped them off.'

'He won't be the only corrupt officer in the force.'

'That's probably true,' I agreed.

'And this Eva person,' asked Graham, 'what did you say her name was?'

'Taal.'

'This Eva Taal, she has her suspicions about Bliek?'

'Er … no,' I said truthfully. 'Not really.'

Now I was tired and the conversation was getting awkward.

'Were you at the raid yourself?' It was a guess.

'Of course not.'

There was a short silence while Graham processed the lie.

'That would have been foolish,' he said. 'If Bliek had seen you, he would know that you would work it out.'

'I guess.'

I was too exhausted to continue the conversation. I knew I'd made a big mistake when I told Bliek I had a photo of the children and the priest. It was an idiotic thing to do when I already had my suspicions about him, and I was glad to be out of Amsterdam.

'Look, Gray, I'm really tired. I'm going to sign off now and try and get some sleep.'

'OK,' he said.

'I just wanted to let you know where I am. I'll continue searching the camps tomorrow. It's all I can do. Unless I get another lead, I'm stuck here in Almería.'

We hung up.

I lay in a sweat, thinking about Bliek. Maybe I was overreacting because Eva Taal was relaxed about him and Graham wasn't convinced either. Which was good because the last thing I wanted was Graham thinking he should get involved. He had always been supportive, but this was my own vendetta with Broekmann.

I stared at my phone, willing Billy to call again.

I DREAMT AGAIN OF SONGOLA. But this time it was different.

This time I was back in Freetown and bartering in the crowded Big Makit where traditional artefacts were sold at high prices to tourists. I was after an ancestral mask of the Sowei spirit, the kind used by the Sande Society, which instructed girls through rites of passage into womanhood. The society was clothed in secrecy, its enigmas known only to those who were allowed inside its hidden spaces, deep in the forests.

The spirit mask I wanted to buy was made of mahogany, its surface blackened with traces of ancient rituals performed long ago. It was sleek and luminous with a full head of hair. The face was a woman's, the forehead bulbous and prominent, the features tiny in comparison: a small, pursed mouth, the nose delicate and sharp, the eyes, with their lower lids half closed, appearing like bottomless slits.

For a reason unknown to me, I had to have the mask and I was bartering hard with the vendor, a faceless man with white hair.

The Big Makit was crowded with tourists, vendors, hawkers, and market women, the din deafening, the suffocating heat pressing down against our sweaty bodies. Eventually, a price was agreed, but when I reached to pick up the mask, its eyes were open and staring past me at something behind.

Turning, I saw her in the crowd, motionless, watching me – everybody else going about their business, brushing past her, unseeing.

It was Songola.

A hint of a smile crossed her face, but her eyes were vacant. I dropped my bags. There was a buzzing in my ears and a lightness in my head, and when she turned to go, I followed. She kept some distance away and I trailed her denim jacket and braided cornrows, moving quickly, elbowing people aside, desperate to touch her and know that she was real. She left the market on the south side, moving down in the direction of Government Wharf and slipping in and out of view. I was concerned I would lose her as she reappeared briefly only to vanish again in the crowd.

Songola was moving as though time was running out, her steps quickening, and I struggled to keep up with her fast strides. She was heading towards the Old Wharf Steps and I followed, reckless as I ran down the uneven eighteenth-century stones, broken and overgrown with weeds, a long flight leading down to the harbour. But when I reached the bottom she was gone, melted away into the mist of the estuary, only water from the Sierra River lapping against the edge of the ancient Freedom Steps.

It was a disturbing dream and I wondered at its meaning. The Sande Society was a secret group among the Mende people of Sierra Leone where girls spent long periods of seclusion for their 'initiation' into womanhood. No outsider was allowed to know what went on in the camps, which were hidden deep in the bush.

A sense of foreboding touched my skin, the hairs rising, a shiver running down my spine ... the Sowei mask and its bottomless eyes staring past me.

I knew there wasn't much time. I had to find those children.

I skipped breakfast, picked up the Fiat, and drove to the camps along the coastal road with my foot against the floor, all the while feeling them slipping away, like innocents on a raft caught in a current that was moving steadily on towards the endless ocean.

NINE
KAREN

Arriving early at the plastic city, I was hoping to catch workers before they left the *chabolas* to start work in the poly-tunnels. I moved from shack to shack, showing the photo of the children, seeking out the English speakers. The camps were difficult to see from the road, hidden behind ugly, graffi-tied buildings or nestled in sparse copses of pine and juniper, some even wedged between the farms – dwellings made of cardboard, wooden pallets and discarded plastic sheeting. Conditions were squalid and unsanitary. I hurried from place to place but no one had seen the children.

I entered a settlement built of cement and tarpaulins, and set on an arid patch of wasteland close to the busy A7. Only a few workers remained in the camp but they directed towards a man called Pedro who was collecting peoples' testi-monies about their experiences in the *chabolas*. He was from a local organisation agitating for better living conditions in the camps, lobbying a disinterested government to respect the workers' rights. Pedro's job was to visit the *chabolas*, take statements from the workers, and advocate on their behalf.

I showed him the photo and he stared at it.

'No, I haven't seen them,' he said. 'Although many

migrant workers here have come from Africa. There is a collective of African workers here in Almería.'

'But these children …' I shoved the photo back in front of him.

'They are too young to work on these farms,' he said emphatically. 'Our authorities are very strict about child labour. I'm sorry, but you won't find them here.'

Undeterred, I decided to come back at the end of the day and talk to more people as they returned from work.

Back at the Maribel hotel, I put in a call to Eva. 'Nothing yet,' I said. 'What if the van has gone somewhere else?'

'Don't give up,' she said enthusiastically. 'We are keeping our attention on the flats at Lang Huis. Surveillance will inform us if a van comes back to the parking lot. They may make a return journey with different people or goods.'

'Drugs, you mean?'

'Yes, we are thinking of drugs. These gangs deal in everything. It's possible Broekmann exchanges the kids for contraband.' At least now CTM were taking Broekmann seriously. 'Keep going,' she said. 'Maybe someone in Almería knows something of Broekmann's gang.'

She hung up.

Later, I ventured out to Roquetas de Mar's small marina, walking across the solid sandstone promenade lined with palms, their fronds rustling in a steadily increasing breeze. I bought a bottle of beer from a street-front café and sat watching yachts bobbing at their moorings, wondering if the children had been transferred to a boat. Maybe I might see them walking the promenade.

But I was kidding myself, and despondency descended.

Locals were emerging from the siesta. Dusk would soon be falling. The light was changing across the little harbour, the sun's weakening rays slanting out across the choppy sea that churned as a steady westerly breeze whipped up the waves. It was time to return to my hotel and get some sleep. Maybe tomorrow there would be a breakthrough.

The wail of sirens started up somewhere in the distance and soon two fire engines hurtled down the waterfront, moving south on their way out of town, the officers inside buttoning up their jackets. A police car closely followed. I crossed the harbour road and made my way back through the alleys now bustling with people, past small boutiques and cheap tourist shops, bars with customers spilling out, and little cafés whose patrons were setting up tables for the evening trade.

Back at the hotel the AC in my room had given up and the heat was stifling. All afternoon the westerly facing room had been baking in the sun's hot rays. I moved to draw the curtains and, in the fading light, I noticed a column of black smoke rising above the plastic city.

I took the stairs two at a time into the lobby, out the front, and down the cobbles to where the Fiat was parked in a bay beneath the seafront palms. An acrid stench was making its way from the polytunnels towards the harbour on the stiffening breeze. I drove towards the fire as quickly as the town's irritating one-way system would allow. Was it a farm or was it a *chabola*?

When I got there, the lanes between the farms were heavily congested. Curious people were walking towards the blaze between rows of opaque white greenhouses that loomed like ghosts in the twilight. One of the *chabolas* was alight. I ditched the Fiat and headed towards the blaze with the crowd of onlookers, covering our mouths against the choking stench of burning plastic, and hearing the occasional blast from exploding canisters. I stood with the others behind the police tapes, officers encouraging us to disperse and go back to places of safety. But people wanted to know what was going on; many of them were residents of the *chabola* themselves.

The fire had spread quickly through the flimsy, uber-combustible dwellings. People's meagre belongings were incinerated in seconds, gas canisters exploding all over the camp, great whooshes of air sucked in by the flames. People stood helpless behind the tapes.

THE NEXT MORNING I returned to find the camp a bleak pile of cinders beneath a cloudless Mediterranean sky, the trees nearby charred and smouldering, the damp odour of inciner-ated garbage clinging to the air. People who had slept in the lanes had emerged to assess their losses, carefully picking their way through the debris, trying to salvage what they could now there was light enough to comprehend the destruction. To my eye, there was nothing left – but a cooking pot here, a metal bed frame there, workers were finding some remnants of their lives.

Pedro, who I had met the day before, was moving around the camp assisting where he could. He came over when he saw me in the lane.

I greeted him. 'Pedro, what a terrible night.'

'This happen all the time. We agitate for better conditions.' He shrugged miserably. 'Sometimes it seems we go backwards.'

We stood observing the steaming pile of blackened dust.

Then he said unexpectedly, 'Some peoples arrive two days ago. Maybe they know about the childrens.'

'Here? In this camp?' I asked excitedly.

'Sí. I speak to them moments ago.'

'Where? Who? Can you take me to them?'

'Please. You wait here.' And he wandered off.

Hope was rising like the smoke from the ruined camp.

He soon returned with a man and woman of middle age who were carrying backpacks and other sparse belongings.

'They arrive in the camp two days ago with other

peoples,' Pedro said. 'They are from Honduras but they dock in Amsterdam before they come here.'

The couple by his side looked weary but resilient, the man, thin and diminutive with a patchy moustache and prominent incisors, his wife more sturdy, her grey hair pulled back off her face with a taught rubber band.

They looked at Pedro, then at me.

'I'm sorry about the fire at your camp,' I said. They were silent. It seemed an inappropriate moment to be interrogating them.

'They speak only Spanish,' said Pedro.

'No hablo Inglés,' confirmed the man.

'Can you ask them if they came to Almería direct from Amsterdam?'

The couple nodded their heads guardedly.

My heart was thumping in my chest. 'Who were they travelling with? Did they travel in the van with these children?'

I reached in my bag for the phone and showed them the photo of the kids. Pedro tried to reassure them, explaining I wanted to help the kids and that I wasn't interested in their situation as illegals. They took the phone warily and discussed in low voices between themselves. There was nodding of heads before they spoke to Pedro who they seemed to trust.

'Were they with you?' I asked.

Pedro confirmed that, yes, the children had travelled in the back of a van with the couple from Honduras. My heart soared with hopefulness.

The woman put her wrists together and said something to Pedro, explaining that the girl had caused trouble and the gang had tied her.

'Please ask them where she is now,' I said, trying to control the rise in my voice.

'Dónde está la chica?' asked Pedro.

I watched their faces as they spoke to Pedro in their native language, shaking their heads gravely and pointing towards the A7.

'What did they say?' I asked impatiently.

'The kids are not here,' he said. 'Many came in the van but not all stay in Almería. They say the girl was put back in the van. The boy, he went away in a car.'

I was appalled. Grateful. Confused. These people had so much information.

'Where have they taken them?' I asked.

But the couple didn't know where the van was headed, or where the car was taking the boy. It was then I realised that my challenge had doubled because the girl and the boy had now headed in different directions.

The Honduran woman was still talking to Pedro.

'The girl went in the van with two African womens,' he said, still looking at the lady from Honduras.

'African women? Who were these women?'

Pedro seemed a bit irritated by my tone, but the Honduran woman was now running her hand round and round her face.

'Please,' said Pedro. 'These workers have suffered much trauma.'

'I'm sorry,' I said. 'Please tell them I just want to help the children.' But I didn't feel sorry. I wanted all the information they could give me.

'The womens who went with the girl,' said Pedro. 'They are young, beautiful. They speak only French.'

French African. My mind was racing, but the Honduran couple wanted to move on.

'Wait! Please! Can you tell me anything about the van?' And to Pedro, 'Maybe they can remember the colour or something.'

'Háblame de la furgoneta. De qué color era?'

The couple shrugged. 'Blanco,' was all they replied.

• • •

I DROVE BACK along the coast towards the hotel. What an immense breakthrough it had been, but I was still in a quandary with no way of knowing where the van might have headed. And now the children had been split up, the girl in the van going one way and the boy in a car that could be headed in the opposite direction. The Honduran couple seemed reliable witnesses, arriving in Amsterdam with promises of a better life and transferring to Almería. I'd shown them the photo of Broekmann, but they said they didn't recognise him, and they didn't know anything about the travellers in the van who had also stayed in Almería. I needed to get a call in to Eva to update her and tell her that at least we knew the van was white and that the children had been at the polytunnels.

But before I could do so, Eva's number lit up.

'Karen, I have more information on the van.'

'You have?' I assumed the vehicle had returned to the parking lot at Lang Huis.

'We have a photo and a clear view of the plate.'

I braked heavily and pulled over.

'A photo?'

'There is much good news, Karen.' Eva's voice was calm and steady. 'You did good work. Maria has come to us … your girl from De Wallen. She walked in the door only a few hours ago.'

'And she has a photo of the van?' I was dumbfounded.

'Not her, but her mother,' said Eva. 'When she left Albania, Maria took a selfie to send to her mother to reassure her. The van is in the background of the selfie.'

'She sent this photo to her mother?'

'Yes. We have been able to put her back in touch. Maria is only eighteen.'

What courage it must have taken for Maria to walk into CTM seeking refuge. I felt humbled by her actions. She was barely more than a child herself.

'The gang took her phone and all her documents,' Eva was saying. 'But of course, the photo is still on her mother's phone.'

'Tell me about the van,' I said. 'How do we know Maria's van is the same one that took the children and the others to Almería?'

'It's a white van with black … I think what they call side-skirts, and a big dint in the back where someone reversed into something. We have the registration number.'

'Yes, but how do we know it's the same van?' I repeated.

'Because we are working with traffic police and Europol surveillance. We're tracking it.'

My heart was racing. This was it. 'It's been spotted in Almería?'

'We have recent footage of the van on the A7, close to Almería, and then travelling all the way to Tarifa where it boarded the ferry crossing to Tangier.'

A hard lump settled in my chest.

'When was this, Eva?'

'Thirty-six hours ago,' she said. 'And now it has just disembarked on the return trip. The authorities are ready to pick it up as we are speaking.'

It had unloaded its cargo in Morocco. Wouldn't it have been easier to take the girl straight there rather than a detour via the Netherlands? What was so important about Amsterdam?

'I'll let you know what they find.' Eva was still talking but I had started the Fiat's engine and was already on my way back to the hotel to pick up my things. The decision had been made for me. I would follow the trail of the girl, not the boy. I needed to see what was hidden in the back of that van, the one that had travelled from Albania to Amsterdam, then south across France and Spain to Almería and then on to Tangier with the girl. What had been the exchange? And where had they left her?

Tarifa port. A four-hour drive south from Almería.

TEN
THE GIRL

The white van with the black skirts edged forward in the queue waiting to board the ferry to Tangier. The two men were arguing between themselves, tired and irritable; their patience had been tested by the troublesome girl and the atmosphere was tense.

Gëzim – the younger and shorter of the two, pale complexion, black studs in each lobe – was the one in control. He realised when he first met Valon in Albania that he, Gëzim, would be making the decisions. Although he was new to the gang, Gëzim had much experience moving whores around Romania and was ambitious. Already, he was eyeing the possibility of going it alone now the Balkans route had closed to refugees making their way to Western Europe from all the war-torn shitholes of the world. Business was picking up. Since the closure of the borders, the only way people could cross them was with the help of people smugglers like him, and he warmed at the prospect of these new opportunities. They would help him build his business and get rich.

Gëzim was the kind of man who was always in control. Whatever difficulties arose in the tricky business of people smuggling, he knew how important it was to appear in command, to show self-restraint and to demonstrate to others that he knew what he was doing. And he prided himself on this quality.

As a child he had suffered from an embarrassing tic – quite pronounced, like an electric current running across his cheekbone that made people think he was winking. It used to spasm violently and was an unfortunate malady for someone in his profession, but over the years he had mastered its control and the worst it got nowadays was a vague flutter that tickled his skin. Any sign of weakness was bad for business; he had the lives of nervous people in his hands. They skittered easily, and it was his job to build their trust and keep them passive.

Gëzim's professionalism, his calm ruthlessness and imperturbable qualities had already been recognised by the boss who had rewarded him with greater responsibility. Like getting that difficult girl to Tangier. They had been warned the stakes were high but they had yet to find out why. All Gëzim knew was that shit would happen if she didn't arrive on time and in perfect condition.

But now he was stuck with the impulsive and violent idiot Valon who was not the right man for a tricky job like this.

Gëzim drew a long drag from his cigarette and blew the smoke out of the window.

'We should tie them all!' blurted Valon, who was slapping a nervous rhythm on the dashboard with the palm of his long slender hand. Spittle had collected at the corners of his mouth and his mulish face was stubbled with beard. A highly strung fellow, Valon, even more nervous since the incident in the mountains. They'd got lucky then.

Gëzim's small grey eyes stared through the windscreen, expressionless and in control.

'It is only the girl who makes trouble,' he replied. 'No need to tie them all.'

'But how do we know she won't influence the others?'

'Because they think they know where they are going. The girl … she does not know.' Gëzim spoke slowly and deliberately to get through Valon's thick skull.

He took a final drag before stubbing out on the dash and flicking the cigarette through the window. The lorry in front belched a cloud of dirty fumes and made a quick run at the ramp onto the ferry.

'I don't trust her,' persisted Valon, even though he had tied her hands and feet for the short crossing over the Strait.

Gëzim pushed the van into gear and edged up the ramp onto the car deck.

'Don't worry,' he said. 'Soon she is no problem for us.'

There had been no vehicle checks at border control. The pair had only to show their green card and personal documents, and hadn't needed the bribe, which Gëzim pocketed for himself. The risk of the van being searched at the Spanish end was now behind them. It was unlikely they'd have trouble on the other side. The boss had friends in ports all over the world.

On the vessel's car deck, men in fluorescent tabards were directing vehicles into tight spots, edging them bumper to bumper, and the van drew up behind the lorry, a people carrier nudging up behind them.

The two men exited from the same side, Valon catching his legs on the stick, swearing as he tripped out of the door. Locking the van, he checked the vehicle was secure and threw a tarpaulin over the roof so fumes from the deck wouldn't enter the vents and poison the women inside. Then he climbed the clanky metal steps after Gëzim, the throb of the ship's engines vibrating through the handrails.

On the passenger deck, the men bought beers and browsed the gift shop for souvenirs they did not want before they settled down in comfortable airline seats of cornflower blue. The sea was calm, and a sultry haze hung over the Moroccan coastline.

'I don't trust the girl,' Valon laboured, his dark eyes hot with fear, the dangling crucifix quivering from his ear. He took a long draught from the bottle. He had heard of traffickers ending up in the Oosterdok for lost or damaged cargo, and the more he thought about that, the more the panic grew. He'd never learnt to swim. What a terrible death.

'Fuck. Shut your mouth,' Gëzim said, tired of the man's ranting. He rested his head back against the seat, his eyes pale, like water under ice. 'What can she do?'

'But the others,' Valon persisted. 'If they remove the rags someone will hear screaming and will come to see.'

'Asshole,' hissed Gëzim. 'The women are illegals with no papers. They won't help the girl. And how do they know they are even on the water, or that for sure we are no longer in the van?'

Silence settled between them as the ferry pulled away and headed across the narrow channel towards North Africa.

'Why is she so special?' Valon asked after a while.

'Who?' Gëzim was drowsy, almost asleep after all those uncomfortable miles in the van.

'The girl. Why can we touch the others but not her?'

'Who gives a shit. By tomorrow she is gone and we are back on the road to Spain.' But Gëzim wanted to know the answer to that question himself.

He rose to make his way to the bathroom, the tic under his eye starting to quiver.

He stood urinating with the roll of the ship, wondering how he could find out more about the girl. She was young, smart and very pretty. Worth a lot of money if a sale was the objective. And Gëzim wanted to know who was buying.

THE ONLY CHINK of light coming through the vents was suddenly extinguished. After hundreds of miles of gloom, with just a glimmer of illumination to delineate night from day, there was now complete darkness in the back of the van.

The women began to panic, moving quickly towards the spot where the light once was, while trying to avoid the girl on the floor, then groping through the slits to find out what was obscuring the vents. But the obstruction could not be dislodged from inside. They would have to wait until the men returned.

The girl, her hands and feet bound and a roll of rags in her mouth, lay still on the floor. The women settled down beside her, holding each other's hands for comfort and noticing that the steel walls of the van were trembling, a sensation of tilting and rolling, the unmistakable rise and fall of the ocean. A sea crossing.

Their journey had taken much longer than the women expected. They were on their way to a better life in the UK but when the van stopped at Almería it didn't feel like the right place for a sea crossing to England.

They had met the smuggler in Côte d'Ivoire who had assured them that professional families were waiting for women just like them to cook and clean and look after their kids. Doctors, lawyers, engineers. Clever people with big money incomes, grand homes, and special quarters for their domestic staff. They would even eat their meals at the family table. There would be educational opportunities, too. Back home in Côte d'Ivoire, neither had finished primary school, but in the UK they would learn English while working as domestics and paying back the vast sums they had borrowed for their transfer to Europe.

Despite their new fears, the women were hopeful. This vessel could still be taking them across the sea to England. But an uneasy dread was creeping in.

The women did not like the troublesome girl who lay quiet on the floor, and they were glad when Valon bound her. Especially now they knew they were on the ocean. The authorities must not open the doors and send them home as illegals.

Even so, they kept a check on the child. The men had filled her mouth with rags to keep her quiet and had bound her limbs to stop her kicking against the side of the van. But the women realised that the gag may now be affecting her ability to breathe in the slowly diminishing supply of air.

One of them leant over the child and listened closely at her nostrils, placing a hand on her chest to feel the rise and fall of her lungs.

'Elle va bien,' she confirmed to her friend. Still alive.

Soon, the ship's engines made a different sound, the tone dropping dramatically, the clanking of chains and the scraping of metal echoing through the deck. They were docking. The women could hear passengers returning to their vehicles, slamming doors, starting up engines, the noise in the steel chamber getting louder. Perhaps they should check the girl again.

Groping in the dark, they felt for the rise and fall of her chest, but this time there was no movement – the women themselves were beginning to feel a little faint. As they knelt over the child, panic started to rise in their throats. Desperately, they clawed at the rags in her mouth, unfastening the tie that secured them, clearing her airways, pressing at her chest. But the girl remained limp.

Light suddenly entered the vents, the door banged shut and the vehicle rocked with the weight of the drivers. The engine fired up and the vehicle edged off while the women slapped frantically on the thin steel panel that separated them from the drivers, pounding their fists as the van shuddered down the ramp and onto the dock.

THE VAN TURNED onto a patch of wasteland at Tangier Ville where construction was underway to form a new terminal that would accommodate the new monster cruise liners. Cranes and shipping containers littered the site, excavators and dumper trucks moving to and fro in sequenced choreography.

Gëzim figured it would be a good place to stop, open the doors, and see who was banging in the back, so Valon turned in, a cloud of dust lifting as the vehicle came to a halt when he jerked the handbrake aggressively.

'Is the girl!' he said defiantly, leaving the door open as he scuttled round the back, his powerful shoulders tensed, ready for the fight.

Gëzim followed with the keys and fumbled with the locks, unease upon him, his tic reacting in a determined quiver. The light flooded in and the women shielded their eyes, gasping for air, hardly able to speak.

'What the fuck you doing?' yelled Valon, grabbing the throat of one of the hysterical women while Gëzim moved in to check the figure on the floor.

'Shit.'

He brought out an army knife and cut the cable ties around her wrists and ankles. Bending low, he brought his ear close to her face, then the back of his hand to her nose, ordering the women to hush, like the touch of the girl's breath was dependent on their silence. He felt no breathing. Then he placed two fingers to the side of her neck and felt no pulse.

Working quickly, he rearranged her body flat on her back, arms splayed, stacking his hands on her chest, pumping rhythmically, wondering if this would work on one so young.

He stopped to listen for her breath as a fresh movement of air travelling across the harbour from the Atlantic pushed in through the doors. Jagged sounds from the construction site stabbed at the air in intermittent bursts and, when they quietened, mournful notes from the muezzin washed across the city.

The girl's chest swelled and she jerked upright, coughing

violently, retching in staccato convulsions that splattered Gëzim's clothing with globs of acrid vomit. Cursing, he encouraged her onto her side and into the recovery position. The women crossed themselves in sanctification, muttering prayers of gratitude into their open palms.

'I said she was trouble,' Valon crowed.

'You are the fuck who stuff her mouth,' Gëzim replied in a low voice and with an icy grey stare, the other man sensing his power. 'We lucky she not dead.'

The girl's eyes opened and Gëzim lifted her head to offer sips of water in a gentle gesture that surprised even himself. Realising his proximity she grabbed the bottle and shuffled away, holding it against her chest, taking small draughts, gradually awakening to the drama she had missed.

'Ok?' Gëzim asked, but she turned her head and curled into a ball. 'Let's go,' he ordered, indicating that Valon should drive while he stayed in the back with the girl.

They lurched off, the vehicle making its way into the evening traffic where a slow-moving caravan of trucks, donkeys, carts and buses encircled the old city like a protective arm. Tangier. Its medina stood bronzed and medieval against the sun's horizontal rays, its high fortified walls washed in the buttery light of the dipping Moroccan sun.

ELEVEN
THE GIRL

It was late in the evening when the van crept through the great Bab Kasbah and into the medina for the drop. They parked in a quiet square under a jacaranda tree, positioning the vehicle so the rear doors were concealed from the street and pointing in the direction of the narrow alleys. Gëzim was first to unload. He would have to carry the girl, still weak from her ordeal.

They had made a diversion to the city's new town to wait until the child had recovered enough to be presented at the hammam. Something about her unnerved Gëzim, the way she looked his way from under her lids as though she still had a plan that would foil him. She never spoke, but he knew how busy her mind was. But very soon she would no longer be his problem.

Gëzim's anger with Valon had deepened after the business with the gag. If Gëzim informed the boss, for sure Valon would end up in the Oosterdok – a deep dock among the canals of Amsterdam where bodies could be reliably sunk. But Gëzim would have to consider this carefully. If he told the boss the full story, it would reflect badly on him and he had no intention of ending up in the Oosterdok himself. He would have to construct a different story to explain the girl's weakened condition. At least now she could stand upright. But he had his answers ready if madame asked awkward questions – it had been an onerous journey from Amsterdam, and the girl had been weakened from some tropical disease picked up in her own country.

Satisfied with his story, Gëzim slung the girl over his shoulder, grabbed her rucksack, and headed off with Valon close behind, herding the women and their belongings down a complicated network of interconnecting alleys lit by lanterns that were set on the ground. The men knew the way. They had been here before.

Nearing the kasbah, the group veered off down a narrow path that opened into a small courtyard where neatly clipped lemon trees grew. A cedar door elaborately carved with Arabic script was set into an otherwise featureless wall and standing by was a man dressed in a black hooded *thobe*, his well-developed muscles stretching the thin cloth.

Gëzim set the girl unsteadily on her feet and rapped on the cedar door. Moments later, the spy hole slid to one side, then slapped quickly back, and the door was opened by a teenage boy wearing a turquoise djellaba and an embroidered white skullcap. He ushered them in, indicating that they remove their shoes and store them in a rack with other pairs of footwear: expensive trainers, leather brogues, colourful pointy-toed *babouches*. Then the boy led the group to a bijou inner courtyard where the heavy scent of jasmine infused the air.

'Wait here,' the boy said. 'She comes now.'

He moved silently under an arch of weeping figs and down a dimly lit passage, at the end of which he ascended a flight of steps tiled with blue mosaics. When he returned, he was followed by a striking but slow-moving woman who entered the room like the Queen of Sheba in an aura that was fragranced with almond oil. She wore a lavish purple kaftan with intricately embroidered panels running down each side, and an elaborately wound turban of amethyst silk.

Madame Toussaint.

The two men stood transfixed. They'd never met her before, but they knew of her reputation. Until now, they had always left the goods with the boy. Regular transactions were never handled by Madame Toussaint herself, but this delivery was special.

Madame was an intimidating-looking woman, tall and handsome, a voluptuous bosom atop a slender frame. Fine jewels hung from her ears and, from one shimmering lobe, an old puckered scar ran diagonally across her throat to her larynx. Rumours were she was related to powerful people in North Africa and an aspect of authority seeped through her pores – a tangible threat that spread like a stain through Gëzim's fragile consciousness.

Unhurriedly, she approached the group. Ignoring the men, she turned her attention to the beauties from Côte d'Ivoire who stood anxiously holding hands, their belongings at their feet, and ran her expert gaze over them. Satisfied, she spoke to the boy and flicked her hand at him.

'Descendez les escaliers,' she said.

'Oui, madame,' he replied, and ushered the two women, who had travelled all the way from Côte d'Ivoire for a better life in England, through a set of heavy curtains and down a corridor to their vastly alternative futures.

It would be the last time the girl would ever see them.

Madame Toussaint turned her attention to Gëzim, noticing for the first time the foul stench emanating from his clothing.

'What is this disgusting …' she asked, testing the air with her chin. There was no denying the telltale acid stink that proceeded from Gëzim's person. He cursed the girl.

'Sorry, madame,' he mumbled, embarrassed but in control. 'The vessel …' But he wasn't allowed to finish. Madame Toussaint's interest was now set upon the girl.

'This is her?' she asked.

'Yes,' he continued hastily. 'We have taken good care of her as instructed.'

Madame looked sceptical and gently pulled the girl into a place where light from a wall lamp illuminated her face. She turned the child's chin this way and that, examining her pretty features, observing her slight frame, her small indistinguishable breasts.

Too young.

'She speaks English, yes?' she asked.

'She speaks good English,' confirmed Gëzim, although he had not heard the girl utter one word himself. According to the gang, she had been mute ever since she left her village.

The girl swayed slightly but corrected herself.

'Why is she weak?' Madame demanded. 'Did you feed her?'

'She has fever from her country,' Gëzim replied. 'And the vessel … the Strait, she is heavy today.'

But Madame's expression was contemptuous. As far as she knew it had been perfect weather for the crossing, although it was not always so.

Unexpectedly, the girl shuffled her feet and cleared her throat. Everyone looked her way.

'Il ment,' she whispered. *Gëzim is lying.*

Madame looked at the child with violent interest. 'Qu'est-ce que c'est?' she asked.

The girl repeated, a little louder, 'Il est en train de mentir.'

Both men looked at her stupefied. *She speaks French?* And Gëzim feared what she had said that he could not understand.

She was now holding both arms in front of Madame Toussaint, pulling back the sleeves of her jacket to expose the vivid welts on her wrists where the ligature had bound her. The woman grabbed her arms, pulling her closer to the lamp to examine the damage.

'What's this?' she asked the dumbfounded men, already condemned by their mortified expressions.

But the girl hadn't finished. 'Et ça,' she said, stooping to roll up the legs of her jeans and exhibiting the similar welts on her ankles.

Panicking, Gëzim moved in to stop her, but madame's arm struck out to prevent him.

'Get back, you mule!' Her voice was strong and powerful.

Gëzim didn't understand the French language, and all the way from Amsterdam he had been oblivious to the conversations between the two women from Côte d'Ivoire and how they had cursed the men, how they hated their abuse and foulness. How they missed their families and were concerned about where they were going.

But the girl had been listening in, and now she felt empowered, speaking in a language the men couldn't understand. Now, she was explaining to madame how they had bound and gagged her, that she had fallen unconscious on the crossing and nearly died.

The men stood impotent and fearful, Valon's mouth agape. The tic on Gëzim's cheekbone shuddered violently and he felt the sting of the woman's palm as it whipped across his face. And the back of her hand when it landed the return.

'Don't you understand the value of this child?' she hissed. 'Get out.'

Gëzim knew her value all too well, and his hatred deepened. Now he had delivered her safely to the hammam, his part of the deal was done. She had been trouble from the start, and now he would find a way to make her pay.

MADAME TOUSSAINT CLAPPED her hands and a hefty woman appeared from behind a curtain to escort them down a curving staircase to the private quarters of the hammam situated on the lower floor. She supported the wobbling girl, a protective arm around her shoulders.

'Did they touch you?' she whispered, close to her ear.

The girl lowered her head and shook it slightly. She sensed the woman's softness and desire to protect her.

In the underground bathhouse a muscular woman threw buckets of water over the girl's body and set to work, whipping up a good lather with a block of black soap. After days in the back of the van, the child wanted to be clean but she would not succumb to the woman's ministrations. Wrenching away the scrubbing cloth, the girl demanded her privacy.

Clean garments had been laid out for her in a small cell-like room – a long pink tunic and hijab – but she refused to wear them. And when the teenage boy brought her food, she ate nothing, though her body was weak with hunger. And when the doctor arrived, she refused to see him and Madame Toussaint did not insist, respecting her wishes, reassured by the assertion of the girl's feisty character.

Night-time, and she lay on the bed staring into space. The room was partly underground, cool air flowing through a grate set high in the wall, which appeared in the street at ground level. She had checked the bars – cemented in – and the gaps too small for her body to slip through.

The place was sparsely furnished. A rug hung on a pole against the wall. There was a single bed with a metal wash-stand at its foot; a striped cotton mat on the floor; and a heavy wooden chest that was empty. There had been a large brass lamp with amber panels, which was the only illumination in the room, but that had been removed by the boy.

Beneath the cotton sheet, she lay fully clothed, her jeans and T-shirt now feeling soiled against her skin, the odour of perspiration unpleasant against her nostrils, but the fresh pink tunic lay folded on the chest, determinedly abandoned.

Now it was time to think.

They had crossed the water from Spain so the girl

concluded she could now be back in Africa. North Africa. And people here may not be as willing to help as in Europe where she had heard there were safe places and different laws that protected children. She knew of people from her own village who had fled to the coast of North Africa, migrating to find work in Europe. But none of their stories had ended well. Most had been unable to get to Europe or even get back to their homes and had been thrown into prison or been worked as slaves. She didn't dare to think what might be her fate if she took that route herself.

Loneliness descended. The air seeping through the grate reminded her there was a world outside. And freedom.

She wondered what would happen to the two beauties from Côte d'Ivoire who had travelled with her to North Africa, and what would happen to the boy Foday who had disappeared in a car from the polytunnels in Almería. And who was this woman at the hammam? She was important for sure because the girl had seen fear in the men's faces, and the hate in Gëzim's eyes when he realised that his lies had been exposed.

She lay exhausted, her mind racing like clouds across the harmattan sky. Outside the grate, she heard a donkey's hooves clip across the cobbles. Was this the end of her journey or would they move her again? Whatever happened, the next time she saw the sky she must run.

The door opened and light entered the room. It was the boy who had come to take away the tray, the food untouched. She eyeballed him defiantly. A young lad, not much older than herself, with a smooth complexion and downcast eyes. When he left, he locked the door. She heard him turn the key, but when she looked in the hole it was still there.

Hours later, she gave up trying to get at it, unable to push out the key with a pencil from her rucksack. Back on the bed she stared between the bars at the scene beyond the window. A long cobbled alley with walls painted blue, columnar trees in terracotta pots, lanterns hanging on the walls. She strained her neck. A waning crescent moon was just visible, and a few stars she failed to recognise.

Eventually, sleep came.

SUDDENLY SHE WOKE, her body drenched with sweat, her heart pounding like the *thabule* drums announcing bad news in her village. Fear rushed through her like the Rokel in full spate.

The alley outside the bars was dark except for a soft glow coming from the lanterns that was too weak to penetrate the room. There was no sound of footsteps or roll of cart wheels on the cobbles outside. All was still, the air cool.

She lay with her eyes wide, holding her breath so she could hear the slightest sound before it became too painful to do so. Then her breathing came in deeper draughts, her lips quivering with the effort to keep quiet, trying to understand what had woken her.

There was a movement outside the door and the sound of the key moving in the lock. But what might the boy be bringing at this hour?

Then the soft scraping of metal turning against wood, the minute sound of pins locating in the barrel. The visitor was taking pains. Then the soft clunk of the lock as it slipped home and the faint squeak as the metal knob turned by an unknown hand.

The door opened halfway, then a shuffle and someone entered, closing it behind them. Her senses were alert, needles piercing the follicles of her skin. There was a movement across the room, then the glow from a cell phone that lit up her face before it was returned to a pocket.

The cotton sheet was pulled around her chin; she dared not breathe.

Then he was on her, pressing a hand against her mouth,

and she recognised his stench immediately. Nicotine on his palm. A weight, his leg, moving across her body to pin her down. Her wrestling was no match for his small muscular body.

The cold tip of a blade against her cheek.

She thought quickly. She had humiliated this man and he was back for revenge.

The blade pressed deep against her skin, his weight heavy against her legs as he pulled the sheet from the bed, furious she was still clothed. With a sharp movement the girl pulled up her knee but he held strong against the pain. Thin slivers of moonlight poked through the grate and splayed weakly across the bed.

She felt for the edge of the washstand with her toes. If she could just edge down, get the sole of her foot against it.

For a moment his weight lifted while he groped with the fastenings of his pants and the girl shifted down, gaining more space, placing her foot against the cool edge of the stand, kicking out with all her strength. It went over, the metal jug and basin clanging against the tiles like church bells.

Straight away there were shouts from without, then voices coming closer and the door swung open. Light poured in along with the muscled guard in the black *thobe* and the boy dressed in sleepwear, a lamp in each hand.

She felt Gëzim's weight lifted off her as he was dragged from the bed to the floor, the guard pinning him down against the tiles, cursing in Arabic as he struggled to keep control of the man's jerking body. The boy stood in the door-way, lanterns high, his mouth agape, eyes wandering over her with concern.

Then a crunching sound like the noise a chicken made when despatched by her father for the pot. He used to call it 'cervical dislocation', breaking the spinal cord to disconnect the blood supply to the brain. She leant over the bed and threw up, the bile from her empty stomach spattering onto the pretty blue tiles below.

In the low light, she could see the unnatural position of Gëzim's head as he lay motionless on the floor. Efficiently, the guard drew his feet together, dragging him across the floor and out of the door where a figure stood calm at the threshold, tall and imperious, hands folded under her kaftan. The child curled herself into a ball, her back pressed up against the wall, her head down and hands against her ears. The door closed softly, the key turned and was withdrawn from the lock.

TWELVE
THE GIRL

Dawn, and sounds in the street filtered through the grate above her head. It was the month of Ramadan, and the traditional *nafar* crier was walking through the street signalling the start of *sawm* on his trumpet – fasting would commence until sunset. She watched him stride out down the street, traversing the cobbles quickly in his long flowing robe, on his head an embroidered prayer hat, pointy slippers at his feet, the long brass horn raised to his lips.

Then followed the mournful notes of the muezzin calling to prayer from the tall minarets of mosques around the city. It was a comforting sound.

Faith in the girl's own country was predominantly Muslim. In fact, her own mother and most of her friends were Muslim. But her father's family was from the Christian tradition and her parents had decided to raise their child that way. Back home in her village, the sound of drumming had announced the Ramadan fast at sunrise and her mother would carry her prayer mat into the small corridor behind their bungalow to pray.

The girl and her father respected the traditions, consuming their own meals away from the house during fasting hours, joining in at the end of the day for the iftar, taking care to be considerate. These were the customs in her country.

The recollection of those comforting rituals, the Ramadan drums, her mother's prayer mat, the communal iftar, brought great sorrow, and a wrenching pain pulled violently at her chest at the memory.

She stood on the bed, her hands around the bars, peering through the window out to freedom and a sea of sapphire blue that was the alley walls. Maybe today would be the day she would run.

There was shuffling outside the door, the key turned and the boy appeared in his turquoise djellaba with a bucket and mop and cleaned up the mess from the night before. Then he moved to upright the washstand that lay where it had fallen at that terrible moment only hours before. He replaced the bowl on the stand and took the jug to refill it, leaving the room and locking the door. A few minutes later he returned with a tray of food and glass of mint tea, which he placed on the mat near the bed.

'Madame says you eat,' he said without ceremony. 'Today you go long journey.'

There was nothing more, and he left the room.

The girl stared at the tray. The last time she had eaten was at the polytunnels, when the group were handed sandwiches by Valon, and now she felt dizzy with hunger. If she was to escape from this place, she would need her strength.

A pat of butter slid across a folded omelette speckled with cumin seeds and parsley. Bronzed flatbread lay on the side. Two spongy rings of *sfenj*, deep fried and glistening with sugar, beckoned. Sliced watermelon on a platter beside them was slippery and pink.

She dropped to the floor and ate eagerly; it was a carefully chosen menu to tempt a ravenous child.

Soon the boy returned with the jug of water and placed it

in the bowl on the washstand. She eyed him suspiciously, sugar from the *sfenj* stuck to her face, but he said nothing and left with the tray and a surly expression.

When the key turned again, she was kneeling on the bed and peering through the grate into the street, confused by the fact that people seemed to be passing through the wall of the hammam, disappearing like magic into a space she could not see, when the alley appeared to her to be a dead end. She deduced there was a tunnel through the building. A place to run, perhaps. She heard bicycles, donkeys' hooves and wheels turning on cobbles when there was no such traffic visible in the alley, sounds that were magnified because they were coming from a tunnel.

She turned from the window and slid down the wall when madame entered the room, curling into a ball, protective of her thoughts.

'There is no need to worry. You are safe now.'

The girl said nothing because, for sure, she knew she was not safe.

Madame continued in reassuring tones. 'Child, the man is dead.'

The girl's head rose a fraction, wondering what had happened to Gëzim.

'It is true. I instructed the guards to dump him in the trash where he belongs.'

Her words were brutal, but the girl was glad he was dead.

'It is a shame you went through that experience,' Madame said. 'I am sorry that it happened.'

The child's eyes remained downcast. She didn't trust the woman, though her manner was kind.

'Get dressed now.' Madame nodded at the pile of clothes the girl had left on the chest. 'The driver will be here for you soon.'

The girl sat on the bed, uncooperative.

'Child, you must cover your hair. It is our custom.'

The girl didn't move, determined not to speak but desperate to know where she was headed and whether this would be the last journey.

Madame sighed and made to approach her with a comforting arm. But the child would not be touched and curled into a tighter ball.

'You may wear your own clothes,' Madame conceded, stepping back and taking the hint. 'But you must wear the headscarf. Do you have clean clothes?'

She indicated the Ghostbusters rucksack that was slumped at the foot of the bed and the girl panicked, reaching to draw her belongings close.

'Put them on. It is nearly time.'

ON THE OUTSKIRTS OF MARRAKECH, they followed a signpost that read 'Route de Fez' and soon after detoured down a quieter road marked 'Tizi n Tichka Pass', a track that headed towards the range of snow-capped mountains that separated the fertile plains from the desert.

The journey from Tangier had been long and hot, heavy with traffic on the highways, the fumes from juggernauts pressing down, vehicles overtaking, the speed of travel disorienting. They had driven along the coast and through the cities of Rabat and Casablanca before emerging into a vast and dustily arid landscape that stretched out to the horizon.

Inside the overheated car, the girl had observed her surroundings with interest; it was a place distinctly different from the lush vegetation and grasslands of home. Everything here was dry and brown with only the occasional patch of greenery where trees and other crops were planted in small farms along the wayside. Out across the plains dust swirled, picking up little tunnels of dirt that sped across the landscape in short bursts, rising vertically, spiralling into the sky, gathering up vegetation and loose stones, spitting debris across the highways and drenching vehicles in the red dust of the Sahara.

They had been travelling south the whole day. The girl knew this because they had set off early in the morning with the sun over her left shoulder and as the day steadily progressed the sun had made its way to her right shoulder. Her father had been right. There was power in the knowledge he had taught her and she took some solace from that fact. Nevertheless, it was concerning to know that she was moving further from Europe with each passing mile.

Two people travelled in front, the driver, a wrinkled man who chewed tobacco, and a bad-tempered woman in expensive clothes – a lemon kaftan with mesh sleeves that were scattered with gold embroidery – clusters of bangles at her wrists. They spoke Arabic in low voices but exchanged few words. They had stopped only once during the journey, pulling in at a filling station where the child had been locked in the roasting vehicle while the man and woman used the facilities and ate a meal at a table close by.

South of Marrakech, they travelled through a more fertile area where orchards of apple, prickly pear and plum spread out across the valley and, after a while, they approached a hilltop village that was framed by snow-tipped mountains rising in dramatic peaks behind. At this point the road narrowed markedly and they were stuck behind a caravan of donkeys trotting on the points of their hooves and weighed down by grotesquely bulging pack saddles. An elderly man in a cotton djellaba and *sheshia* reed hat walked leisurely at their side, tapping on a convenient rump with the tip of his long willowy stick.

The wrinkled driver cursed at the stunted progress of their journey, chewing aggressively on his tobacco.

The girl clutched her rucksack. The village looked poor – dwellings made of red clay bricks and large rocks and built into the side of the hill, their flat roofs held up by thick timber supports. She could smell the open cooking fires. Pomegranate trees were lavish with fruit and people squatted on mats under arbours of heavy vines.

Casually, she eyed the handle of the door.

But the lemon kaftan woman was no fool and ordered the driver to stop while she moved into the back, wedging herself hard against the girl, her jangly bangled hand grasping firmly around her arm, nails digging in.

Several miles further on, they turned down a track towards a huge horseshoe arch built of pink stone. Beyond it stood a magnificent building that resembled a small palace. Two sets of iron gates barred the way and security personnel stood ready with AK47s slung over their shoulders. Carved into the horseshoe arch were the words 'Alqasr Al'ahmar'. The Red Palace.

The girl sat wondering what place this could be and whether it might be her final destination. The Kalashnikovs drew chills up her spine and she sat back, pressing her body into the cloth of the interior. A thuggish type in a black *thobe* leant in at the window and spoke quietly to the driver in Arabic before waving them through.

The driveway was lined with palms, shady gardens on either side, then an enormous house that looked like a Moorish palace where fine arches framed long terraces dotted with ornamental fountains; lush vegetation sprang from vast terracotta pots and colourful blooms trailed from pergolas.

Beside the front portico was a wide turning circle but the car did not stop; instead it followed the route to a single-storey building situated to the rear but connected to the house by a long covered walkway where a small reception committee was awaiting them – a well-dressed woman in a pink kaftan, an older stooping woman in black burka with sleeves rolled up, and a plump boy in striped djellaba, sandals on his feet.

The girl sat rigid as the man and woman got out of the car.

In her gut she knew that this was it. Morocco, her final destination. She looked back towards the gates and the armed guards, then at the palace's fortified boundary topped with razor wire, and considered how she might run from a place such as this.

The bangled woman in the lemon kaftan reached in the car and yanked her out, presenting her unceremoniously to the woman in pink, who the girl deduced was her senior. An aggressive exchange took place between the two – undignified behaviour for ladies such as these, but then the lemon was younger and prettier than the pink.

The black burka woman was staring hard, eyeing her up and down, making her own judgements.

The girl took a moment to survey the gardens, dotted with tall palms and jacaranda, Cyprus and almond trees, and the familiar bougainvillea of home. A heavily turbaned man moved through the borders with a hoe, his eyes firmly set upon his task.

THIRTEEN
KAREN

By the time I arrived in Tarifa, the van had been impounded. A group of Moroccan women had been travelling in the back on their way to work as labourers in the strawberry fields of Andalusia. The driver had been arrested and Eva was now on the phone.

'They also found hashish,' she was saying. 'So we can make the charge for both human trafficking and drug smuggling. The driver is in the cells awaiting a lawyer.'

'Has he said anything about the girl?' I said. 'Where he left her in Tangier?'

'Nothing yet. He denies all knowledge of transporting women in the other direction. We are hoping for CCTV at the port in Tangier, but there is limited coverage of the town.'

'Any chance I could speak to the police?'

'None. Let them do their job. The Europol people are involved in this also. The Gibraltar Strait is becoming the main entry point for drugs into Europe.'

'OK.'

'Karen, what are you going to do now?'

I was headed for the next ferry to Tangier. I couldn't wait around hoping the driver, now in police custody, would confess to where he'd left the girl. But I wondered why there had been only one driver on the return trip, especially as he had a cargo of people as well as drugs. There had been more than one, I was sure of it. Billy referred to 'the Albanians' and 'bad men'. And the Hondurans had mentioned that the drivers took turns so they didn't have to stop and rest. Where was the second driver if he hadn't returned to Spain – could he still be with the girl?

What I knew so far was that the van had left Almería with one girl and two women in the back, and that the next sighting was when the van boarded the ferry at Tarifa. I wanted to know if there had been any sightings between those two points – whether cameras had picked it up between Almería and Tarifa – so that I could rule out the chance that the girl had been dropped off along the way. I knew how long it took to drive the distance because I'd just done the journey myself. I wanted to know whether the van had driven straight to the ferry with the girl still on board, or had it stopped to drop her off.

But I couldn't wait to know for sure.

'Eva, can you ask the Spanish police to check their cameras along the route?' I asked. 'I mean, do the timings fit? We have an approximate time the van left Almería, so maybe they could work it out.'

'Yes, I'll ask them,' she replied. 'They also work closely with the port authorities in Tangier who we hope will have something on their side. This is a good haul for them. Well done, Karen.'

The realisation dawned that I had helped in an arrest. If I hadn't been chasing the girl or visited De Wallen and met Maria, the van would have driven back to Amsterdam full of hashish, having dumped a number of illegal migrants at the strawberry fields in Andalusia. This was a good start and I considered how much more I could achieve once I had the evidence to trap Broekmann. Had the news yet reached him –

that his van had been impounded, his driver arrested and the hashish seized? And would his driver be persuaded to give evidence?

'I'll be on the next ferry,' I said to Eva. 'It leaves in an hour.'

'What will you do when you get there?'

'I'll work it out,' I said. 'Maybe you'll find some CCTV footage that will give me a steer. There must be something from the port.'

Eva went quiet for a moment.

'You still there?' I asked.

'Yes …' she said, her voice tentative. 'If you are intent on going to Morocco there may be someone who can assist you there.'

I waited, but she seemed reluctant to give more details.

'Who is it?' I asked.

'Let me make some calls,' she said. 'It's sensitive but I'll get back to you either way.'

We hung up and I headed off towards the port's booking office to buy a ticket for the crossing to Tangier. I was at least one day behind the girl and I had no idea how far ahead I was of Lucas Bliek.

I GUIDED the Fiat down the clanking ramp into the fierce Moroccan sun and joined the line of cars and trucks edging towards the barriers that lifted and dropped with every passing vehicle. Ferry traffic was filtering out onto the city's circular route and I wondered which way I would turn when I got there. As yet, I had no plan.

I wound down the windows and a pleasant breeze passed through. Ahead, a port official was making his way along the line and speaking into a walkie-talkie at his chest. When he spotted the Fiat, he looked directly at me and signalled for me to wait. Moments passed while he checked the Fiat's registration, the drivers behind manoeuvring awkwardly in an effort to circumnavigate my car. Leisurely, the port policeman approached the window and leant in, his arm resting on the side of the car.

'Tout va bien?' I asked, slightly concerned. My fingers were tight around the steering wheel, knuckles pale, sweat starting to prick the back of my neck.

'Bonjour, madame. Êtes-vous Karen Hamm?' His breath smelt of cigarettes.

'Oui,' I answered in a voice barely audible.

'Oui?' he confirmed. 'S'il vous plaît, sortez du véhicule.' And he stepped back to let me out.

I swung my legs round, bile rising in my throat. Had Lucas Bliek got here already?

'Laissez les clés,' the officer said as I reached for my bags and made to remove the keys from the ignition.

'Les clés?'

'Oui, laissez les clés,' he repeated.

I left the keys and the officer took my place behind the wheel. By then, a second man had appeared ready to march me back to an official-looking building in the direction of the ferry. I protested, but he gently took my elbow and guided me from the line of traffic and across the busy car park already filling with vehicles waiting to board the return to Tarifa.

We arrived in a stuffy office on the second floor of the terminal building where I was asked to sit, sweating hard, in front of a desk behind which a port official in an important cap was busy with his papers.

'I demand to know what's going on,' I said, my clothes now sticking embarrassingly to my body. 'Does anyone here speak English?'

The two men ignored me, speaking to each other in Arabic and nodding in agreement about something. Eventually, the man in the cap looked up and said, pleasantly, 'Of course we speak English. We are not desert nomads.'

The two chuckled, amused by their joke. When they had recovered from the hilarity the man in the cap asked for my passport.

'Why am I here?' I asked, handing it over. 'Where is my car?'

'*Your* car, is it, madam?'

'Yes. Well, no. It's actually a hire car, but …'

'Exactly. You have driven the car out of Europe illegally.'

'What?'

Relief spread across my body, my heart rate slowed and my temperature cooled.

'The agreement with the hire firm does not allow you to cross borders,' the man said importantly.

'Right.' I said, compliant and grateful. *Is this all?*

'When you boarded in Tarifa our systems were alerted. These things are very sophisticated.' He spoke in a tone that suggested I would find this notion perplexing. 'And,' he added, 'your hire company has tracking on their vehicles.'

Do they really? I hadn't thought of that.

'What will happen now?' I asked politely, trying not to let them know how elated I was at this happy development.

'The vehicle will return to Tarifa. But there is a penalty to pay.'

'I see,' I said, wondering at the man's smile of satisfaction and how much might be in it for him. Unnecessarily, he once again shuffled the documents, pretending to look for the figure that he must already know. Then he pointed to the relevant spot on the paper.

'Six hundred euros.'

There was silence as he allowed me to consider the figure and prepare himself for bartering, or a protest or denial.

But after asking to examine the papers myself, I concluded, 'Of course. How can I pay?'

Cash. And one of his officers would escort me to the cash machine conveniently located in the corridor outside.

· · ·

'ENJOY TANGIER,' called the officer as he pulled away from the kerb.

The police car dumped me at a busy roundabout by the port's enormous mosque – a modern building, its minaret and arched colonnades ornate with carved orange stucco and green ceramic tiles. On the esplanade in front, slender palms towered against the cobalt of the Mediterranean sky, their fronds pointing eastward in the stiffening Atlantic breeze. Traffic roared past in a fog of fumes and clamour of horns.

Sunlight bounced off the old city walls and the concrete approaches of the port. I hitched my rucksack and carefully worked my way across the lanes of traffic in the direction of the Bab el Bahr – an ancient castellated gateway that faced the sea and gave direct access into the medina. Crowds of tourists milled on its steps.

A good-looking man in his twenties with wide smile and gestures suddenly appeared beside me. He wore a traditional blue striped djellaba and Nike trainers.

'Welcome to Morocco!' he said, exuberant. 'I am Khalid. I am here to guide you!'

All around, touristy types were being similarly swooped upon by would-be guides who congregated near the famous Bab el Bahr. Young and old in traditional dress, they brimmed with cheerfulness, all blessed with the same enviable skills in parleying and negotiation. The pressure was intense.

'No, thanks, I can find my way,' I said, heading off through the gate in the same direction as everyone else.

Undeterred, he followed, walking close to my shoulder. 'Madam,' he said gravely. 'Please, is not safe for nice lady to walk alone.'

'I'm fine,' I said. 'Please leave me alone.'

But this was only his first line of attack. He stayed close beside me like a shadow and after a short distance he said,

'Let me show you my beautiful city.' He was gesturing his arms as if to embrace the charms of the medina. 'I can take you to the souks, the grand kasbah …'

I wasn't listening and strode purposely on towards nowhere. Then, realising I would need a map to find my way around the city, I asked, 'Where is the nearest tourist information?'

'No tourist information,' he said with an air of authority, his happy blue eyes holding mine beguilingly.

We slowed to negotiate a mass of tourists, vendors, and would-be guides that had bottlenecked in the narrow alleys.

'What d'you mean "no tourist information"?' I said.

'No, madam. No tourist information.'

Obviously, he was lying.

We emerged into a small square.

'We are personal guides here in Tangier,' the man was saying, his smile still confidently wide. 'Please, madam. Let me show you my city. I was born here. I am Khalid! Every new body gets lost in the old town. No one knows Tangier better than I!'

Khalid could tell I was weakening. 'Five hundred dirhams,' he said. 'And you have personal guide for the day.' It was already afternoon, so I looked at him hard. 'The medina, the markets, the palace, the bazaars,' he said. 'Everything you want!'

Then I realised Khalid was exactly the person I needed to guide me through Tangier. Tourist information could find me accommodation but they were unlikely to point me in the direction of the brothels, the Moroccan Mafia, or the under-world of narcotics and criminal gangs. What I needed was some local lad with expert knowledge.

'Ok,' I said. 'I'll pay you five hundred dirhams, but I don't want you to take me to the tourist places.'

'No tourist places?' He looked suspicious.

'No tourist places,' I confirmed, deciding to be upfront

with him in a vaguely duplicitous way. 'I'm not a tourist, Khalid, I'm a reporter from a newspaper in the UK and I am researching people trafficking across the Strait of Gibraltar. I want to learn why local people take the risks.'

At first he was taken aback, but as he began to understand what I was saying, a shadow passed across his handsome face. But it quickly faded. He was cautious, but interested.

'You are reporter?' he asked.

'Yes.'

'Freedom of the press is a wonderful thing,' he replied, as I started counting out the dirhams.

I hitched my rucksack in preparation.

'Madam,' he said, eyes on the money. 'I will take you wherever you wish.'

FOURTEEN
KAREN

The sun was dipping and casting a pink glow across the sloping cobbles of the Grand Socco, a palm-fringed plaza just outside the medina with a huge marble fountain at its centre. The westerly breeze had picked up, and fronds were rustling madly in the tall palms above our heads. Waiters scuttled to and fro folding away parasols at the street cafés.

Khalid and I sat at an iron table in awkward silence. A waiter approached with an ornate Moroccan teapot and poured from a height into small chunky glasses, little splashes of pale green liquid catching the sun's last rays, landing silently on the paper cloth.

I took a sip of the sweet mint tea while Khalid stared at his.

'You don't like the tea?'

'Not yet, madam.' He averted his gaze.

'Not yet?'

'Is Ramadan. We are fasting.'

I followed his stare towards the horizon where the last light was fading.

Embarrassed, I pushed away my glass. 'Of course. I'm sorry.'

We sat and waited, but it wasn't long before the iftar cannon fired across the city and Khalid made a grab for his glass.

He had already taken me on a tour of the bars and restaurants popular with tourists looking for the 'exotic' side of Tangier. The idea of a woman entering such places he found most offensive, but he had borne the challenge well. A devout Muslim, he had remained outside the alcohol-serving establishments while I wandered in looking for two vulnerable women and a girl from West Africa. A futile endeavour, to be sure, but an opportunity for me to get a feel for Khalid and what I might safely ask him to do, get a sense of his trustworthiness, whether he might be willing to help me when he knew my plans in more detail, or whether he even had the information I was seeking to conduct a proper search. Instinctively, I felt he was ok. What could be safer than a serendipitous meeting with a young man trying to earn a living on the streets of Tangier?

Khalid sat in a tense arrangement of limbs at the end of the *socco*, arms and legs crossed as though the temperature had dropped and he was conserving heat. His discomfort was palpable.

'Madame is English?' he said, and I confirmed that I was.

'Is good,' he replied. 'Some time, the Americans … they do not pay.'

I had already secured his services for the next day.

'Look,' I said, aware of the tension and deciding to pay upfront, 'five hundred extra dirhams right now.'

He pocketed the money without hesitation.

'I will need accommodation,' I said. 'But not in the tourist places. Do you know of a family that will take a foreign guest?'

'Of course,' he replied. 'I can recommend.'

He made a call on his cell phone, speaking quickly in Arabic. 'Is all arrange,' he said.

It was time to give Khalid more information about my search for the girl, so I told him about the two women who I believed had been smuggled on the ferry to Tangier, and of the group of Moroccan women who had been found in the same van on the return journey to Spain.

The story seemed all too familiar to him and he seemed keen to recount his own.

Khalid explained that he had a friend whose sister had taken a great risk and paid smugglers to transport her by small boat across the Strait. She had borrowed money from friends and family to pay the smuggler – twenty thousand dirhams. When she got to the meeting point on the beach it was the dead of night and she found there were thirty people waiting to board a small inflatable boat that was built to hold ten. The sea was calm with only a light wind and everyone hoped the fourteen-kilometre crossing would go smoothly. From where she stood on the beach in Tangier, the girl could see headlights across the water, moving along the Spanish coast.

The crossing went smoothly, but when the boat reached a point where the distance to the beach was swimmable, the smuggler turned the vessel around, ordering the travellers into the water to swim the rest of the journey. This way the smuggler could be halfway back to Tangier by the time the group reached the Spanish coast. They had no choice but to get in the water and swim to the beach.

Khalid described how the sister of his friend was lucky because she was able to swim, but others could not and she saw horrible things. Eventually, she reached the beach and dragged herself up onto the shore, only to find the Spanish Guardia were waiting to pick up those who had successfully made it.

It was only days before she was back in Tangier.

'But why would your friend's sister take such a risk?' I asked. 'She could have been killed.'

'People here are desperate,' Khalid explained. 'They are poor. We do not have opportunities as in Europe.' He spoke quickly and quietly as though we were being spied upon. 'My friend's sister is clever,' he said. 'She has a university educa-tion … bio-sciences … but there is nothing for her here.'

'But there are official channels to seek work in Spain?'

He nodded. 'But the visas get taken up quickly. There is corruption and people don't get a fair chance.' He looked over each shoulder again, then said in a low voice, 'Everyone knows someone who's made an attempt.'

Khalid slurped the rest of his tea. I refilled his glass and ordered more. The square was emptying of everyone but tourists, fasting Muslims hurrying home or into restaurants to celebrate iftar. Khalid made no attempt to leave to break his own fast.

He had been confident telling me his story and I thought we were getting along well, so I carefully asked, 'Khalid, can you tell me about the brothels in Tangier?'

He sat back shocked and deeply embarrassed, looking around to see if anyone else had heard. He didn't know how to answer, so I encouraged him.

'It's ok. Remember I am a reporter and I need to ask these questions. I know that women smuggled across the Strait often end up in brothels in Tangier. That is why I need to know.'

He wasn't convinced. Perhaps he was afraid he might shock me, but from his reaction, for sure I knew he had the answers.

'Prostitution is illegal in Morocco,' he whispered, pausing to sip his tea in noisy slurps. Maybe he thought I was trying to catch him out so I tried a different tack.

'Khalid, you were telling me about your friend's sister. Suppose she made it to Spain and hadn't been picked up by the coastal patrols.' He was watching me keenly. 'And maybe once she was landed the smugglers had different ideas for her, and maybe they claimed she owed them money.'

His expression changed because what I was saying resonated. He knew this scenario could be true.

'Maybe the smugglers took her passport,' I continued. 'All her papers. Maybe she was forced to do work she didn't want to do.'

He said something that sounded like a curse in Arabic.

'You know it happens, don't you?' I said, pushing my point.

No answer.

'If that had happened to your friend's sister, you would want someone to help her, wouldn't you?'

I could tell he was softening. He looked nervously around the *socco*, then stood up.

'Now we walk,' he said, dialling a number on his cell phone and putting it to his ear as he set off across the cobbles in quick strides.

I left a pile of dirhams on the table and followed him through the massive keyhole of the Bab Fass gate and straight back into the medina.

THERE WERE no registered brothels in Tangier because officially prostitution was illegal. That much was true. But it was common knowledge that girls and women worked alone, in bars and clubs and small hotels called *pensions*. But brothels also operated in the city disguised as something else. Tea shops, coffee shops, masseurs, *petites pensions*.

I walked with Khalid back through the chaotic souks of the medina, down the alleys of the claustrophobic labyrinth where vendors pitched at tourists proffering spices, carpets, lanterns, ceramics, leather goods, babouches, copper pots, woodcarvings. Khalid offered me little protection. It was his job to lead tourists through the tightly packed souks into the clutches of such vendors, and most of them knew him well.

Soon we emerged into the Petit Socco, a square lined with restaurants and cafés, where Khalid stopped to take a call, standing with his back to me, speaking Arabic in a low voice. Straight away the vendors pounced, magicking from behind their backs jars of spices, lanterns, and babouches of many colours. I plugged in a pair of earphones to appear somewhere else and stuck close to Khalid, who finished his call and said something to the hawkers that successfully persuaded them to move on. Then, without a word, we were headed out of the *socco* and up the hill towards the kasbah.

'Where are we going?' I asked, a little breathless with the incline.

It was almost dark and I wondered what Khalid had arranged for my overnight accommodation and when he was going to break his fast. The call to evening prayer echoed through the streets, but he seemed to be on a different mission, climbing higher towards the kasbah.

'I have spoken to a friend,' he said as we walked. 'You tell me the women are from Africa?'

'Yes,' I said. 'Does that make a difference?'

'Some establishments,' he said, his skin darkening with embarrassment. 'You know … they specialise.'

'Specialise? You mean in African women?'

He nodded, ashamed to be having such a conversation. 'I take you there,' he said.

'Now?'

'There is a place,' he said. 'A hammam … many of the hammams … they offer extra services.'

'A hammam?'

'We will take the route through kasbah. This one … it is far side of kasbah. Is exclusive.'

We walked quickly taking various shortcuts along narrow alleys and moving in the direction of the great citadel that crowned the old town medina, up a flight of stone steps and through the stuccoed horseshoe gate of Bab-el-Assa that was set in the crenelated walls.

On the other side we moved through an uneven cobbled street lined with terracotta urns, clipped orange trees and date palms that stood in wooden planters painted blue. Then we hurried across the leafy walkways of the palace's lush gardens planted with palms and eucalyptus, and on through a tenth-century maze of narrow streets where cascades of bougainvillea trailed from the overhanging floors of ancient houses. Trickling fountains and stubby palms filled the tiny courtyards and trailing geraniums hung from pots beneath the windows. We moved quickly down a white stuccoed alley, dim lanterns illuminating walls that were covered with blue-painted flowerpots filled with damask roses.

When we arrived at an alley painted blue, we stopped.

'What is this, Khalid?' We were breathing heavily.

'There are many, madam.'

'Many what?'

'Many hammams, madam.'

'Call me Karen.'

'Yes, madam. I show you this one because I am told this one, they …' he whispered, 'specialise.'

I couldn't see any obvious hammams down the alley, although I didn't know exactly what I was looking for. There were no hints that an establishment of any kind resided in the street whose vivid blue walls shimmered in the half light. There was no signage, just an ornately carved door shaped like a keyhole set into a stone Moorish arch overhung with a massive lantern. I assumed that must be it.

'Ok,' I said. 'Shall we take a look?'

I started down the alley but Khalid hung back.

'No madam. Is not permissible. You cannot enter.'

'Why can't I enter?'

'They won't let you in.'

'Why not?'

'You are woman, madam. This is male hammam. There are no female bathing pools or saunas. Is all male. Please, I show you … now we go.'

He seemed deeply anxious, and I wondered whether Khalid knew to whom this 'specialist' hammam belonged.

It was quiet in the alley, situated in an exclusive part of the medina, just behind the kasbah and not an obvious tourist attraction. Locals had already disappeared indoors to celebrate the iftar with friends and family.

There were no windows along the street, but grates were positioned at ground level. The solitary door, massive in its proportions, was ornate with intricate carvings in Arabic script and surrounded by stunning *zellij* tile work illuminated by the lantern – tiny mosaic patterns in shimmering shades of yellow, rust and green.

On either side of it, conical Cyprus stood sentinel in pots. At first glance, the alley looked like a dead end, but in the corner a narrow tunnel cut straight through the building, from where a man on a bicycle emerged, his robes flowing out behind him, the bell rattling on the uneven cobbles. He passed us without looking up.

'It's ok,' I said to Khalid, and made my way towards the door where I stood up on the step and knocked. Then I noticed the tapestry bell pull and gave that a tug. The step below my feet was tiled in a complicated multicoloured miniature of mosaics. Turquoise, pink, gold and green. Exquisite tiling.

I stared at the door, willing it to open. Then a small wooden panel slid back behind a lattice grill and a young man's face peered through, just a teenager, wisps of an immature moustache gamely breaking through. He wore an embroidered white skullcap and looked surprised to see me.

'Good evening,' he said in English. 'Can I help you?'

But he looked doubtful and his gaze moved past me to

where Khalid stood a short distance away. I felt unexpectedly protective of him.

'Good evening,' I replied. 'I wish to visit the hammam.'

His eyebrows raised and he smiled benevolently, showing even gaps between his small teeth.

'I am sorry, madam, but we do not allow lady visitors. This is a male hammam. I can recommend a very nice hammam for ladies, the Ciel Bleu, but it will be closed at this hour.'

'Oh, I see,' I said, trying without success to look past him into the building. Behind his head was a fixed wooden screen that was positioned precisely to obscure the interior from view.

'Your guide will take you.' The boy was looking at Khalid again.

'Yes, thank you,' I said. 'Goodnight.'

'Goodnight, madam.' The wooden panel slid firmly shut.

FIFTEEN
KAREN

Khalid's family lived in a one-bedroom apartment situated in the centre of the medina, approached through a series of alleys and tunnels that cut straight through neighbouring buildings. It was on the second floor of a flat-roofed house squashed between others in a poor quarter of the town. There were three occupants: Khalid, his mother, and his sister Amina. It was a neatly kept home and welcoming.

The room prepared for me was usually shared by Amina and her mother. There were two single beds, a striped cotton rug, a large chest of drawers and a rail for hanging clothes. A ceramic wash bowl sat upon a wooden table, a metal pitcher inside it filled with water. A worn tapestry bearing Islamic designs and shrivelled tassels, its colours faded, hung from two pegs on the whitewashed wall. There were no bathrooms in the building, only a communal toilet on the landing. In poorer quarters such as this, families bathed at the hammam, as they had done for millennia. I unpacked some things from my washbag and freshened up with cool water from the pitcher. I checked for messages from Eva, but there were none.

Khalid had dashed off to evening prayers, leaving me

with his family in their home's small living space where we sat together awaiting his return, me upon an embroidered pouffe, the others cross-legged on the sagging cushions of a low ottoman. Spread out before us was the iftar feast that we would share when Khalid returned.

He arrived sweating and gasping for sustenance. None of the three had eaten since sunrise, fourteen hours before, but the meal was served with ceremony: a green salad with vast bowls of hummus, pastries filled with smoked cheese, a tagine bearing couscous spiced with cinnamon, platters of glistening roasted vegetables and fluffed rice. For dessert, watermelon and yoghurt and a salver of sugar-coated sweets. And to wash it all down, two silver Moroccan teapots brimming with sweet mint tea.

There was no talking as we ate, just great intakes of air and accompanying kissing sounds as the tea was slurped with relish. Khalid threw me a glance, a warning not to talk about the nature of my visit to Tangier. I had been sworn to secrecy to save his family a cultural shock from which they may never recover – according to Khalid. But I wondered how embarrassed Amina might be if she discovered I was seeking trafficked women in Tangier. Perhaps she was the 'sister of Khalid's friend' who had herself attempted an illegal crossing to Spain.

After the meal, Khalid said goodnight and made his way up a ladder through a trapdoor to spend the night on the roof. His mother settled to sleep on the ottoman, Amina palmed off to a family member who lived nearby.

I lay awake with mosquitos humming and dogs barking, the sharp sound echoing down the alleys. Outside the window, a crescent moon allowed a weak luminescence to penetrate the room, landing on a pair of sparkly purple babouches that had been laid on the floor for my use. The heat was intense, pressing down on my exhausted body. There was an underlying stench about the place, an odour created by the combination of ancient drains and scorching temperatures.

Eva had not yet called with news of any CCTV at Tangier port, but I needed to know where the van had headed after disembarking the ferry. There were hundreds of hammans in the medina itself and in the new town, and plenty of expensive villas, clubs and casinos dotted across the rocky outcrops of its environs. My plan was to start my search at the 'specialist' hammam Khalid had shown me, but what if I then drew a blank?

The next morning I awoke to the sound of a cannon firing across the city from the port and a trumpet being sounded in the street below my window. I checked my phone – 4.30 a.m. and still dark. I lay listening to the strident notes of the horn, gradually diminishing, as the trumpeter moved away through the lamplit alleys. I dragged myself out of bed and filled the water bowl, listening to the clatter of pots and pans that was coming from the flat's tiny kitchen.

There was a tap on my door, Khalid announcing that the predawn feast of *suhoor* would soon be ready. A banquet of harira soup, pancakes, boiled eggs and dates. But I felt nauseous at the thought and made excuses to stay in my room and check for emails from Eva.

Nothing.

But an hour later the screen lit up with a message directing me to email.

Have been trying to reach you on phone. Poor coverage your end? I have information from port authorities. They have footage of van after ferry docked. Please call as soon as you can.

I flew out of my room.

'Khalid, where is the best signal for me to make a call?'

His mouth was filled with pancake but he gestured with his fork and I climbed the ladder to the roof, stepping out through the small opening, the predawn light barely splitting the horizon. I dialled Eva's number and she picked up straight away.

'Eva!' I said. 'What can you tell me?'

'Did you get the email?'

'Yes, just now. The internet is sticky here.'

'Ok. We have the van at the port. It stopped on waste ground and the drivers got out.'

I held my breath.

'They are building a new ferry terminal,' she said. 'So there is good coverage in that area for security. We can clearly see two drivers getting out of the van and checking the rear.'

Two drivers.

'They spent some time in the back,' she said. 'But the camera is at the wrong end and we can't see in the rear. So, no sign of the girl or the women. We're guessing they were still inside.'

'What were the men doing?'

'No idea. But they were in the back about fifteen minutes, then one got out and started driving.'

'And the other stayed in the back?'

'Correct.'

'Anything after that?'

'Yes,' she said. 'The van was seen driving into the new town, then it gets lost for about three hours. After that, a camera at the Avenue Mohammed picks it up again before it turns into the medina.'

The medina.

'And after that?'

'A few minutes later it was seen crossing the Grand Socco – do these names mean anything to you?'

'Yes, yes. Go on.'

'The last sighting was on the Rue de la Kasbah. There is no coverage in the medina itself.'

Rue de la Kasbah.

'The van was lost for about an hour,' Eva continued. 'Then

it was picked up travelling back through the Grand Socco to the Avenue Mohammed, and then heading south. From there we have nothing until it boards the ferry the next day.'

Khalid had walked me through the kasbah gardens to get to the hammam last night. But that would be too easy. I was quiet, processing everything she had said.

'What do you plan to do?' Eva asked cautiously.

'I've made a contact here already,' I said. 'A local guide. In fact, I'm staying at his family's home. He knows the city well and is sympathetic to my research.'

'Your research?'

I lowered my voice. 'I've told him I'm a journalist.'

'I see how that might help.'

It was good to hear Eva's voice. Her approval meant something to me. Over the past few days she had become more than a colleague – she was a sister crusader just like Dorothy. Eva thought like me and trusted me. She had faith in my instincts and I knew I could not have come so far without her.

'But Eva, I don't really know what I am doing.'

'Has that stopped you so far?' she replied. 'You are strong, Karen, but be careful. The trafficking Mafia are scumbags. Barely literate, most of them, and that makes them ruthless. You don't want to mess with them yourself. If you find anything, you call it in to me straight away, yes?'

I acquiesced immediately. But I still needed her help.

'Eva …' I had to ask because she wasn't offering the information herself. 'You said there may be someone in Morocco who could help me. Have you been able to make contact with them yet?'

There was a brief silence. Perhaps she was deciding the best answer to give me.

'Not yet,' she said. 'But I hope to do so soon.'

'Thanks,' I said. But who was she talking about? 'Can you tell me more?'

'Not at this point … but I promise I will be back to you as soon as I can. Keep checking in, just in case I can't get hold of you.'

She hung up.

I opened Google Maps and found Rue de la Kasbah straight away. The idea that the girl might be so close brought blood to my veins in a violent rush of heat. I contemplated the possibility of finding her. Even with the heaving mass of tourists in Tangier, the hundreds of tiny alleys, coffee shops, restaurants, bars and hammams, I refused to let the likelihood of success dampen my euphoria.

I would start at the hammam we visited last night.

KHALID WOULD HAVE to return with me. The maze of alleys had been disorienting and I couldn't be sure I would be able to find it again myself, and if I wanted to discover what was happening on the other side of that impressive door, the only way to do it was to send him in.

If Khalid could visit the place officially, maybe he could ask the regulars about the extra services and what the girls were like. But even as I hatched the plan, I imagined the shock on his face, the look of moral indignation, so I had to convince him that the stakes were very high.

We were sitting on the roof of his home among the sprawling mass of similar rooftops with their satellite dishes, TV aerials and birdcages. Chickens pecked at seed that was scattered in a fenced-off area on the roof next door. Rows of static washing hid us from view.

'This is her,' I said to Khalid, showing the photo of the missing girl I had taken at Lungi Airport.

'She is just a child,' he said in horror.

'Just a child,' I agreed. 'She was travelling with the two African women, and nobody knows what they have planned for her or where she will end up.'

He looked upset and perplexed.

'I took this photo myself, Khalid. I know the girl arrived in Amsterdam and then travelled all the way to Tangier in the back of a van. My sources are good. I can be sure the information is correct. I wouldn't be here if I didn't believe this child was in trouble. If I didn't fear for her safety.'

He was hesitating, not at all happy with my plan, but emotionally engaged with the situation. I explained to him that the van she was travelling in had been picked up on CCTV in the area of the medina.

'I need to eliminate this hammam before I can move on to search others,' I explained. 'You said yourself that African women are working there.'

'Not me!' he said defensively. 'My friends give me this information.'

'I know, I know,' I said softly. 'You are a good man. You come from a good family and they respect you. But, Khalid, will you help me save this child?'

I offered him an additional five hundred dirhams, ashamed that I was exploiting a good man who was desperate for work. He took the money and tucked it into the pocket of his djellaba.

Later, we approached the alley of the previous night, distinctive because of its sapphire blue walls, luminous with early sunlight slanting across them. The street was called Der ash Shems.

'It means Alley of the Sun,' Khalid said, remembering that he was once a simple tourist guide.

This was the location of the Hammam Palmier, on the face of it a traditional bathhouse where people came to bathe in accordance with Moroccan culture. It may have a reputation for something else, but Khalid accepted that there was also the innocent, everyday side of the business, a legitimate place for men to come and bathe.

A long lemon headscarf was draped across my head and

shoulders, loose clothing covered my legs and arms, and I wore flat leather sandals. The modest apparel made me feel more confident in these environs. Laden donkeys clattered up and down the cobbles, traders moving to and fro, using the tunnel that cut through the building. Vendors had set up stalls selling babouches, rose water, colognes and fragrant oils close to the entrance of the hammam. A good spot to service the clientele.

The centuries-old cedar door was now open and offered me a glimpse of the lavishly tiled interior. While I waited by the vendors, Khalid bobbed his head and entered the building, speaking to a young man in a turquoise djellaba, a beautiful flowing garment that covered him from head to toe, and the same embroidered skullcap that I'd seen the night before. The boy passed Khalid a towel and a phial of oil and soon they had disappeared to be replaced in the doorway by two middle-aged men who were exiting the hammam deep in conversation, moving leisurely past me in a cloud of strong cologne.

Khalid would be some time at the hammam, especially if he was going to find out all the information I needed to know, and we had agreed to meet later at the Petit Socco. So I decided to explore the surrounding area and assess the hammam's proximity to the Rue de la Kasbah where the van had last been seen.

I followed the Der ash Shems through the tunnel, intrigued to know where it led with so much foot traffic moving to and fro. It was narrow and in parts there was just enough room for a donkey and handcart. The air was cool beneath the stuccoed arches where donkeys' hooves echoed against the stone. When I emerged on the other side I found a noisy covered marketplace set in a cobbled square lined with palms and thick stone colonnades on either side. I crossed over and continued through a similar passageway down a series of short alleys into a heavily congested area where cars, scooters, bicycles and donkeys were parked haphazardly under the jacaranda trees. Now I was outside the medina walls in an ugly square surrounded by tourist cafés, shops and restaurants, vendors selling fruit and vegetables direct from the back of their carts beside the Moorish arch of the giant Bab Kasbah – the gate that led back into the medina.

The western side of the square opened out to a busy thoroughfare congested with traffic that was travelling in one direction. Google Maps wouldn't open on my phone so I could only guess my exact location. I walked up the hill in the direction of the flow hoping to find a better signal and stopped on a corner waiting for the app to load.

In an instant a turbaned hawker appeared with a sheaf of rugs slung over his shoulder asking which one I wanted to buy.

'Non merci,' I kept repeating, but then I thought to ask, 'Monsieur, où est la Rue de la Kasbah?'

He looked at me dully, then raised his eyes to the sign above my head. We were standing on the Rue de la Kasbah.

I retraced my route back through the chaos of vehicles parked under the jacarandas in the square outside the medina, then the alleys that passed through the medina walls and into the covered market square, then through the tunnel that led directly to the Hammam Palmier.

I HURRIED through the giant Bab Kasbah where I had seen a number of tourist shops and bought a map of Tangier, from which I was able to identify my location exactly. A clutch of would-be guides was headed in my direction so I started walking assuredly towards the Petit Socco to wait for Khalid.

Much later, I saw his tall slender figure striding towards me across the square.

'Well?' I said eagerly, before he could sit down.

The iron chair scratched noisily as he pulled it across the

cobbles while a waiter appeared like a genie with more tea. I looked apologetically, knowing Khalid couldn't drink with me.

I leant across the table. 'What did you find?'

'I didn't see the girl,' he said bluntly, backing off a bit. 'No young people in the hammam. Only the youth at the door who is the owner's son.'

'The one in the turquoise robe? The same one as last night?'

He nodded.

'Why do you think he's the owner's son?'

'It's obvious to those who understand these things.' He looked aloof.

'Do you know the owner of the Hammam Palmier?'

'She is called Madame Toussaint. She is well known in Tangier.'

'Madame Toussaint … is she French?'

'Many people are French in this town.' He was talking down to me. What had he found out?

I wafted a determined fly from my glass of tea and covered it with a paper napkin, taking my time, allowing Khalid to settle. It wasn't like I had just asked him for a quick tour of the Mendoubia Gardens.

'Are you ok?' I asked.

He shrugged, staring at an orange seller who had parked his cart in front of us.

Eventually, he said, 'There was talk among the men.'

'Talk?'

'New women have arrived. French-speaking African.'

My heart rate quickened.

'But I saw no one like that,' he added quickly. 'The masseur who look after me was male person. They are always the best. If you want female masseur in male hammam you are asking for a different service.'

'OK. Good.' I tried to contain my excitement. 'These African women. Did the men say when they had arrived?'

'No. But maybe it was not long. The men, they were still excitable.'

He sniffed in a righteous manner, not really wanting to have this conversation, and I realised this might be a good time to offer my gratitude – knowing what else I was to ask of him.

'Khalid, thank you, thank you so much for doing this. Can you see how much you are helping? We're getting closer and closer to finding that girl.'

'We?'

He didn't look convinced, but managed a weak smile. 'Inshallah.'

'I also have news,' I said.

He raised an eyebrow.

'You remember I told you about the van that brought the girl and the women to Tangier …' He eyed me suspiciously. 'And that the CCTV cameras lost it when it turned off into the medina?'

'Yes.' His guard was up.

'Well, today I found the point where it turned off … it is a route that leads directly to the Hammam Palmier.'

Khalid's eyes widened in amazement, then narrowed as the implication of my words sank in. He didn't like the cadence of my tone.

'She could still be there, Khalid.'

There was an awkward silence as we sat looking at each other, me hopeful, him fearful.

'No, no. Please, I can no go back. Madam, please. I have helped you. That is it.'

His phone started ringing and he leapt to his feet in gratitude. 'Excuse. I must take.'

He put the phone to his ear and wandered off across the *socco*.

I paid the bill and followed him. He was speaking in Arabic, his back towards me, and when he finished the conversation he apologised.

'Sorry, madam. I have to go. There is an urgent matter with my sister.'

With that, he disappeared south through the alleys.

SIXTEEN
KAREN

I returned alone to the blue-painted alley of Der ash Shems. Intense heat bounced off the cobbles, the sun now at its zenith, its reflection off the walls giving the place an ethereal feel – the impression you were on your way to heaven. It was quiet at this hour, the crush of traders gone to secure their spots in souks and markets around the medina. Life had ground to a halt in the stupefying heat of the alley and the door to Hammam Palmier stood invitingly ajar, lush palms and cool green tiles visible in the interior.

The stall selling oils and cologne was deserted, its elderly owner dozing in a shady spot, his feet resting in a bucket of water. The man looked dry as a dead leaf. This was Ramadan, and people everywhere were weak and dehydrated, only the sense of communal martyrdom making their ordeal endurable.

A barrow of oranges and pomegranates was parked at an angle against the wall, the Berber vendor squatting between the handles, seeking shade. He sat hunched, watching me with dispassionate eyes under a complicated turban that wrapped around his head and fell in loose folds across his chest. It was sapphire blue like the walls of the alley.

I stepped into the shade of a tall potted palm, waiting and watching. The noonday call of the muezzin drifted in on the dry air as the sun burned with a frenzy, sweat slipping between my shoulder blades in a steady tantalising trail. The heat and the fear were making me weak.

The girl was close, I knew it. But the warnings from Eva echoed in my head.

There are watershed moments in life when you know, for sure, that the next choice you make will be immutable. That whatever decision you take, right at that moment, will be wholly consequential, the point after which there will be no going back and nothing will ever be the same. Like a moment of existential crisis, when the decision you take defines your future. When the steps you make, forward or back, will determine the rest of your life. This was one of those moments.

The blue walls seemed to close in around me and with every heartbeat there came the violent longing to run. The Berber's eyes were watchful, waiting for me to decide what to do. Like he knew something of consequence was bound to happen. Inshallah.

AT THE ANCIENT CARVED ENTRANCE, an elegant middle-aged man wearing a white djellaba and carrying a briefcase appeared from inside and stood on the step. He paused and a woman dressed in a shimmering purple kaftan joined him. After a short conversation, she extended her hand and the man shook it, offering a slight bow before he left. She caught my eye before turning back into the hammam's shady interior.

I stepped in and cool air greeted me. A forest scent of eucalyptus. To one side was an intricate cedar desk, its panels dressed with gold inlay, substantial lanterns casting a glow. In front, two ottomans facing each other with lavishly plump velvet upholstery, plum red. Between them, a low copper table and an assortment of richly embroidered pouffes. Lush potted palms stood by. Along one wall, a row of stained-glass keyhole windows gave out to a colonnaded terrace and interior courtyard that was furnished with plentiful greenery and cane furniture scattered with plum and ochre striped cushions.

Beside the desk, a horseshoe arch led to a corridor laid with green and white tiles, where lamps were set in recesses along the walls, and beyond which a large stone urn was illuminated in a golden glow ~ the entrance to the inner chambers of the hammam.

The cool air caressed my neck.

The boy in the turquoise djellaba was rolling plump white towels into long tight cylinders, lining them up along a green tiled bench, placing a phial of oil within the folds of each. Would he recognise me from the night before?

He looked up. 'Madam, please. Can I help you?'

'Yes, thank you. I am looking for someone.'

'Who is it that you seek?' He moved towards me with a pleasant smile, his hands resting abbot-like across his chest, his height belying his youth.

'A child has gone missing,' I said, and I took out my phone to show him the photo of the girl.

He glanced at it briefly, but I couldn't read his expression.

'Madam, you will not find her here.' He tilted back his head and looked down his nose at me.

I was not deterred by this bumptious lad's air of confidence.

'I think she may have been brought here recently … in the last few days. Maybe she was travelling with others.'

A momentary flash of panic, then calm.

'No, madam. She is not here. Perhaps she is in some other place.' He was taking more interest in me now. 'I must ask you to leave as we are for male persons only. No ladies allowed. There is no reason for the girl you seek to be among us.'

Someone else had joined us. She spoke in a low-timbred voice with a heavy French accent.

'Thank you, Nuri. I will handle this.'

She jerked her chin and Nuri disappeared into the corridors beyond.

Madame Toussaint was equal to my height and she looked directly at me with smart black eyes that were edged in kohl. Her features were angular, like an Egyptian king's. An interesting old scar was drawn across her neck.

'Perhaps I can help you,' she said, her manner slightly combative.

'Madame Toussaint?'

'What do you want?'

'I'm looking for a girl,' I said, trying to keep the tremor from my voice. My heart was thumping, my temperature suddenly cold.

'Who is this girl? There is no one here.'

I showed her the photo and she glanced at it.

'Have you seen her?'

She replied with a question of her own. 'And, might I ask, who are you?'

I explained I was a journalist from the UK following a story about trafficked persons into Morocco.

'And you expect me to answer your questions,' she said, not unreasonably.

I pressed on. 'Have you seen her?'

'Where are your credentials?' Her eyes flicked over me.

I passed her my university card to which she raised a manicured brow.

'I am sorry, but I am unable to help you.' She took my elbow resolvedly, guiding me towards the door. It was difficult to resist the pressure of her hand. Things were slipping away.

Back in the blistering heat, I had nothing to lose. The old Berber's gaze shifted our way.

'I know she was brought here in the last few days,' I hissed, a tightness developing in my chest, an increased palpitation. 'She's young. But you know that, don't you?'

Madame was unperturbed. 'Karen Hamm.' She was reading from the card, rolling my name around on her tongue to test its legitimacy. 'You are taking quite a risk asking questions such as this.'

'Where is she?'

'Who is this girl to you?'

I could not draw an answer from my muddled head. I wanted to say she was Songola, because in my desperate mind, she was. But she was more than that. She was my witness. A weapon to avenge the death of Songola, and I needed her to trap Hendrikus Broekmann.

Madame's voice was barely audible, and I had to lean in to catch her words.

'The Hammam Ciel Bleu. It is close to the new town quarter. Outside the medina. Meet me there at five o'clock.'

She turned and moved back inside the building, the silk of her kaftan brushing silently against the dark green sentinel Cyprus.

I ENTERED the Hammam Ciel Blue through a discreet door in a windowless façade down a back street and stepped into a dark space, cedar screens cut out with Koranic text and an arched colonnade lined with intricate *zellij* tiling. A young woman took the charge of fifty dirhams and handed me two towels, a block of black soap, and a rough textured glove with a plastic sleeve that contained paper knickers. Through an iron gate I made my way into a small anteroom that served as a changing area where I was met by a short stocky woman in a lilac tunic, matching trousers, and grey hijab. She indicated that I should strip and put on the paper knickers. Then she took my towels and washing equipment and beckoned me into the next room, which was intensely hot and dry, and lined with a circular stone bench, the domed ceiling covered in shimmering tiles of blue and green.

She left me alone while my body became accustomed to the heat and my mind became accustomed to the fact that Madame Toussaint was nowhere in sight. What did she want to say that she could not say earlier in the Der ash Shems?

Before long, I was moved along to the next chamber, which was humid and wet, steam rising, condensation dripping from the low domed ceiling. It was hard to breathe, the temperature burning my lungs as I searched the darkness for Madame, but I was the only person there. Maybe she was playing a psychological game because the agreed hour of five o'clock had long passed.

The final chamber was the washroom itself; bars of soap and wooden buckets lined up on the marble surrounds beneath a low vaulted ceiling, the walls sweating with condensation, a heated floor adding to the suffocating temperature. I was invited to lie on a stone bench and then slewed with *sabon beldi*, the woman working it into my skin with violent sweeps. Then the mitt was out and she was scrubbing my body with vigour, turning me over, standing me up, sitting me down, cleansing every gaping pore until my skin shone brightly pink. Buckets were filled and thrown over me, followed by more scrubbing. One more iced bucket and I was done.

A fully naked woman entered the chamber with her masseur and lay down prone on the hot stone awaiting her own punishment.

I was ushered into a cooler room where I was wrapped in a cotton robe, and a towel twisted round my head. Women lay relaxing on the beds, reading, sleeping, chatting together.

Where was she?

Soon I was led through a tiled arch and encouraged to advance through another door into a smaller chamber where the fragrance of sandalwood filled the air.

Only one person was resting in this room.

'Good afternoon, Karen Hamm. How did you enjoy our hammam experience?'

I ventured in and sat down on the bed next to hers.

'Can I offer you mint tea?'

Without waiting for a reply, she poured me a cup, lifting the silver teapot with elegant hands, allowing the green liquid to flow from a distant height with practised skill.

'Why am I here? Where is the girl?'

She shared a gentle smile.

I sat stiffly on the bed, scowling, expectant.

Madame was dressed in a similar robe, towel twisted around her hair. But she was unmistakable, the fine architecture of her face, the dark kohl around her eyes. Her voice was deep and lilting, unmistakably French.

'The hammam in Moroccan culture is a safe and private space for women. We can relax here and socialise. We find that it purifies our souls as well as our bodies.' She appeared completely relaxed, leaning back, sipping her tea. 'We meet our friends, conduct business, we even arrange our daughters' marriages in the sanctity of our own hammam.' Her smile was enigmatic as she looked directly at me and her words were heavy with nuance. 'Women's business can be very different from that of men.'

Her comment was loaded, but she was not to be hurried. I sipped the tea, sweet and hot, fragrant with fresh mint.

'You are French?'

'I am French-Moroccan,' she said. 'My father came from Rabat. He was a minor aristocrat, one of many who did the bidding of the king. He came to Paris on diplomatic affairs, met my mother, and seduced her in the style of the Don Juan.' There was bitterness in her tone. 'My family had homes in both Paris and Rabat. I still own property in Paris, inherited from my mother.'

'She is dead?'

'Both of them are dead. My mother killed herself, and my father had a heart attack copulating with an underage girl.'

Her face was impassive despite the violence of her words, and a short silence descended between us.

An underage girl.

'You own the Hammam Palmier,' I said slowly.

'Yes, I am the owner. You will find that the Palmier has the best reputation in Tangier.'

'Reputation for what – underage girls?'

She barely flinched.

'I'm sorry to be direct,' I said, 'but I know you run a brothel and that your business is illegal.'

'You seem to be very well informed, or so you think.'

She leant forward for the teapot, her robe gaping to reveal a full breast. She refilled the glasses with less flourish this time.

'Is it true there are African women working at the Palmier? French-speaking? Two that arrived in the last few days?'

'Why do you think that?' she asked.

'The women were travelling with the girl, and I have informants here in Tangier who frequent your establishment. There is talk of new women.'

'There is?'

'Was the girl travelling with the women?' I leant in and lowered my voice, although we were the only people in the room, which I suspected was reserved for her alone. 'You know where she is, don't you?'

'Who is this girl to you?' she asked.

'She is an innocent child who needs rescuing.'

'I suspect you lie, Karen Hamm. There are many innocent

children who need rescuing.' Her eyes were deep pools of sorrow, but her jaw was strong and controlled.

'Tell me what you know,' I insisted.

She put down her glass, a gesture full of significance. 'The girl was with me for one night only. I took great care of her. She left early yesterday morning.'

I felt sick with joy. 'Thank God,' I spluttered, trembling with relief.

'What is she to you?' Madame asked again.

'Where is she now … what have you done with her?'

I felt like putting my hands around her long and disfigured throat and squeezing to extract the truth.

'I have done nothing with her,' she said, backing off. 'Why do you think I invited you here? To pass the time of day? Don't you think I am taking quite a risk myself?'

I hadn't considered that. More calmly, I said, 'So why are you telling me this?'

Madame hesitated, as though she were searching for the words, wondering how much to tell me. 'Let's just say I have an interest in her well-being,' she said.

'Where is she?'

'She has moved to Marrakech. She is safe at the moment, but that won't last.'

'Marrakech? Where in Marrakech? What are your plans for her?'

'They are not my plans,' she said, bristling.

'Will she be moved from Marrakech?'

'No. She stays in Marrakech.' Her mood had darkened. She feared for the girl.

'Then tell me where she is.'

'You must take the night train. Someone will meet you in Marrakech.'

'Who will meet me? You want me out of the way – the girl could still be here for all I know.'

'Karen Hamm,' she said slowly. 'If I wanted you out of the way I can assure you there are easier ways than this.'

She leant over the tray and rang a silver bell, its sharp tinkling ringing out in the quiet of the room. A woman appeared from behind a curtain and waited for instructions.

'It has been good to meet you, Karen Hamm,' said Madame Toussaint, rising and tightening the robe around her body. 'You have what you English call "balls". But I can say no more. Now, go. You must find your girl.'

SEVENTEEN
THE GIRL

The girl sat by the window staring out at the night sky; the opening was too small for her to identify any of the known constellations with confidence. She thought she could make out the North Star – which her father had called Polaris – because she thought she could see the cup of the Big Dipper, which her father had called Ursa Major. She knew that two stars on the cup of the Big Dipper pointed directly to the North Star but she could not be certain she was looking at the Big Dipper. So she sat waiting for Earth's rotation to shift the stars universally westward.

But, even then, there was to be no clear view of Big Dipper. She needed to get outside for a better look.

There was more sky here – vast expanses that the girl was not used to. The 'palace' was surrounded by a wilderness of dry earth and brittle shrub – very different to the landscape back home where much of the sky was obscured by the forest canopy and the many hills and mountains that crowded out the view. Therefore, it was necessary to drive some distance from their village to get a proper look at the night sky. But here at the palace, it was different. If only she could stand outside and see the full heavens she could identify her exact location.

But the door to her miserable room was firmly locked and there would be no escape from this window, barred and meshed as it was.

The room was situated in the servants' block. A tiny space with a thin foam mattress atop a wooden frame, a stained cotton sheet, a striped blanket, a table with a broken leg, and a wooden chair on which to hang her clothes and where the precious Ghostbusters sack was slumped.

It was her second night in the room and she was expecting one of the servants to escort her to the washroom as they did the night before. Tonight she would refuse, planning instead to call out in the early hours when the servants were half asleep and witless – an opportunity for escape or at the very least a chance to get outside and see the stars.

The escape plan was not yet fully formed. She would need to understand more about her location and precise situation, and she would have to establish what kind of environment she would be escaping into. Thinking carefully and methodically in this way, meditating on the wider plan, was exactly what her father would expect her to do.

There were the mountains to meditate upon – a magnificent range of snow-topped peaks like those she had seen when the van stopped in the pass. These new mountains were visible from the window of the servants' bathroom, which was situated on the opposite side of the corridor to her room. From this information she deduced that if the North Star was visible from her window, the mountains must be to the south.

They were beautiful, to be sure, and so immense they blocked a swathe of the southern sky. What were these mountains, and would she have to cross them to find her way home? And what then when she emerged on the other side? Would the Sahara Desert stretch for a thousand miles beyond in an ocean of sand?

The girl knew enough about the Sahara Desert to know it was not a place to get lost. And even if she found her way home to her village, she could not be sure what would happen to her then. Would the authorities arrest her aunt for abetting human smugglers, or would they send the girl back to be sold once again to the traders in human misery that passed through their village? For sure, she could not trust the authorities to make good decisions on her behalf.

No, she would not be crossing any mountains or deserts. She would be travelling north to find her way back into Europe. To be specific, Scotland, which was where her father had promised to take her. To the place of his beloved alma mater – the University of Glasgow – where he had studied medicine and made many friends.

She slumped on the bed, momentarily confused, her excellent brain overcome by a different feeling she could not identify. An ache – like her stomach or her heart or another organ, maybe lungs – had swollen and was pressing against her ribs. And there was a thickness in her throat that made it difficult for her to swallow.

She knelt on the bed craning her neck for a glimpse of her beloved stars scattered so prettily across the heavens, her loneliness and grief dulled only by thoughts of imminent escape. The constellations were still there, reminding her that some things never change. That if she could only get outside and follow the stars she would be secure in the protection of her loving father's arms.

THE RED PALACE was aptly named due to its palatial size and vermillion hue. A white dome rising from its centre gave the impression of a mosque and, on the roof, low castellated brickwork gave the house a fortress quality. Fountains and terraced walkways, orchards, palms and abundant flora – they all implied a rich and powerful resident.

Who might own a house such as this? Its size and opulence reminded the girl of the American Embassy in Freetown, a splendiferous and fortified edifice perched atop the deforested foothills of the lush Leone Mountains. Security at the palace was similar to that of the American Embassy: high fencing, impenetrable walls, razor wire, barriers and sentries at the gate, and guards armed with Kalashnikovs.

On her first day, the servants had taken away all her western clothes and she had been instructed to wear a cotton tunic over long baggy pants and a headscarf that made her scalp itch. She wanted to know how much had been paid for her and why they had gone to so much trouble to get her all the way to the palace. And would she see the inside of that building or was she to live her life in her miserable room where she couldn't see the stars and was treated like a slave?

But these questions were hypothetical. She had no plans to stay long enough to find out.

As soon as she arrived, the girl had been put to work in the kitchen to slave for the cook – a broad-shouldered woman with bad breath and a quick temper who dressed head to foot in a burka. She was a violent person, similar in temperament to the girl's brutish aunt who had sold her without qualms to the traffickers.

Auntie had always been jealous of her brother, Doctor Jacob, who was clever and rich and revered in the community. His bungalow was luxurious in the context of their village and he had a car, two bicycles, and even a good plot of land to grow vegetables. Mariame, his wife, was intelligent and educated and had fancy manners. Their girl was smart and pretty.

Auntie's depressing circumstances only compounded her envy. So it was no surprise, when Jacob and Mariame died, that she grabbed everything for herself, moving into the bungalow with her vengeance, her bitterness and her weapons of violence, beating the girl for the slightest misdemeanour.

And there were plenty of misdemeanours, slight and otherwise, because the child had within her the spirit of resistance.

THE KITCHEN WAS ATTACHED to the servants' quarters and connected to the house by a short covered walkway that passed through the gardens. The layout was thus: the girl's miserable room; the main servants' quarters; the kitchens; the garden; the house.

The kitchens were hot and dark and hazardous, and infused with the aroma of rich spices. Along fires of glowing charcoal, rows of strange-shaped pots were upturned, and steaming underneath were couscous and vegetables, the fragrant scents of cumin and turmeric reminding the girl of home.

The servants spoke Arabic and, occasionally, French. Others conversed in a language she did not know but later learnt was Berber, the language of the people who lived in the mountains. In all conversations, she noticed one word was repeated – *sultan* – the name used in deference to the master of the house. Whether he was an actual sultan or just some *big man* who terrified his staff was not clear, but he was still out of town and the girl had yet to catch a glimpse.

His wife, *la femme du sultan*, had already made an appearance. She was a statuesque woman – the older and uglier wife – who dressed in fine robes, twisted turban, and nasty scowl, and came to the kitchen to give orders and cast hostile glances at the girl, who spent most of the time daydreaming and making plans for her escape. This attitude enraged the cook who shouted a lot, repeating 'Dépêche-toi, idiote!' or 'Écarte-toi! Vite! Vite!' dragging the girl round the kitchen, giving orders in French, which the girl pretended not to understand.

A chubby and docile lad, shaped like a teddy bear and wearing thick glasses, worked alongside her in the heat. His rotund mid-section pressed firmly against the cotton of his djellaba, which was once royal blue, his plump hands dimpled at the knuckles. He had a pleasant and deferential manner, his posture permanently stooped ready to duck when the cook let fly; despite his rotundity, he could move quite quickly when the need arose. The lad worked side by side with the girl but never spoke or glanced her way. His nature was kind, covertly correcting her mistakes when the cook's back was turned.

Eid was approaching and activity in the kitchen was frantic. Many guests had been invited to the palace for an extravagant celebration when the sultan returned so the girl was set to work peeling, chopping and slicing sacks of onions that would surely feed a thousand mouths. It was a simple task, but still beyond her means, the juice-releasing enzymes irritating her eyes, remnants of peel and root finding their way into the pot, slices of all different sizes. Maddened by her ineptitude, the chef threw chilli in her eyes. But the boy chopped onions like a ninja, covering for the girl's lack of progress, made worse by her temporary blindness.

More items to chop for the stew – chilli, garlic, thin strips of meat to dry in the sun on lines strung out across the yard. The scrubbing of pots and cutlery, and the worktops where cook prepared the food. The cleaning of the servants' latrines, the shovelling of chicken shit from the yard. And all the time the girl was encouraged by the heel of chef's shoe, or a lash from her belt.

There was a hen house in an area of dust a short walk from the kitchen and a little distance from the servants' building. It was enclosed by a wire fence, the gate left open during the day so the birds could wander and peck dirt in the spaces around. They were the most attractive fowl the girl had ever seen – iridescent feathers of green and purple, red and orange, and even some hens with white and black stripes. They reminded her of home. Everyone in her village kept hens and the sight of the simple creatures gave her comfort.

The best part of her day was when cook put the basket in her hands and sent her to the coup to collect eggs.

THE CHICKEN COUP was close to the boundary of the palace and near to a section of high fence that was topped with razor wire. From here, the girl could observe the surrounding area and consider the viability of different escape routes. The palace estate was an oasis in the landscape, surrounded by semi-desert and scrubland that was dotted with dry palms and wizened shrubs, the occasional green argan tree defying the elements.

On the road from Marrakech, they had driven past people who were dressed in strange clothing as though wearing blankets lifted straight from their beds. They wore reed hats with conical domes that had colourful pompoms dangling from their brims – perhaps to keep off the flies. These people populated the hill villages and their homes were built of clay bricks, stone and wood; materials drawn from the natural landscape like the houses in her village back home. When she ran from the palace, it would be in the direction of these hill villages rather than taking a chance on the lonely winding road.

A donkey caravan was kicking up dust as it passed the perimeter fence where she sat on the roof of the chicken coup. It moved across the scrub at a slow, steady pace, the animals' packs swaying from side to side in rhythm with their strides. Close by, a herd of black goats grazed unperturbed on dead twigs, their goatherd's head swaddled in a turban to keep out the dust.

There were many goats and donkeys in Morocco. Goats she was familiar with, many families in her village had at least one. But donkeys were scarce where she came from. They had all been killed and eaten during the war. But one day, her schoolfriend's brother had brought a donkey-type mulish-looking creature to their house and everyone stepped out to marvel at it. It was strange looking, but docile, and the children were allowed to climb on its back and ride for several circuits of the *barrie*. Her father had explained that nowadays, donkeys were killed for the sticky glue found in their skin. There was a market for it and high prices were paid. In particular, the Chinese couldn't get enough of it. So it wasn't very long before the donkey-type mulish creature disappeared from their village without a trace.

There were plenty of comings and goings at the palace, and from the roof of the chicken coup there was a clear view back towards the entrance. Fancy four-by-fours – the kind driven by aid workers in her own country – pulled up at regular intervals and were then waved through the gates by the guards. She had seen a motorcycle draw up, its rider dressed in black leather jeans and jacket, and a red and white striped helmet. He had dismounted to chat to the men with the Kalashnikovs. She could hear their laughter from her position on the roof. The motorbike looked big and powerful and she considered how difficult it might be to ride. It would surely cover a long distance at great speed.

These thoughts kept her going and helped suppress the grief that smouldered just below the surface of her consciousness.

THE FOLLOWING DAY, the cook dragged the girl out of the kitchen and marched her off to the vegetable garden where leafy raised beds were carefully laid out in a grid pattern. Along the paths, water flowed through a complex web of hissing pipes.

A man of African descent was digging with aggression in

his patch of legumes. He had seen the couple approaching but had wisely averted his eyes from the girl. He knew she had just arrived and was intrigued by her story and her youth. There were rumours she was special, that she was being watched by very senior members of the household, and that there was a secret camera in her room.

But he kept his head reverently low as she moved around the garden, all the time digging at the same patch of ground, his gaze sneaking out from under his brow, gathering to himself an impression of the child. The girl was uninterested, but the cook pulled her along, pointing out the different varieties of vegetables and herbs that grew in his neatly tended patches. His beds were lush and green, irrigated by a sprinkler system that pumped water from an underground spring.

The gardener's gaze discreetly followed their progress. He guessed the child was also from West Africa.

Near the artichoke patch, the hefty woman came panting to a stop, her legs astride, gesturing at this and that, sermonising her vast knowledge of the legumes, while the girl stood gazing at the mountains.

'Voilà les légumes que nous utilisons dans la cuisine,' the woman was saying, explaining that this was the kitchen garden and that any item not grown here had to be collected every morning from the market in town. This was the case for fruit, also. The palace had orange and olive groves but most of the fruit consumed by the family was brought in fresh every day from the market in Marrakech.

Cook then stopped to address the gardener, who straightened up. He wore a pink and white striped cap that had been knitted for him by a pretty admirer who worked in the laundry. His T-shirt and jeans were covered in dust. He rested on his spade, looking determinedly at the woman, his smile easy but his eyes alert.

There had been talk that the one who had just arrived was not for servant work and that all male eyes were to avert whenever she passed. This had confused him because the girl was living in the servants' bungalow – in his opinion, the least protected environment in the palace. All male servants had access to that space, and the child was slaving at the mercy of this devil woman. But, while the sultan was away, irregular things occurred under the slack supervision of his lazy, jealous wives.

'C'est Abdullah,' the cook was saying, by way of introduction. 'Tu ramasseras les légumes de chez lui quand je t'y envoie.'

The girl nodded vaguely. She was to be sent to Abdullah to collect vegetables and herbs for the kitchen. She pulled at the small gap in the fabric under her chin, trying to loosen the headscarf, her eyes now very firmly set upon him, studying the man with a strange intensity, like she hadn't really noticed him till now.

With sudden interest, Abdullah stared towards the snow-capped Atlas, aware the girl's eyes were now transfixed upon the tribal marks etched on the skin across his cheekbones, and he knew then that they must be familiar to her.

EIGHTEEN

THE GIRL

Later that day Abdullah arrived at the chicken coup to collect a bucket of manure. The afternoon sun was slanting in through the wire creating a thatched pattern on the henpecked ground. He unwound the latch that held the gate and entered the enclosure, the bucket in one hand, a shovel wedged beneath his arm.

Unexpectedly, the girl emerged from the hut, her head-scarf askew and loose around her chin. She was carrying a basket of eggs laid by the prized rare breeds, which Abdullah himself had a strong affection for. The sight of him waiting in the dirt with his bucket and shovel surprised her and the corners of her mouth raised slightly.

'Bonjour, mademoiselle,' he said, turning his head to the side, feigning a sudden interest in the goats beyond the fence.

'Bonjour, monsieur,' she replied, and straight away Abdullah knew she was not from a French-speaking country like his own.

He allowed her to pass and entered the coup himself, ducking under the roosting perches and placing the bucket down, ready to scoop the precious substance shatted across the floor. The stuff contained essential nutrients for his garden so he visited the coup most days for its retrieval. He set to, scraping at the green-brown faeces topped with white crusts of uric acid, dropping them deftly into the bucket. The process released a strong odour of ammonia and he had to raise his neckerchief to cover his mouth and nose. It was serious business. Not only was the substance good for his vegetables, but removing it from the coup improved the health of the chickens because it allowed them to breathe without inhaling the fumes from their own foul excrement.

A solitary hen nestled broodily in the straw of her box watching him with her beady eye, and he imagined her expression was one of gratitude. The rest of the brood were out of the hut, pecking at the seeds that had been scattered by the girl.

Abdullah was of diminutive stature but, even so, when he stood in the coup his cap touched the roof, so he hunched himself to exit with bent knees.

He hadn't noticed the girl standing watching from the door.

'Mademoiselle,' he said in alarm, lowering his eyes immediately.

'Comment vous vous-appelez?' she asked, even though she already knew his name.

Surprised at her boldness, the gardener gazed around the hut at everything but her. 'Abdullah,' he said.

'Vous êtes de la Salone?' she asked, and he suspected she had identified the tribal marks across his face and was trying to make a connection.

'Non, mademoiselle. Mon pays est la Guinée.' He daringly glanced her way.

So she was from Sierra Leone – the neighbouring country to his own.

Her expression brightened and Abdullah saw she was a rare beauty. Perfect skin like silk, and a pretty heart-shaped face, her eyes glittering like the gemstones in the sultan's onyx rings. A tremble of fear fluttered in his chest.

He smiled back showing a chipped front tooth among otherwise pristine enamel. Then they squatted and chatted in excited whispers discovering they were almost neighbours, their villages situated on either side of the Sierra Leone–Guinea border.

Then Abdullah remembered with a terrifying jolt that he was not allowed to talk to this child. He should leave the coup before anyone discovered them, so he retrieved his bucket of manure and exited, striding across the dust and through the gate, refastening the latch mindfully.

He would be back for more shit soon.

THE NEXT TIME the gardener met the girl it was in a quiet corner of the garden where he was kneeling barefoot, his rear end pointing towards the sky, his forehead resting on a worn *muslaiyah* intricately woven in bold Islamic patterns and carefully positioned on the grass facing east.

Prostrate and distracted, he muttered, 'Oui?', with no way of knowing it was the girl who had disturbed him.

'Pardon, monsieur,' she said, her tone respectful.

Abdullah knelt back on his heels, hurriedly finishing his prayers, turning his head right and left before rising. He stood and rolled his mat into a tube, then slipped his feet into his dusty trainers.

The girl looked embarrassed to have interrupted his prayers, but she was eager to talk and discover how he had travelled to North Africa all the way from Guinea and why he had not already escaped from the palace. Had he just arrived, like her?

Abdullah sighed to himself. The child had so many questions. It had not occurred to her that he was working at the palace willingly as a respected member of staff. That, over the years, the family had come to value his expertise. That they paid him a fair wage and that life at the palace was much easier than it had been in Guinea where all Abdullah could look forward to was joblessness, insecurity, and deep, deep poverty. There had been no future for him back home. It was a place of constant searching for non-existent work, and he had left to save his family from a life of destitution.

Over the years, he had wired home money that he had saved up and stored in an old turban that he securely stashed beneath his mattress. Because of this, his wife and children were now well fed and living in a hut with electricity – although they still had to walk some distance to fetch their water. His son even attended secondary school. The family's lot had improved immeasurably and this made him proud.

If Abdullah had not left Guinea to find a better future, none of these good things would have happened and this knowledge heartened him. Inshallah, it would not be long before he could return home to his family. He had not seen them for five years, a fact that gave him much pain. But his wife had been supportive, continually thanking him, grati-tude and praise moving in a constant flow from her lips to his ears. To be sure, she was a thankful woman, acknowledging the sacrifices he had made, the risks he had taken when he crossed the desert to search for a better life for their family.

But every time he phoned home to see how they were doing and plan his return, his wife seemed determined for him to stay in Marrakech to preserve the flow of cash. Some-times, he wondered why she did not miss him as much as he missed her. She was in no great hurry for his return, not even a short visit let alone a permanent homecoming.

He had tried to convince her that he could now establish himself in their village and improve the productivity of their own tiny farm. Maybe buy more land. His experience in Morocco had vastly improved his knowledge and skills in farming. He had learnt so much, especially the power of herbs (which grew profusely in his raised beds), and their ability to cure all manner of ills and diseases. In fact, he had become quite an expert on the subject, developing a deep understanding of how to blend curative plants and herbs. He was regularly consulted by the palace servants, and even the family itself, to provide medicinal remedies for all kinds of ailments. Indeed, Abdullah had made quite a name for himself. He knew all the plants that contained the mysterious properties to heal (or otherwise), depending on their precise preparation and dosage, and his knowledge was in demand.

Abdullah had therefore decided that one day he would surprise his wife. He had no intention of remaining an economic migrant forever. He yearned for West Africa from the bottom of his heart, and one day he knew he would return.

'Mademoiselle,' he now uttered quietly, his heart still full from the intensity of his prayers.

But when she launched forth with her tirade of urgent questions, he held up both his hands. 'Non, non,' he said. *Not here.* There would be eyes from the house and the kitchens.

'Que faites-vous ici?' he said, but the girl's expression was blank, trying to remember the purpose of her errand to find the gardener. Ah yes, she remembered. She had been sent to bring coriander for cook's stew. So they walked together to the green and healthy patch where he produced a small machete and cut several bunches for her basket.

'Merci, monsieur,' she said. And they agreed to meet later in the coup.

THE GIRL SAT in the straw, cradling a hen whose plumage was barred with white and black feathers. Abdullah was on his knees, scraping every last drop of shat from every corner of the hut as they conversed in urgent, whispering voices.

Wrapped around his head today was a yellow T-shirt arranged in the style of a hijab-cap turban.

He was keen to share his experiences with her and explain how, at great personal risk and under heroic conditions, he had travelled across the Sahara from Guinea along a new western smuggling route that followed the coast of North Africa from Mauritania all the way through the ungoverned spaces of Western Sahara into Morocco.

The girl concentrated hard. She seemed very interested in potential smuggling routes.

Because the route from Mauritania was new, the smugglers had taken several wrong turns and everyone was close to starvation all the time. The vehicle in which they travelled was unfit and overcrowded, and it had broken down miles from any town or settlement in a vast expanse of dunes where there had been no shelter from the blistering sun and their water supplies had run out. After many desperate hours, the men fixed the fan belt and the vehicle limped over the border into Morocco.

Abdullah's final destination was to be Spain, but when he arrived in Tangier he found that economic migrants like himself were being detained at the border for several years. While people waited in limbo, all the time enduring squalid and dangerous conditions, the smugglers demanded more and more money.

One day, Moroccan security forces launched a hunt for all irregular migrants sheltering in the hills and forests around the Spanish enclave of Ceuta where Abdullah had been hiding with many desperate others close to the triple barrier of razor-topped fences – impenetrable unless you tried to scale them, or swim around them and approach via the beach, which he had not attempted on account of the fact he could not swim. When the security forces struck the camps Abdullah had managed to escape, but hundreds of migrants were not so lucky and found themselves in even worse conditions.

After that, Abdullah had decided he could not risk waiting any longer for an attempt on the European mainland, so he concluded it would be best to try his luck in Morocco. It was many months since he had left his family in Guinea and they would be waiting for remittances to compensate for the cash they had raised to pay for his journey to Europe, the immense risks he had taken crossing the Sahara, and for the abandonment of his family.

The girl listened to Abdullah's story attentively, asking about the geographical location of the palace, in particular the signpost 'Tizi n Tichka Pass' which she had noticed on the journey there. Abdullah confirmed that the sign pointed to the road that led up the mountains of the High Atlas and disappeared into the desert, a difficult and treacherous route south. She nodded, as though she had already deduced this herself.

The child hung on Abdullah's every utterance and her spirit impressed him. She emitted a forceful, hopeful, purposeful life essence, and he could not help but be affected by it. She reminded him of his own daughter, and his village, and he felt drawn to her, protective of her, like she was home.

Now she was asking him about the family who lived at the palace. Who it was who had bought her and why had they gone to so much trouble to get her here, but Abdullah could not share the conclusions he had already drawn for himself.

'Ah, mademoiselle. Je ne sais pas,' he said, half truthfully.

There were soft clucking sounds from the hens nesting broodily in their boxes.

How could he give this child details of the man who was now in control of her life? For sure, she must be for something special because she was being guarded in such an overt way. He knew there was a camera in her room and that the men were not allowed to look at her, or escort her to the bathroom. That there was a fearful undercurrent among the male servants in case they were caught with their eyes in her direction. She was kept under lock and key during night-time hours and watched closely during the day, and he did not believe this was solely to stop her from escaping. Her innocence was being preserved, and he feared he knew what for.

A shrieking sound startled the pair from their reverie. The girl was late with the eggs and the cook was now marching in a brisk rolling stride in the direction of the coup. The child dropped the hen, picked up the basket, and followed the clucking creature out of the hut.

Abdullah lay low in the coup, waiting for the fuss to die down.

THE NEXT DAY, the girl was roughly woken by the cook who told her to rise and dress quickly. It was early and the child rubbed her eyes, peering out of the window where the breath of dawn fell lightly on the landscape beyond the wire. A herd of black goats were grazing on some thorns while their young goatherd sat on a stone waggling his willowy stick absently, his pale skullcap luminous in the dawn. Maybe she could follow the well-worn tracks of goatherds when she made her break for freedom.

The cook returned in a temper, screaming in Arabic, and the force of the slap caused the girl to stagger, the ringing in her ears disorienting. Taking up the bundle of clothes, the woman yanked her out of her room and into the bathroom, then shouted some more – from which the child understood she was to dress, urinate, wash and pick her teeth.

Outside the window a car was parked, the same one that had brought her all the way from Tangier. She returned to her room and grabbed the rucksack, tied the headscarf in an amateurish knot and left the room, emerging into the dim light with a sense of expectation as dawn hovered on the horizon splaying warm tones across the gardens.

The engine of the car was idling. It was the same driver who had brought her all the way from the coast and in a moment of hope she believed she was to make the return trip, so she gazed at the mountains, their white slopes rosy-pink as the sun struck their peaks. Would it be the last time she would see them?

The cook was shouting, stacking baskets into the boot of the car and waving her arms at the driver. She moved around the vehicle to grab the girl, shoving her into the back then easing in beside her, sweating profusely and emitting a strong odour, even at this hour. The kitchen boy sat up front beside the driver.

The car pulled down the long track towards the gates where the guards waved them through. Back on the highway, they retraced the route they had taken from Marrakech but after several miles, they turned into the city – a chaotic place where trucks and cars, donkeys and handcarts, pedestrians and cyclists, all vied for position on the three-lane highway. Soon they slowed and turned into a narrower street that was rammed with pedestrians and traffic; the driver mounted the kerb and parked on the pavement.

Bending her body with a grunt, the cook hauled herself out of the car, dragging the girl behind and loading her up with empty baskets, yanking the rucksack from her arms and handing it to the boy so he could return it to the car.

For the first time in her life, the girl began to scream, the terrible sound surprising her, reminiscent of the wandering spirits that entered her village to issue threats of ancestral vengeance upon unsuspecting residents. She was going nowhere without her rucksack. It contained one hundred US dollars and a priceless gift from her father.

Her screeching was attracting attention and slapping the girl only made it worse. So the cook grabbed the boy and attached the rucksack to his back to keep her quiet. He stood bemused and acquiescent, his white skullcap askew, then he went ahead, leading the way into the bustling souk, baskets dangling from a yoke across his back, the Ghostbusters sack wedged tight between.

When the girl realised they were headed for the crowded markets of Marrakech she panicked with joy at the prospects this might offer for escape. Excitement flooded her veins, as well as another feeling – hope.

But where exactly was Marrakech? She had seen signs to the city on the highway, the same highway that had brought her from Tangier, which she knew was by the sea, but she was not sure how many hours she had travelled in the car. When they had set off from Tangier it was early morning. When they reached the palace it was dusk. She tried to get her bearings, trying to decide how to get to Europe from here. If she ran from the market, maybe she could hide in a truck that was headed to the coast. But she would need to be sure the truck was heading in the right direction when it turned onto the highway.

As she pondered these important questions, her arm was lifted by the lad and a leather cuff slipped on to her wrist. It was attached to a chain that bound her to a similar cuff attached to his own wrist. Her captors did not trust her. It must be possible to escape. Maybe someone had done it before.

The bondage arrangement restricted her movement around the market, the kitchen lad pulling her along as they moved as one body through the crowd, following the cook from stall to stall, collecting dried fruit, fresh spices, strawberries, plums and apricots.

They stopped at a stall weighed low where the vendor dropped what he was doing straight away and loaded his very best produce into the baskets of this important customer.

'Salaam alykum!'

'Alykum salaam!'

The cook turned to the girl to discuss the subject of legumes, the communication of which was complicated by her total deficit of attention, the rucksack now in the hands of the vendor and being loaded with melon and prickly pear.

The woman presented the girl with a pomegranate, holding it up, caressing its red, leathery skin, tapping it with her nail, gently squeezing to check for yield, calculating the weight by holding it in her palm and affecting and up and down motion. The girl scowled but was curious to know what she was being trained for. Maybe she was to progress from onion chopper to fruit buyer.

'Prends-le!' the woman squealed, and the girl took the fruit, looking at it with a dull expression. The headscarf was itching her neck. She squeezed at the fruit aggressively.

'Non, non!' The woman slapped her head and pulled her in for a closer look, the lad dragged in with them.

'Regarde ça,' the woman said, taking another fruit and shaking it at the girl. 'Pas bien, pas bien.' She was doing the weighing motion again and shaking her head.

The child took both fruits and realised the first was heavier than the second.

'Ah! Bien, n'est-ce pas!' the woman said, satisfied that she had now got the message.

The crowd pressed in. It was hot and claustrophobic.

Were they close to the sea?

The girl could not smell the sea. The people in this town did not pull fish out of the ocean and sell it from the quay as they did in Freetown. She looked around, trying to gauge which way she would run when she got the chance. Which would be the best direction to disappear straight away and to have this nasty woman gawping in disbelief as she vanished from the crowd. The leather bond was no deterrent. Next time they drove to the market, she would conceal a knife from the kitchen and slit the strap when she got her chance.

NINETEEN
KAREN

It was first light when the night train from Tangier pulled into Marrakech and I had spent the journey wrapped in a thin blanket, propped in an uncomfortable, lightly padded seat. The service had been full of sleeping passengers and my neighbour – an elderly man in a crocheted skullcap – had slumped against me, his mouth agape, yellowing teeth and smelling of garlic. He had settled in, nestled against my shoulder, the weight of his head like a stone. In Rabat, the train had to wait for dense fog to clear, and when we eventually lurched away from the platform the man had woken with a start, mumbling an apology before turning to face the other way.

I had missed the first call from Billy while dozing on and off with the rocking rhythm of the tracks. The vibration of my phone had woken me only to find a missed call message from an unknown number and, for the next hour, I stared at the screen willing him to try again.

Billy's voice was barely audible when he called the second time and I imagined him hiding somewhere, finding a place where his conversation could not be overheard.

'There is talk among the men,' he muttered.

I flattened my ear against the phone, the rattle of the tracks making it difficult to hear.

'They say is special delivery … she arrive in Marrakech.'

'A special delivery? What do you mean?'

'The one you seek,' he said. 'She payment for something. She special delivery.'

'In Marrakech, did you say?' I repeated it to be sure I had heard him correctly. 'What are the men saying? Who has her now?'

'Yes, Marrakech. She payment for something.' Then the line went dead.

Before I received that call from Billy, I was contemplating my sanity – travelling all the way south to Marrakech with only the word of Madame Toussaint to sustain me. A woman unknown to me and with a dubious reputation, hundreds of miles into the heart of Morocco on the say-so of someone who wanted me out of Tangier. So before I had spoken to Billy, I was beginning to question my judgement, clouded by my obsession to find the girl and trap Broekmann.

When Eva learnt of my plans to get to Marrakech she had warned me off. 'Maybe this is the end of the line for you, Karen.'

She sounded genuinely concerned, but Eva didn't fully understand my motives. She did not know about my need to avenge Songola. To atone for my mistakes. So I had mumbled something about being careful, not doing anything stupid, and reporting to her as soon as I arrived in Marrakech.

Still she warned, 'Karen, I don't think it's worth it.'

Eva could give me no updates about the contact who might help me in Morocco and she was evasive when I pressed her, promising to let me know if anything changed, but my hopes of help were fading.

The knowledge that Billy from Club VG and Madame

Toussaint from Hammam Palmier were both connected to the gang that brought the girl to Marrakech spurred me on. The connection could not be a coincidence. After all, the original tip-off from Billy had led me all the way to the door of Madame Toussaint.

I ALIGHTED from the train into the easy Marrakech dawn, not knowing who was to meet me, where I would find them, or what was their connection to Madame Toussaint. Sleepy people were making their way along the platform towards the exits and I waited until the crowd had dispersed, wondering who I was supposed to look for and how they would recognise me. I felt vulnerable with the unfamiliar sense of dependency. So much was at stake if the word of Madame Toussaint turned out to be unreliable. Would she come good, or would I still be here when the next night train pulled into Marrakech?

The platform emptied and the train stood idle, the air thick with diesel fumes, cleaners boarding to do their work for the return to Tangier. When there was no one left on the concourse I hitched the rucksack and made my way into the station hall, lined with shops and cafés, natural light falling through huge windows in the vast domed ceiling that was supported by mushroom-shaped columns. It was noisy in the echoey space, people shouting in French and Arabic, luggage clattering along the marble tiles, phones ringing and unintelligible announcements over the loudspeakers. Strong aromas of spice and incense filled the space and mingled with the sterile stench of cleaning fluids still wet on the mopped marble floor.

I stood in an open spot and scanned the crowd.

It wasn't long before a round-shouldered man with an uneven gait moved determinedly in my direction, his walking stick tapping against the tiles. He was dressed in a white djellaba and a traditional red fez whose tassel dangled over one brow. He unfolded a sheet of paper which he smoothed and held up for me to read, the words 'Karen Hamm' written across the page in sloping black capitals. He scanned my person with his milky eyes hoping he had picked the right one. When I showed him my passport he seemed satisfied and without further ado he set off towards the exit. I followed, shortening my stride to match his lumbering steps.

We emerged onto the station's wide esplanade, its yellow clay and red-brick façade luminous in the sun's slanting rays. In the centre of the square, tall palms stood among dramatic black and white mosaics encircling a flagpole where the green star pentagram of the red Moroccan flag fluttered in a slow-moving breeze. In the distance behind it, the striking peaks of the Atlas Mountains shone like porcelain.

We crossed a busy intersection and headed down an avenue carpeted blue with the fallen blossom of late jacaranda, then down a back street to where an ancient motor-cycle was resting at an angle on its side-stand, two helmets dangling from the bars.

The old man hitched his djellaba and flung his good leg over the seat, passing me a helmet before fixing his own and giving me his stick to hold.

The streets of the city were already congested but my companion was unfazed as he wove in and out, crossing multiple lanes of moving traffic, sharp diagonal approaches to the junctions, mounting the pavement at an overcrowded section. There was a pleasant sandalwood odour issuing from his dried-out skin that was wizened as a roasted nut.

Soon, we passed through the thick walls of the medina and found ourselves among pedestrians, handcarts, donkeys – a similar scene to those in Tangier – and we meandered down an indistinguishable maze of alleys, across the expanse of the Jemaa el Fna, past the Café de France already rammed with tourists enjoying their breakfast in this famous square.

More alleys before eventually we drew to a halt and I dismounted, my companion murmuring something in Arabic and propping the bike up on its stand. It was a tiny alley with a shady courtyard where the name on the wall read Derb Lalla Chacha. A pretty name and a pretty street that was lined with potted cedars and trailing pink geraniums that hung against the white stuccoed walls. A wooden door studded with metal rivets stood half hidden behind a bushy fan palm. We approached and the old man magicked a solid-looking key from somewhere in his robe and let us in. The internal door required a different key and, beyond that, a wrought-iron screen that made a grating sound when he pushed against it.

A sumptuous home lay beyond, fragrant and deserted. I was instructed to remove my shoes and select a pair of embroidered babouches from a row of colourful items that were stored on a low shelf inside the screen. I drew a pair of sparkling turquoise slippers from the rack, noticing that my palms were clammy and my heart was thumping. How quickly this stranger had brought me to a place where someone else held the keys.

The old man gave me a quick tour, his only concern being to educate me on the operation of the overhead fans and, in particular, the AC unit which was situated in the master bedroom. He spoke in Arabic but his instructions were clear, gesturing at the windows and shutters (painted blue), opening and closing them purposefully, pointing at the AC unit, giving the 'plenty dollar' sign with thumb and forefinger. From this I understood I was to close the windows when the AC was running. Then he shuffled back through the gate, handing me the keys and indicating that I should lock up behind him.

The house was lavish in the traditional riad style, unrevealing from the outside but inside rich colour and texture, ornate tiling and ironwork, fountains and palms. Opening onto the courtyard was a long colonnaded gallery with keyhole arches whose stone was decorated with intricately carved stucco. Lattice screens bordered the garden where citrus trees and date palms stood in terracotta pots and jasmine climbed the walls unrestrained. A basin-shaped fountain strewn with rose petals gave the impression someone had left moments before. Two spouts jutting from the walls filled small pools beneath, the trickling sound adding to the tranquil mood that permeated the building. Beautiful geometric tile work in ochre, terracotta and all earthy shades was everywhere.

Someone took great care of this home. There was nothing out of place, as though someone was expecting visitors.

A long formal salon ran alongside the courtyard. It was sumptuously furnished and arranged with handcrafted arts. Ornate cornices ornamented its ceiling. On the opposite side there was a kitchen and a modest area for washing. Access to the upper and lower floors was via tight winding staircases lit by brass lamps, down to the hammam and up to the bedrooms and a further, informal salon, more like a TV lounge, with comfortable wicker seating, a writing desk, and padded ottomans.

A final flight of steps led to the terrace where the rooftop garden was planted with every kind of succulent arranged around a central fountain. Wooden loungers, a dining area, and a shower to cool off. A breathtaking view across the medina's flat rooftops towards the Atlas Mountains.

But there was nothing in the home to distinguish its ownership. There were no photographs, no paperwork, nothing personal. No clothes in the closets, no books that would denote an owner's preference, only maps of Morocco and guides to Marrakech and travel books about North Africa in general. No appointments were stuck to the fridge, or artwork drawn by a child.

But it was hers. I knew it. And I wondered once again why Madame Toussaint was helping me. Could she be the person that Eva couldn't talk about? But if she was, then why had Eva tried to warn me off?

I sat on the bed in the master suite – blue and white *zellij* tiles on the floor, the walls covered in detailed plasterwork – and pulled out my phone hoping to find a signal in the house and grateful to find full coverage. I could check in with Eva and tether my laptop to research Marrakech.

But as I looked at the phone's screen, I hesitated. The familiar wallpaper of a smiling me and Graham astride a stile on the Yorkshire Moors, the busy columns of apps, lists of missed calls and messages. Email alerts.

It was quiet in the house, noise from the bustling medina cut out completely by the thick stone walls, only the gentle trickle of water as it entered the pools in the courtyard below.

Full coverage.

I switched off the phone and ran down to the kitchen to find something that would help remove its sim.

WHEN I ENTERED the Jemaa el Fna, half of its expanse was filled with men kneeling on prayer mats and facing east in veneration. Flip-flops, trainers, slippers of every kind, lay abandoned to the side; foreheads were pressed to the ground and the air was filled with the mournful drone of a thousand voices chanting sacred prayers. Tourists were milling around, some intrigued by the spectacle, others oblivious.

I moved along the stalls at the periphery of the square where the overhanging canopies gave respite from the heat. The yellow headscarf was wrapped around my head, its long ties slung over my shoulders; I wore loose pants and a tunic, my whole body covered, and I felt comfortable edging with the crowds.

I was looking for a stall that would sell me a burner phone, the kind criminals throw away when the crime has been done. Anonymous, untraceable, disposable. Because anyone with the right technology and the mind to do so could track my whereabouts through my mobile phone. Somebody like Lucas Bliek.

The new phone purchased, I sat in the Café de France with a glass of mint tea, and made a call to Graham with pay-as-you-go credit.

'It's me.'

'You've got a new phone.' Tension already in his voice.

'Yes,' I said, sounding breezy. 'The iPhone's been stolen. Some pickpocket in Tangier.'

'Tangier?'

The last time we had spoken I was calling from the poly-tunnels in Almería.

'Things have moved on, Gray.' I was buoyant, reminding myself how far I had already travelled on this journey of speculation and hope. 'The van was picked up on the ferry leaving Spain, so I took the initiative and got myself to Tangier. I'm working with Eva so don't worry. I'm on the phone to her every day.'

A futile attempt, and disrespectful to someone who knew me and could work things out for himself.

'Right,' he said in the tone he used when he knew I was lying. 'Then you must have identified the van?'

'Somebody gave Eva the heads up – CTM works with informants, a bit like the police do.' Graham was still thinking, so I said, 'I thought I'd ring to let you know I'm now in Morocco.'

This was more than I ever used to do. It was not my habit to inform Graham of my every move, and he was OK with that. In my mind it was a way of protecting him. He rarely knew where I was or where I'd been until I returned home to Yorkshire. It wasn't something that usually bothered him because he knew it was a method I used to manage his anxiety. And perhaps, my own.

'Where are the children?' he said. 'Do you know for certain they are in Morocco?'

'The child,' I corrected him, lowering my voice. 'It's just the girl I'm following now. The boy was taken in a car somewhere else. Eva's working on that … they know about a Dutch network operating out of Costa Blanca.'

'So it's just the girl who has gone to Morocco.'

'I can feel she's close, Gray. I know she's here. Don't ask me why.'

There was a pause.

'When I find her I'll have what I need to lock that bastard up.' I was speaking in hushed tones, hunched over my tea.

'How so?'

'Because she will be able to identify him.' It was obvious, really.

'Do you know where she is?'

'Not exactly.'

'Then how will you find her?'

'Eva knows someone. She has a contact here.' I felt a little exposed in the café, but the neutral space was better than the riad and there was a buzz to the atmosphere. It was crammed with tourists ticking off the Café de France from their list of essential things to do in Marrakech.

'A contact?'

'Yes.'

'Local?'

'Hmm.'

'Karen, I think it's time you came home.' His tone had changed so I knew he was serious. 'I know you want to catch him but I'm not convinced this is the way.'

'And what other way do you suggest?'

'Come home.'

'I can't.'

'Let Eva handle it.'

Graham seemed to have great confidence in Eva Taal although he had scant information about her from me. He would have checked her out online. He had access to data and resources denied the majority of internet users due to his experience in the industry, and I had no doubt he would have done a proper trawl on Eva.

'She doesn't have the resources, you know that, I've told you.'

I was thinking of a way to end the call without making things worse. Perhaps it had been a bad idea to let Graham know where I was when there was so much work left to do.

Then he said, 'There are too many what-ifs.'

'What d'you mean *what-ifs*?'

'What if you don't find the girl but you only find trouble for yourself? What if she doesn't want to be found? What if you find her, but she won't talk? What if she doesn't know Broekmann? What if you find her and she can identify him but he gets away with it anyway?'

'What do you mean "she doesn't want to be found"!' I was incensed. 'Of course she wants to be found. What on earth are you saying?'

'I'm saying that maybe you need to think carefully about the reasons you're trying to find her.'

The anger was bubbling, a confusion of emotions. Graham was intolerable and I was tempted to tell him more than he needed to know, but I was in a public space and he would only react more erratically if he knew the whole story.

'I have to go,' I said. 'I need to speak to Eva and get in touch with her local contact.'

I hung up.

People were staring with teacups halfway to their lips. I drew some dirhams from my wallet and left them on the table. Gathering my things, I headed off across the Jemaa el Fna where the worshippers had now dispersed and only tourists wandered the bazaars, one group standing in a semi-circle mesmerised by a snake charmer sitting cross-legged on a pile of rugs, the cobra weaving seductively from the basket.

I entered a small bar, bought a beer and decided I would make a call to Dorothy Turay to see if there was news about missing children from Freetown. Dorothy was a true comrade, a fellow agitator. She had faith in me and I trusted her completely.

'It's Karen.'

'Yes.'

Dorothy was a friend, but tricky.

'How are you?' I said.

'Why are you calling me? I'm busy.' I could hear some beat-bop music in the background and she was slightly out of breath, like she was walking uphill.

'I need your help.'

'What can I do?'

'Those children. I sent you their photos.'

'Yes,' she said. 'You have found them?'

Her confidence in my abilities was encouraging.

'Not yet, but I'm close. It's just the girl now. They've been split up by the gang. The boy has been taken somewhere else, but I'm close to finding the girl.'

'Where are you?'

'Morocco … North Africa.'

'I know where Morocco is. This is my own continent of which we speak.'

'Yes, yes.' I was reminded to get straight to the point with this woman. 'Look, when I find this child I'm going to need your help identifying her family and contacting them. I suspect the gang will have her papers and I will need to have confirmation of ID from you before she can be repatriated to her family.'

'That may not be the best idea,' she said wisely. 'Not if it was her family that sold her.'

Of course, I knew that was a possibility.

'OK. I know. But she will still need ID-ing for travel papers and a passport out of Morocco back to Amsterdam.'

'That makes sense. But I will need a name.'

'Sure,' I said, a little panicked. But I knew in my heart it would not be long before I knew her name.

'What is she to you?' Dorothy demanded. The beat-bop music had died down and her breathing had returned to normal. She was off the street.

'That girl is my ticket to Broekmann,' I said. 'You saw his "shopping list" of children for yourself. You were the one who explained it to me.'

Surely Dorothy, of all people, must understand my motives.

There was no response from her and a silence ensued. She was waiting to hear a more plausible answer.

'Are you still there?' I asked.

'I am here.'

Dorothy spoke in a flat monotone, no nuance to her voice. Information exchanged without any embellishment such as joy, or fear, or anger. She had seen the photos of the children and I wondered if she had also noticed the girl's strong resemblance to Songola, but I dared not ask her. Dorothy had been closer to our murdered friend than anyone – they were like blood sisters, born in the same rebel camp during the country's civil war, and growing up in the bush together. If anyone wanted to avenge Songola's death, it was Dorothy.

She was quiet on the other end of the line, and I imagined her equine profile and the little furrows on her brow as she waited for my reply.

Eventually I said, 'Can you do some more digging? Someone must have noticed these children are missing.'

'If you give me a name I can investigate,' she said without

pushing me further. 'Then I will find out how she got into the hands of these people. That I will do. For sure.'

Dorothy was an undergraduate law student and was teaching at the mission school. She was a confident and capable woman, and I had a deep respect for her. But time was running out. That girl needed my help and I prayed she would survive until I found her.

TWENTY
KAREN

Thirty-six hours later I was beginning to lose hope. I had spent all my time time wandering the souks and drinking tea in the cafés around Jemaa el Fna hoping to see the child walk by. The situation had now reached an impasse; without news from Eva I was on my own with no more leads and no more information. The old feeling of recklessness was approaching. Something I had experienced before – when there was nothing left to do but the obvious.

Several times I had telephoned the Hammam Palmier in Tangier, but it seemed Madame Toussaint never took calls or was away 'on business'. I still didn't know why she had sent me all the way to Marrakech just to lose track of the girl. But there was something about her that I trusted. Whatever Madame Toussaint's motivation, she had taken a risk sharing information about the girl. The riad in Derb Lalla Chassa was deep within the medina's maze of alleys, squashed between a patchwork of high-value residences and commercial properties and it felt like a safe house. But things did not add up. It seemed like I was waiting for a starting pistol, biding my time until the real race began.

It was evening and I sat alone in the riad's terrace garden planning my next move and gazing across the disorderly rooftops of the medina, pitched at different heights and different angles, pierced by the occasional minaret. Beyond the city walls there were immense palm groves and, further still, the pink-hued mountains of the Atlas, luminous in the evening light. A sliver of crescent moon hung like a bauble against the indigo sky, the heavens beginning to reveal their hidden flickering gems.

Nights in Ramadan were special. At sunset, the cannon fired and the muezzin began their call to prayer. The streets and alleys soon emptied as people dispersed to celebrate the iftar. No cars, no carts, no pedestrians. Even the dogs stopped barking.

I had not seen the old man since he had handed me the keys when I arrived at the riad. He had not returned with a message from his boss or any information that might help me. So I decided that the next day I would return to the Jemaa el Fna and the labyrinth of alleys that surrounded its immense plaza and show the girl's photo to whomsoever I met. I would attempt to find another Khalid, someone who might have local knowledge that would help me find her.

Then my phone lit up with an incoming call from Eva.

'Don't ask all your usual questions,' she said straight away, 'because I can't answer them. Not because I don't want to but because I don't know the answers myself.'

'OK.'

'I am still waiting for clearance,' she said. *Clearance?*

'So you will just have to trust me.' She was speaking quickly as though the words were eager for her to spit them out. 'If you keep asking all your questions you may jeopardise the lives of others.'

'I understand. What *can* you tell me?'

'I can tell you that help is coming soon.'

'You know where she is, don't you, Eva?'

'I don't have clearance for that.'

'What's all this about *clearance?*'

She went quiet.

'Sorry … I forgot.' But I wasn't expecting what came next.

'Karen, what you need to understand is that nobody cares about this girl as much as you do. This is the hard truth you need to know. There is more going on than you can know about – things that I can't know about, even. And that fact makes you her only friend.' Her words were as sharp as knives. 'There are other lives to consider, not just hers.' She was getting it all out before her natural kindness took over and prevented her. 'Important operations are at stake that make your girl only a small consideration.'

'But human trafficking, Eva. That's your fight also.'

'Can't you trust me?' There was an uncharacteristic harshness to her tone.

'Of course I trust you.'

'What I can tell you now is that someone will make themselves known to you very soon, so be ready. That's all I can say.'

'Thank you, Eva.'

She hung up.

THAT NIGHT HE CAME.

At three thirty I awoke to the sound of a key turning in the inner door and the scraping of the gate. I sat upright straining to hear over the thumping of my heart. Movement on the courtyard tiles, a heavy object being dropped on the floor, something else rolling around. Footsteps moving into the kitchen.

I swung my legs over the bed, pulled a robe around my body and padded out of my room. Down through the canopy of citrus I could see to the courtyard below; the scent of jasmine floated up, sweet and heady. A large duffle bag and a red and white striped motorcycle helmet had been dumped on the tiles. The kitchen lights were illuminated, a shadowy figure moving around, the clink of bottles being removed from the fridge, a metal top fizzing open, rattling on the counter.

Fear held me and I tried to rationalise. Who else would have the keys to Madame Toussaint's home other than those whom she could trust?

A scraping on the tiles as the duffle was lifted, but I couldn't see him clearly. Then footsteps getting louder as he made his way upstairs. I moved back into the room, knocking against a rustling palm, and watched him walk along the gallery opposite, dropping the bag by the second bedroom before entering the first-floor salon. A low lamp was illuminated before he opened his laptop and flopped against the cushions of a low cane armchair, taking a slug of beer from the bottle.

The night air was cool. I drew the robe closer, bare feet moving stealthily along the tiles, stopping at a spot behind a palm so I could get a good look at him through the salon door. A lanky frame, floppy brown hair. Untidy beard. Mid-thirties.

He took a long pull from the bottle, his eyes focused on the screen, and when he looked up I recognised the cobalt blue of his irises.

'Karen,' he said, rising to greet me, 'Finn der Weese … you may remember …'

I remembered, and his familiar face brought a gasp of relief from my constricted throat.

'Yes … Finn.'

Mimi's brother. The only time we had met before was on Eva and Mimi's houseboat near the Schinkel dock in Amsterdam.

'Sorry to wake you,' he said. 'I'll be leaving in a couple of hours so it might be best if we talk now.'

Finn der Weese was an officer working for the Koninklijke Marechaussee, an elite branch of the Netherlands armed forces that focused on national security. This much I knew from my conversation with Eva and Mimi after Finn had left the houseboat – Mimi so proud of his commission to the Criminal Intelligence Unit.

What was he doing in Marrakech? Was he after the trafficking gang himself?

'I'm sorry but there is little I can say about the reasons I am in Marrakech,' he said gently, reading my mind and indicating that I should sit opposite. 'But what I can tell you is that I am not here in an official capacity for KM and that you must not disclose our meeting to anyone. It is a matter of national security.'

I nodded assent, perching on the edge of an embroidered pouffe. He looked exhausted, like he hadn't slept for days. He leant forward, his arms resting on splayed knees, cradling his beer.

'I can help you with the girl.' There was a slight Dutch inflection to his voice. 'But you must understand that nothing you do can jeopardise the work I am involved in here … which is not connected to this child.'

I had so many questions, like how did he know Madame Toussaint? And what was he investigating if it wasn't trafficking? But I focused on the reason he was here, which was the whereabouts of the girl.

'Have you seen her?'

'Yes, I have seen her. And I can tell you that she is living in a house owned by the head of an organised crime network here in Morocco. He is a very dangerous man, and the people around him are the kind you must not anger. The man, let's call him the sultan, he is greatly feared by anyone with any intelligence.'

'Where is this house?' I was ready to hit the road.

'I can't tell you the location of the house. It is heavily guarded and has razor-wired boundary walls and fences. You must never go there.'

I let him continue.

'But I *can* tell you that I have seen the girl for myself,' he said.

'You have been to the house?'

He ignored the question. 'She is living with the servants doing menial tasks, cleaning, clearing out domestic animals, and working mostly for the cook. She spends time in the vegetable patches with the gardener.'

Relief surged through me. Somewhere in my soul I was convinced she was to be sold for prostitution. So young and beautiful, the kind that certain men desire.

Finn continued. 'She is to become the fourth wife of the sultan. The man is travelling at this time but preparations are being made for his return for Eid celebrations. Soon after, there will be a "marriage" ceremony. The other wives are jealous and are making her do all the shit in his absence.'

Forced marriage had never crossed my mind. But why not? In many parts of Africa it was rife. Young girls – innocent – forced into marriage, even within their own families, but more often travelling long distances for the substantial extra bounty they could bring for the traffickers.

'It seems she was trafficked to order,' Finn was saying. 'The sultan wants her as part payment of a debt.'

'What sort of debt?'

'That I cannot say. But the girl is well educated and innocent. This is a condition for the sultan's wives.'

I felt sick with apprehension. 'When will this happen,' I asked. 'How long have we got?'

'We? No, I am afraid I can take no part in the rescue of this child, even though I may want to help you. I am sorry to say the work I am doing is more important and is unrelated to the sale of this girl.'

'Yes, of course.'

He could see the disappointment on my face and smiled weakly. 'I'm sorry, but is true.'

How am I going to find her without his help?

'But I have some information that might help you.' He leant in as though ears were listening through the walls. 'Every day the cook takes the girl to the souks to collect provisions for the house. Fruit and vegetables from the market at Mellah. This is your opportunity.'

'The market? Here in Marrakech?'

'It is not far from this house.'

'This house!'

'Not far.'

'And she goes there every day?'

'This is my understanding. They set off early. The wives are demanding, and violent if they don't get the best.' He drained his beer and put the bottle on the table. 'I hope you find her, Karen.'

I showed the girl's photo to Finn, just to be sure.

'Yes, that's her.'

My heart was in my mouth. How long did I have to rescue her before time ran out?

'I won't be here when you wake in the morning,' Finn was saying, but I couldn't imagine I would be sleeping any more that night. 'If you're lucky and you get her, bring the child to this house. It is safe and the last place they will look for her, but you must be vigilant and get her out of the country as quickly as you can.'

He picked up his leather jacket from the chair where he'd slung it and gathered the rest of his things. In two hours he would have left the house, and the country.

'Now I must bid you goodnight and good luck.' He made

his way to bed. The light was soon extinguished, and then a gentle snore.

I climbed to the roof, my mind whirling with hope and gratitude. Looking east across the city, the glow of sunrise was creeping against the horizon, the sound of distant trumpets signalling the *suhoor*. To the west, a shard of crescent moon still hung low above the hills.

TWENTY-ONE

THE GIRL

Abdullah was late. He usually entered the coup towards the end of the afternoon but today he was nowhere to be seen. The girl scratched her neck and loosened the headscarf; she could not wait much longer or cook would come looking for her eggs. The hens were already crowded into the hut and starting to roost, their happy chattering filling the space with sounds of contented poultry. If Abdullah did not arrive soon she would have to go, then try to slip away later, because she could not risk the woman marching across the yard to find out why she was late. No one must know of her meetings with Abdullah. It would be bad for them both if anyone found out.

But before she could leave, he arrived.

'Mademoiselle,' he said, smiling, kneeling down and scraping at the dirt with jerky movements.

She greeted him excitedly, telling him all about her visit to the market and the opportunity it presented for escape. Abdullah listened carefully. He explained that he knew about shopping trips to the vegetable souks. Occasionally, he had to accompany the cook himself when the kitchen lad was needed for other duties.

Her features alive with excitement, the girl presented her plan to him: that, on the outskirts of the city, near the ten-lane intersection, there was a vast lorry park where trucks pulled out onto the highway going north and south. When she escaped from the market and found her way to the lorry park she must be sure she boarded a truck headed north to Tangier. She recalled that the journey south to Marrakech had taken a whole day, at the end of which the white peaks of the Atlas Mountains were on the left-hand side of the car. So, she must make sure the truck she chose to hide in was travelling with the mountains on the right – headed north. She did not want to end up on the south side of the mountains moving towards the desert or some other unknown destination where she would be truly lost. She had noted that many of the trucks had flatbed trailers with curtains hanging down their sides and decided that this kind of vehicle would be easier to board than a fixed-sided trailer – difficult to scale – after which she might find who knows what to sit on for the long journey north.

So the main concern was knowing which way a truck would turn when it exited the lorry park. She could ask around and pay someone to take her to Tangier but this was a risky strategy. She had heard of the fate of lone girls travelling the highway with inadequate information and little money and she was sure Abdullah would know the answers to these questions.

The gardener sat back on his heels and gaped at her with a wondrous expression. Such a determined child. But he was not keen on the plan. Trucks in the lorry park could be headed anywhere with any deceitful person at the wheel, and everything you could think of could go wrong, and he would not allow the plan as it stood.

Then he asked about the straps that bound her tightly to the boy, restricted her movement in the market and would prevent her from running.

But the girl already had a solution for that part of the plan.

'Je vais voler un couteau dans la cuisine,' she said confidently.

But his expression was doubtful. Would the kitchen knife be strong enough to cut through leather, he asked, and how easy would it be to steal it, hide it in her room, conceal it upon her person, then retrieve it from where she had hidden it under her clothes before sawing away at her bonds?

The girl sighed noisily. Negativity was a curse, her father used to say.

'Connaissez-vous un camion qui se dirigera vers Tanger?' she was asking now.

Yes, Abdullah knew of trucks leaving for Tangier, but he suggested she might be safer on a bus. After all, buses usually had the destination written all over them, but then the bus station would be the first place they would look for her.

The girl noted Abdullah's mood was not as buoyant as her own.

'Qu'est-ce qui ne va pas?' she said warily.

The chickens were murmuring softly. She had picked up a hen and was cradling it against her body.

Abdullah smiled at her affectionately. 'Rien,' he said kindly. He would speak to friends who drove to Tangier from the lorry park.

THE NEXT DAY, Abdullah was scraping shit from the boards of the coup when the girl dipped in her head and beamed at him, hoping for information about his friends at the lorry park, but his body was tense.

'Ça doit être bientôt,' he said under his breath. *It must be soon.*

The girl noticed the change in him. There was no chipped smile on his face today. His happy features were now serious and watchful. Something was up and it made her nervous.

He took her hand and sat her down beside him on the wooden slats. A hen eyed them from her nesting box, clucking nervously.

'Demain,' he said simply.

She asked him what was wrong. Why was he telling her she must escape tomorrow.

He explained that it was time to get away from the palace, in fact at the first opportunity, which would be the following morning on her next trip to the market. That the sultan was due to return for the Eid celebrations, and that his guests would be participating in a ceremony to mark his new marriage. A fourth wife to add to his portfolio. Young and beautiful and clever and chaste.

Her.

She felt like her insides were vibrating and her mouth became dry as she recalled her cousin Fatima who had been forced to leave their village and marry a toothless old man of immense ugliness who was chief in the northern provinces. He already had several wives and many children, most of whom were older than Fatima herself. It had been a terrible fate for a young girl, but it was not uncommon in their country, and now it seemed the same was planned for her. She reached for the restless hen, taking care not to disturb the dozing poultry, and embraced it lovingly, resting her face against its feathers, feeling the warmth and security of its body.

Abdullah explained his plan quickly. He had friends who drove the A3 and A5 highways to Tangier. They were men he had met in the camps in Tangier who had decided to stay in Morocco and try their luck, ending up as drivers, hauling all manner of merchandise up and down the country in trucks and vans. Among this group, there was someone he could trust to help the girl. But the man would need paying, and the timing of the escape would be tricky.

Abdullah's friend worked for a company that hauled

textiles between Marrakech and the ferry port at Tangier. The following day, the man would delay at the lorry park so that the girl could find him when she ran from the market. He would be taking a serious risk and Abdullah had agreed to pay him two thousand dirhams for his trouble, but he did not mention that to the girl. The truck – it had a yellow cab and blue wagon – would be loaded with rugs, blankets and other textiles, and would have the name Tariq Textiles painted in Arabic on the side. He showed her a paper with the name and asked her to memorise the script. The truck would be waiting in the lorry park and would leave no later than 10 a.m. so it could get to Tangier in time to board the ferry to Tarifa. It would not be possible for him to delay any longer, but the girl would have plenty of time to get from the souks because the cook arrived early, around 7.30 a.m.

The girl was nodding enthusiastically, excited that she may be riding a truck that could take her all the way back to Spain, and Abdullah wondered from what depths this child drew her resilience, the girl with skin like midnight and a heart full of hope and courage. Something he'd lost long ago. He would miss her companionship. The solid link to his homeland.

There was only one real weakness in the plan, but Abdullah would take care of that himself.

TWENTY-TWO

KAREN

I arrived early at the Mellah as market vendors were setting up their stalls. Sacks of fruit and vegetables, bags and jars and trays of spices, crates loaded with herbs of every kind, were being offloaded from donkeys, carts, and trucks. When the first customers trickled in, I picked a good spot to observe the crowd and take photos of the scene and everyone in it.

The covered market at the Mellah was accessed through a pink horseshoe arch and was surrounded by smaller stalls on its outer periphery. There were many improvised stands made from tarpaulins spread out on the ground where farmers brought their single crop to sell; others were trading straight from the back of their carts, and still others setting up stalls all along the edges of the street where they were shaded in the overhang of covered walkways. The stands were a riot of colour, herbs, fruit, and vegetables of every hue, vendors erecting wide parasols to protect their merchandise from the unforgiving sun that was steadily rising behind the dome of a nearby mosque.

I absorbed myself among the shoppers, searching for a young unmistakable heart-shaped face. At a dried fruit stall I bought dates, apricots and figs, and a jar of olives at another.

Women, swaddled in hijabs and carrying large baskets, hurried through the markets gathering ingredients for the day's meals, including fresh meat. Live chickens – which were kept in precarious multistorey cages set on trolley wheels – were being blessed by the butcher before slaughter. It was a local custom demanded by their customers but an upsetting spectacle to witness.

Hours later, I was still wandering the stalls, picking up goods and examining them, returning them to the displays, resigned to the continuous pressure of aggressive vendors and batting them away as best I could. I fingered the note in my pocket – all morning I had been ready for the moment that I found her, when I would slip it into her hand.

I am a friend and want to help you. I saw you being taken at Lungi Airport. I will look for you again. Please come with me. Karen.

But I had not seen the girl, or anyone like her, and as midday approached I knew the opportunity had gone, that she and whoever brought her to the market would have already purchased their goods and returned to the palace. Resigned, I sat on an upturned crate and ate a slice of honey-soaked almond cake watching the vendors clearing away, sweeping rotting fruit and vegetables from the cobbles, stacking jars of spices back onto their carts to be hauled away ready for the next day's trading. I would be back, for as long as it took.

I joined a trail of tourists in Jemaa el Fna who were roasting in the heat and moving in a slow column behind a noisy tour guide shaded under a parasol and shouting into a mobile amp. Large crowds had gathered beside the lush gardens of the Koutoubia Mosque waiting for a closer look at its famous arch motifs and the spire and metal orbs atop its minaret. Further on, a Syrian whirling dervish – surrounded by tightly packed tourists – was beginning to rotate, arms splayed akimbo, faster and faster until the skirt of his garment formed a circle around his body. It looked as though he was levitating. He appeared in a trance, like his audience, and I watched for a while, absorbed in the moment, trying to put the disappointment of the day into perspective.

After a while, I returned to the riad to study the market photos.

TWO DAYS after Finn der Weese had visited me, I was still searching for the girl and vendors at the market were beginning to wonder about my intentions, this tourist taking photos all day long, not buying much. Desperation was setting in and I had started working on an alternative strategy.

Where was this sultan's house? If I could locate it, I could do a recce. Obviously, I would not attempt to get inside the place, but maybe I could watch the gates, get there early for a glimpse of the girl as she left for the market.

Thoughts such as these circled in my head as panic and despair began to engulf me. I knew that time was running out. The moon was now invisible and I was unsure how long it took before a sliver of new moon announced Eid. For sure, there was tension in the city – everyone waiting for permission to live again.

It occurred to me that Madame Toussaint would know where to find the sultan's house. And surely it wasn't a secret here in Marrakech. Local people would have heard about the Maroc Mafia and must know the location of the boss's mansion. These things were known in close-knit communities. Maybe I could ask around, take the bus, dress in a hijab, mingle with the locals.

I sank into the upholstery in the riad's upstairs salon, grateful for the coolness of its interior, and uploaded the latest photos from the phone. Maybe there would be something new today. But the pictures were indistinguishable from the hundreds of shots I had taken on previous days in the market. What was I missing?

I took a cold beer from the fridge and moved upstairs to the terrace garden where a welcome breeze blew across the rooftops. The only thing to do was start again from the beginning. Scrutinise every photo until I found her.

The files loaded on the laptop.

I positioned myself in the sloping shade of the date palms and started to search again from the very first shot, meticulously analysing every image, zooming in on any girl of African descent who could be her – short, a slight frame, hair in cornrows. Skin the shade of an indigo sky, much darker than most people that had visited the market.

Hours passed and the cannon struck for the end of fasting, restaurants reopening and people rushing home to share the iftar together, spicy aromas wafting over the rooftops. The heat of the day lingered on, drawing the sweat from my body, and the first stars flickered into view as the muezzin started their wailing, a distressed resonance echoing across the city and up into the Atlas Mountains.

Something in one of the photos caught my eye, an object vaguely familiar for reasons I could not immediately determine. I enlarged the picture as much as possible without over-pixelating the image into a blur, and checked the photos either side of it. Yes, it was there, and my heart thumped with excitement.

I pulled up the original photo of the girl at the airport and checked it against what I now saw on the screen.

A rucksack with a Ghostbuster's logo.

She had been carrying a rucksack with the same logo – a red and white 'no-ghosts' image – that stood out strikingly against the black sack, a throwback to the eighties, and it seemed very dated. I stared at the image. What were the chances of such a distinctive Ghostbusters rucksack and the girl I was searching for being together in the marketplace Finn der Weese had sent me to?

Sick with excitement, I started to panic, imagining the photos would suddenly disappear before I could identify who was wearing the rucksack. I zoomed in on him.

A young man, rotund, wearing a white skullcap and grey djellaba. He had a yoke across his shoulders bearing large wicker baskets at either end, and the Ghostbuster's sack was wedged in between. Beside him were two women in hijabs who were buying pomegranates from a massive fruit stall. One of the women was large, swaddled in layers of black cloth, sleeves pushed up her forearms. Next to her, a much slighter figure dressed in a pink headscarf and oversized white tunic that swamped her body. Frantically, I scrolled through the photos to see if I had taken a closer shot and maxed up the magnification.

There she was. Staring through the crowd, the headscarf slipped a little. A direct gaze straight at me, just as she had at Lungi Airport. It was her. No question. And she had been there on my very first day at the market.

I stood and gazed up into the velvety sky. Many more stars emerging from the blue. Still no sign of the new moon. Not yet Eid.

TWENTY-THREE

THE GIRL

That morning, the girl did not hesitate to dress quickly when the cook arrived to wake her for their trip to the market. She now had her route to freedom carefully planned and was ready to make her escape. The alternative was beyond contemplation.

But, on the journey into town, an overloaded truck stacked high with bales of hay had overturned on the highway and traffic had ground to a halt. Tensions immediately flared, the cook shifting her bosom out of the window to shout and curse at the upturned bales of hay as though they might get up and move themselves, all the while imagining all the best pomegranates being sold to an inferior customer. The girl remained calm. There was plenty of time. She knew the way and the truck would be waiting.

Later, the vehicle parked up in its usual spot on the pavement and the cook, the gardener and the girl hurriedly alighted, leaving the driver unwrapping the *pastilla* he had packed for his breakfast.

The girl had been surprised to find Abdullah in the car that morning but the kitchen boy had been unfit for travel. During the night, there had been a commotion in the servants' bungalow. Someone rushing to the bathroom – the door flung open, then banged shut – the disturbance continuing all through the early hours. Unpleasant sounds emerging from under the door. Groaning, vomiting, excessive effluence hitting the pan.

The voice sounded as though it might belong to the boy although, when she thought about it, the girl had never heard him speak. It transpired that he had food poisoning following the servants' iftar the previous evening – although everyone else had enjoyed the feast without any consequential up-chuck. Perhaps some indigestible herb had been concealed in the lad's portion, or maybe rancid goat had been present in his serving, but, whatever the cause, the boy had not emerged from his quarters that morning.

Abdullah placed the leather cuff on the girl's wrist and bound her to his own in the usual manner, making a point of it so that the cook could see he was obeying the rules to prevent the child from running. Their original plan had been to wait until a moment when the woman was distracted – perhaps engaged in her usual argument with the vendor – then Abdullah would loosen the bind and the girl would run. But now they had been too long delayed on the highway, and the girl would have to make a run for it at the very first opportunity. The yellow and blue truck could not wait past the agreed hour of 10 a.m. and Abdullah did not want to think about the consequences if she missed that safe passage to Tangier and was left alone in the lorry park, hungry eyes upon her.

The plan was that she would run all the way from the market to the edge of town. The girl was confident of the way because the palace car had passed the truck stop every day. Heavy vehicles came and departed continuously, drivers resting or taking refreshments from the bustle of vendors who were hawking the site. When she got there, the girl would look for the truck with the yellow cab and the blue wagon and the Arabic script on the side. The driver would be waiting for her. His name was Ajamu, and he would take her safely all the way to the coast.

Under her tunic, she had fashioned a sling-like receptacle and strapped it around her waist. Inside was her secret stash of US dollars, seven hundred dirham given to her by Abdullah, a bottle of water, some bread and two hard-boiled eggs stolen from the kitchen. And the precious item from the bottom of her Ghostbusters sack. It was easy to hide things under the oversized flowing robes.

The market was busy and the crowds pressed in, separating briefly to allow an empty handcart to pass through before closing in again more tightly than before. Moving through this throng would be difficult today. The place seemed more crowded than previously. Perhaps people were stocking up for Eid. And now the girl felt a pain in her stomach, an aching cramp in her abdomen that she recognised from before.

At their regular stall, she waited for the cook to turn her back and offer the usual greetings to the vendor.

'Salam alaykum,' the woman screeched over the hubbub.

'Wa alaykum salaam!' the vendor replied.

Abdullah unlocked the chain and slid the cuff from the girl's wrist. She slipped her hand in his and felt the comforting warmth.

He edged them out of the crush, but it was difficult manoeuvring the yoke of baskets in the crowd. Under the flowing garment, sweat poured down the girl's body. Fear and excitement gripped her as she stood wedged in, her heart pounding, the uncomfortable headscarf scratching her neck.

'Good luck, little sister,' Abdullah whispered, squeezing her hand, the words catching in the cacophony around them.

She stood motionless, staring into his face.

'Maintenant! Allez vite!' he hissed, pushing her away from

him, encouraging her to go. The truck would soon be leaving on its journey to the coast. Inshallah.

She stepped back to absorb herself into the crowd and move with it away from her jailers. When she saw a gap she would run. Gradually, she increased the space between them, keeping her sights on the broad back of the cook who was now leaning over the vegetables, her bosom resting on the yams. The child touched the belt around her waist for reassurance, feeling her father's presence, her breath quickening, matching the rhythm of her heart.

She pushed in the direction of the alley that she knew would take her east towards the lorry park, bumping into shoppers with hostile stares, slipping on spoiled fruit that littered the cobbled ground. She clutched at someone's djellaba and fell heavily among the mess, and when a shriek went up, she recognised the fearsome voice. Dizzy and disoriented, she scrambled to her feet, wondering which way to run, panic and confusion crushing in. She looked for shadows to identify the direction of the sun but there were too many people, no clear line of sight, no identifiable alley that she had been running towards. Now she would have to run in any direction that would take her away from that woman.

A hand slipped into hers. But it wasn't Abdullah's.

Someone whispered, 'Trust me.'

Then the girl was running again, but not alone.

They ran together through the crowd and out of the market into a maze of alleys that the child didn't recognise but sensed was not in the direction of the blue and yellow truck. She followed willingly, allowing herself to be led, sure that once she had her bearings she would break free and find her way to the lorry park where the driver would be waiting for her – there could still be time. As soon as she could see the angle of the shadows clearly, she would know the location of the sun and that would help her determine an easterly direction. But for now she was running and sweating, the precious

belt bouncing at her waist, the pain in her abdomen inten-
sifying.

The hand in hers belonged to a woman. Pale slender
fingers wrapped around hers, urging her on.

They ran for some time, dodging in and out of
gawking tourists, taking a complicated route through the
narrow streets, avoiding the huge expanse of the Jemaa el
Fna. The sky was obscured by tall buildings that filled
the streets with shadow and the girl set her eyes overhead, searching for the sun, trying to get her bearings
and colliding with a turbaned vendor who had been
carrying a tray of pearly teeth, hundreds of individual
items, and full sets that were attached to pink gums, all
now scattered across the ground. He stared angrily into
her face and cursed in Arabic, his breath rank with hali-
tosis from the fasting, deep lines etched into his crispy
skin.

But the woman pulled her on, no time for politeness.

Down the next street, they slowed. Their speed in the heat
was attracting attention and suspicious stares, so the woman
slackened their pace, her grip on the child firm, pulling her
along the street. Arab pop music radiated from a small,
shallow grocery store, where the vendor shouted into his
phone over the noise. In the shop next door a mechanic was
fixing the spokes of an upturned bicycle. Across the street,
rows of imitation Premier League football shirts hung from
horizontal poles.

The pair stopped for a moment, standing aside to allow a
donkey cart to pass, the animal defecating as it clipped along
the cobbles. But straight away a shopkeeper appeared to
sweep away the mess.

Then through a dim passage that cut between two buildings and out into a garden planted with orange and lemon
trees. The sound of a gurgling fountain. Then out again
through a Moorish arch into the sunlight where rich aromas

wafted through the streets, the noise of handcarts on cobbles and donkeys braying.

Turning left and right, the hand holding hers confident of the way.

The girl's heart was full of hope for no reason she could muster. Who was this woman with the lemon scarf, its tassels swaying down her long straight back as they hurried along the streets? There was something about her that seemed familiar.

The child kept glancing back, expecting the cook to be following with a stream of others, brandishing shoes or belts or other weapons, intent on her recapture. But then she remembered that the cook found difficulty walking, let alone running along the cobbles.

The pain came again, viscous cramping in her womb.

As if she knew, the woman put an arm around her shoulders.

'Keep going … it's not far.' Her voice was reassuring.

They pulled up against the cool stucco of a shaded wall and the woman drew the child in close to her, looking behind to check who may be following.

No one.

So they turned down a tiny alley with trailing pink gera-niums and paused to unlock a huge studded door where they slipped unnoticed into the cool shade of the interior.

'DO YOU SPEAK ENGLISH?' the woman panted at the child.

The girl said nothing. She needed time to work things out.

The woman led her into a courtyard garden heavy with the scent of jasmine, where water flowed in a gurgling stream from taps that stuck out from the wall.

'I'm Karen,' the woman said. There a flush to her cheeks. She was perspiring rapidly and removed the lemon headscarf to reveal thick dark curls that were stuck to her head.

'Please, let's sit down.' The woman indicated a wicker armchair with padded cushions, but the girl remained standing.

'I've been searching for you ever since I saw you at Lungi Airport,' the woman said, the words coming out in an excited rush. 'Let me show you.'

She produced a photo which the child recognised as herself standing beside her abductor who had dressed himself as a priest. With them stood the boy, Foday.

Foday.

Something clutched at the girl's heart when she recalled his name, but the photo explained where she had seen this woman before.

The girl moved around the garden, looking up through the foliage to the upper floors and the sky. This would be an easy place to escape from after the high walls and fences and armed guards at the palace. There had been many twists and turns on their route here from the market so she could not be sure of her new position and would need to check the sun and the location of the mountains to have an idea which way to run to find the lorry park. She had the dirhams from Abdullah and would pay someone else to take her to Tangier. For sure, Ajamu in his yellow and blue truck would have gone by now. But there would be others.

Right now, she had a different concern. She could not run far with the pain.

'Do you understand?' the woman was asking her. 'I think you do speak English?'

The girl nodded vaguely, peering at the woman from under lowered lids in a manner that did not suit her character but, on this occasion, suited her purpose.

'I've followed you all the way from Amsterdam,' the woman was saying, joy in her voice. 'You and the boy. I want to help you … if that's ok.' Her breath had calmed and she stood beside a lemon tree glowing with delight.

The girl was suspicious but impressed to know that this woman who called herself Karen had followed her all the way from Freetown. But what for? And why was she so keen to help her?

The child stood on the pretty tiles in the quiet courtyard listening to the water trickling out of the walls into shallow basins and wondered what sort of 'help' this woman was offering. Goodness shone in her wide green eyes. It was the same expression she had observed in her friend, Abdullah.

'Are you hungry? There's plenty of food.'

Without waiting for a reply, the woman made for the kitchen and returned with a glass of milk and a plate laden with flatbread and cheese. She gestured for the child to sit, but she remained standing, reaching for the glass and sipping at the cool, sweet liquid.

'What's your name?' the woman asked, but the girl turned her head to gaze at the ferns. 'I'm from the UK.'

A flicker of interest in the child's dark eyes.

'I've visited your country many times. I am a friend of Sierra Leone.'

The girl doubted that very much. She just wanted to get her bearings and see the sun.

From the columned gallery adjacent to the garden, steps led up to the first floor and she ascended, scanning the various rooms until she found the second stairway that led up to the roof. Perhaps there would be a good view of the city and the sky and the mountains from there.

The woman followed behind with the plate of bread and cheese.

'Please,' she said. 'I think you should keep out of sight. They will be looking for you and eyes could be anywhere.' Her face was riven with concern and she made a move to encourage the child to descend from the roof. 'I don't think they will give up easily … they will be angry now, and searching.'

The girl turned her gaze from the sky, recognising that these words were true. She nodded her understanding, the skin on her body turning cold at the thought of how angry the palace staff would be. What they might do to find her. If her first plan had worked, she would now be on the road to Tangier and out of their reach hidden inside an anonymous vehicle.

She descended from the roof, aware of the embarrassing stain now spreading across her garments. The woman noticed it too, and like a broody hen from the palace coup began fussing over her, encouraging the child into the bathroom where she drew water into the tub and indicated for her to remove the tunic and get in.

The woman disappeared to another room and returned with fresh clothes.

'Please, take these,' she said.

She handed the girl a pair of jeans, a shirt and fresh undergarments. 'They will be too big but I'll go to the market for clothes that will fit you better.'

The woman was considerably taller than the girl.

The child examined the woman's face. Kindness, concern, fatigue.

'I'll give you some privacy.' And she left, closing the door behind her.

TWENTY-FOUR
KAREN

'I have her!' Relief covered me like a blanket. I was speaking to Eva from the riad's garden and it was a long time since I had felt so happy.

'You have the girl?' Eva's voice had the edge of caution. It was always present in her tone.

'She's here at the house. She looks well, Eva. How do we get her home? They will be looking for her ... there's not much time.'

Now I had found her, a tight ball of pressure had settled behind my sternum with the responsibility to keep her safe.

'You took her from the marketplace?'

'Yes. It was complicated, but yes.'

'Has she given you her name or details of her family? Do you know how she came to be abducted?' She was slightly out of breath, and said she was cycling to a meeting at the Ministry for Social Affairs.

'No, she hasn't spoken yet. Not a word. I need to build her trust.'

I had left the girl on my bed, curled up in a ball and nursing her abdomen. She had refused painkillers, but I knew that rest would help her feel more comfortable.

'Sure,' said Eva. 'You must take it slow. But I will need her details to get temporary travel documents – then we can get her on a flight to the Netherlands.'

'I'm sure she'll talk to me after she's rested. I'm going to ring Dorothy next, see if there's any progress on missing persons, but she hasn't much reliable data to work with. Really, I think it all depends on the girl … building her trust to tell me her story.'

'If you could send a head and shoulders photo, that would help the process along.'

'Yes, I'll do that.'

'There will be some angry people looking for her,' Eva warned.

'Yes,' I said, the ball of pressure building in my chest, my voice a little shrill. 'The most dangerous man in Morocco has just lost his bride.'

Eva went quiet. I could hear her steady breathing, the clanging of trams and the rattle of bicycle wheels. I wondered how much more she knew about the sultan and the reason Finn der Weese was here in Marrakech. Did she know about the connection between him and Madame Toussaint? But I knew better than to ask.

'Sorry,' she said. 'Just crossing the intersection.'

She had stopped now and I had her full attention.

'Thanks for sending Finn,' I said.

'Let's just focus on getting the child to safety.'

'Of course,' I agreed. 'But Eva, can I be sure this house is safe?'

'It's safe, actually. No question.'

'Finn said it was the last place they would look for her, but I don't know why he would say that.'

'I don't know either. But you can trust him. As soon as you send me her details I'll get the documents processed,' she was gulping water from a bottle. 'Then I'll come to meet you in Marrakech myself – smooth the flow in my official capacity.'

'Thanks, Eva.'

'Keep me informed,' she said. 'Well done, Karen … you're nearly there.'

She hung up.

I dialled again. This time Dorothy Turay in Freetown.

'Dorothy, it's me.'

'Have you found her?'

'Yes. She's with me in the safe house.'

'That's good. What's her name?'

'She's not talking yet. What is happening at your end?'

'There have been no reports of missing girls who look like her. But people don't always report the missing, especially when they know where the missing have gone.'

Dorothy spoke plainly, just as it was. I loved her for it.

'I'm sorry it's so frustrating for you.'

'The pastor is helping,' she said. 'He has many contacts.'

My heart quickened at the mention of his name, and I wondered if Dorothy had told him it was me she was helping. I couldn't speak. The old yearning clawed at me despite all that had gone wrong.

'Get her to talk,' Dorothy demanded. 'Tell her that if she wants to speak to someone in her own language – and I don't mean English – she can talk to me.'

I absorbed the rebuff as I had absorbed so many before from this fine friend who had taught me so much.

'Thanks, Dorothy. I'll find a way to make that happen.'

'Will she identify the Dutchman?'

'For sure,' I said with optimism.

'And if she doesn't?' But I didn't want to think of that possibility.

There was silence then; unspoken words hung between us.

Then she said, 'You are not responsible for the murder of our sister.'

I could think of no response.

'You did not kill her yourself.'

Was Dorothy angry with me? She must be hurting so much herself.

Something lodged in my throat but she waited patiently for a reply. Of course I didn't kill Songola myself. It just felt that way.

Eventually, I said, 'The girl looks like her, don't you think?'

'So this is why you want to rescue that child. A life saved for a life lost.'

It was a good point.

'Does it make sense to you?' I asked.

'It makes no sense at all. Our sister was killed because she was brave and got in the way of big people. It is not unusual in our country. But that will change.'

'But she took me to the plantation,' I said. 'I spoke to the villagers and whipped up the tension. The people were energised and believed they could get compensation for their land. Everything kicked off after my visit, and it was Songola who paid for it.'

'Hah!' Dorothy blurted. 'You think the white woman arrives and something changes. No, my sister. Have you learnt nothing? You were just a passenger on the bus that overturned.'

THE GIRL WAS SLEEPING SOUNDLY. When she woke I would have to find a way of getting her to talk to me so that Eva could arrange her travel documents. I was sure she would recognise the photo of Broekmann, just as Maria had, but I didn't want to frighten her and would have to choose my moment carefully. After everything she had been through it might take time to win her confidence.

The girl was snoring gently as I watched her and I wished Eva was with me. This was her domain. She knew exactly how to care for people who had been traumatised and God knew what the girl had been through at the hands of the gang.

After speaking to Eva, I was now confident the house was safe. But what about the journey to the airport, and the airport itself? This so-called sultan would be searching for his bride and the obvious places would be the city's transport hubs. Eyes could be anywhere. The girl would need new clothes; there would have to be nothing recognisable about her.

I took a pair of blue linen pants and descended to the ground-floor salon in search of cutting and sewing materials to shorten them. There was nothing to be found in any of the drawers or consoles, cabinets or bookshelves, so I opened a heavy trunk that was filled with blankets, fine silks and tapestries. I took everything out and at the bottom I found a photo frame and lifted it out. Gold-plated metal with intricate cut-out detail in the Moroccan style – a picture of a handsome woman, dark kohl around her eyes, chiselled cheekbones like an Egyptian king, sitting beside a boy under an orange tree in a pretty tiled courtyard, water flowing from spouts in the wall.

So the boy in the turquoise djellaba was Madame Toussaint's son, just as Khalid had said.

I put the photo back where I had found it and piled the blankets on top. Madame Toussaint's home in Marrakech was a safe house. And I wanted to know the reason why.

I RETURNED to the bedroom to check on her, hoping the pain had eased off and that she might feel ready to talk. But the bed was empty. I hurried around the gallery to the salon opposite and found her sitting at the writing desk drawing on some paper. When I approached she turned over the sheet and stood up quickly.

'Hi. How are you feeling?'

She said nothing, her pretty pointy chin tipped upwards, her gaze focused determinedly on the ornate stucco of the ceiling. She was wearing my jeans, rolled up several times, the baggy striped shirt hanging down below her hands.

'Can I see?' I nodded at the writing desk. I moved to turn the paper she had been working on and discovered she had drawn a map of the city.

It looked like a plan of the market and the busy circular road around Marrakech. She had included a number of prominent mosques as points of reference, and details of the market itself, accurate as far as my own memory served me. There were arrows pointing in different directions and illustrations of trucks and cars parked together in one spot. And a house. Very similar to the one we were standing in and circled in heavy pencil. She had drawn the sun in different locations with question marks next to them.

Is she planning an escape?

I moved to the sofa and smiled at her, patting the cushions, but she would not join me.

'It's a good map,' I said pleasantly.

Her expression was impassive. She took the paper from me, folded it, and pushed it into the pocket of the jeans.

'Will you let me help you?' I asked, trying to keep the pleading from my voice.

She shuffled her feet, but seemed willing to listen, a half-cocked ear in my direction.

'If we return to Amsterdam there are good people there who can help you.'

Silence, but her gaze had moved to the wall behind my head.

'If you want that,' I went on. 'We will need to get travel papers for you. You can't fly without a passport.'

There was a flicker of interest at the mention of a passport, and her eyes moved to examine the tousled curls on my head.

'When you are back in Amsterdam we can locate your family and friends.'

At that, her face went blank again.

'Let me show you.'

I sat and charged up the laptop while she lowered herself onto the edge of the cushions peering sideways at the screen. I opened the home page of Eva's organisation, CTM, and explained about the facilities and support they gave to trafficked people.

Her eyes were steady on the screen.

'Their job is to help children who have found themselves in the same situation as you,' I said. 'You can be sure they will protect you from the people who brought you here.'

I had her full attention now, and pulled up a smiling photo of Eva Taal.

'This is Eva,' I said. 'She is my friend and is the one who can help you. She will get travel documents for you and come to meet us here at the airport in Marrakech.'

The girl was computing quickly, her eyes darting about the screen. I knew she understood every word.

'Do you want us to help you?' I asked lightly, aware of the escape plan now sitting in her pocket.

Unexpectedly, she took the laptop from me and started scrolling through the information on CTM's website, working the laptop like a pro. She stopped to study various sections before moving on.

'Maybe you want to know a little more about me,' I said lightly. 'Can I show you?'

She didn't want to relinquish the computer, so I said, 'OK. Google Karen Hamm.'

Up popped all the recent media coverage on the arrest of

Nigel Hurt, UK minister, and embezzler of international aid. Her eyes widened and she leant into the screen, reading through the reports about how I had blown the whistle on Hurt's operations with his corrupt friends in the palm oil sector. The girl opened each page and read voraciously. I guessed the subject of palm oil corporations would be of interest to someone from a nation so exploited as hers.

'And this,' I said, indicating the university photo that had appeared at the top of the Google search engine.

The link took her to my university website, my academic profile and details of my PhD research in her country. Once she had finished reading, her eyes slid my way, looking at me properly for the first time.

I LEFT her studying the computer and made my way to the bathroom to wash her clothes, sensing that she needed a break. I filled the tub, sloshing clothes from bucket to bucket, rinsing them before plunging everything into hot suds to scrub. What was it going to take to break through to her? Maybe she was mute and couldn't actually speak. Maybe it was shock – perhaps I could ask her to write things down. Clearly she was literate.

I pummelled away, the tension and fear clawing at my chest. I wanted to shout at her – we had so little time and I felt protective, solely responsible for her safety. I wished Eva was with me with her expert ear and sound judgement. How was I going to get through to this child? I sat back on my heels with my head in my hands, seeking inspiration, suds sliding down my wrists and dripping onto the floor.

Then she padded in and knelt beside me, slipping her hands into the water, scrubbing at the material with a prac-tised technique, the suds in the water now twice their volume with all the additional pummelling. After a few minutes she got up and stood behind me.

'My name is Kaidi Owuso.'

I didn't move.

'I am twelve years old. I come from a village that is situated in the northern province of Sierra Leone, close to the town of Kabala, where I go to school with my friend Aminata, and where I am a first-class student. Top in maths and science. My home is a beautiful place. The land is rich for rice farming and for the cultivation of vegetables. At night, if you ride five miles east from the hills, you will see the magnitude of the heavens quite clearly. It is a good place to live because most of our country is mountainous or forested, and in those places the night sky is almost totally concealed from view.'

The magnitude of the heavens?

She paused briefly. I was dumbfounded, suds still clinging, hoping she would continue, afraid to look at her in case I broke the spell.

'I am an only child,' she continued. 'The daughter of Dr Jacob Owuso and Dr Mariame Owuso. My father is the only clinician for the whole of our district and my mother is the head teacher of our prestigious high school for girls. My family is respected in our community. My parents are loved by all who meet them.'

Her voice was strong and proud, and I thought how desperate her parents must be, worrying about what had happened to their daughter. I glanced behind. She stood there like she was making a speech at the prestigious girls' high school herself, hands clasped in front of her, head high. So small and vulnerable, the jeans now unravelled and trailing on the tiles, her previously tight cornrows starting to unwind, the ribbons crushed. But the light of defiance was bright in her eyes.

I opened my mouth to speak, but she interrupted.

'Miss Karen. I hope this gives you enough information for your friend to bring me a passport.'

I scrambled to my feet, joy overwhelming. 'Thank you, Kaidi,' I said. 'Let's call her now.'

She followed me back into the salon where I pulled the burner phone from my pocket.

As I searched for Eva's number, Kaidi said, 'I saw you, Ma.'

'You saw me?' I uttered, my voice a little unsettled at the sound of her speaking her local vernacular for mother.

'When you took the photo,' she clarified.

'Ah, yes.' She must have seen me taking photos in the market. After all, I had been there for days and when I eventually spotted her, she had been looking at the camera probably wondering about my motives. The girl was bright.

'I have been trying to find you for days,' I explained. 'Someone told me you might visit the souks for fruit and vegetables, so I have been there every day looking for you.'

'No, Ma,' she replied. 'Not at the markets.'

'Not the markets?'

'I saw you at the airport.'

Her eyes shifted about the space, not looking at me directly, but I knew now we had made the connection, and I wondered whether Kaidi remembered me from Lungi Airport when I grabbed her in the market. Was this why she gave little resistance when I guided her out, even though she had plans of her own to escape?

'I wanted to help you when I saw you at the airport,' I explained. 'Because I knew the man you were with was not a priest.'

'How did you know?' she asked.

'Because I had seen him before and I knew that he associated with criminals.'

When I said the words out loud, I wondered how accurate they might be. Would they stand up in court if I had to give evidence.

I needed Kaidi to identify that photo.

'It was the Ghostbuster's backpack that I recognised at the market.'

'The backpack?'

'You were wearing it at Lungi Airport.'

'Yes.'

'I recognised it on the shoulders of the boy you were with in the market. It was the same one.'

'My father gave it to me,' she said, emotion cutting her voice.

'You must thank him.' I smiled at her. 'It was the Ghost-busters pack that saved you.'

SHE WOKE in the night screaming, piercing howls that filled the riad and I thought the Mafia had come to take her.

I rushed to her side. Her body flailed like she was possessed, and she beat at my chest, the blows striking my breastbone with surprising force.

'Kaidi, wake up. It's Karen.' I held her shoulders, shaking her firmly, willing her to wake.

Her eyes were wild, their whites vivid in the darkness. Sweat glistened, silver streams pouring down her face.

'Kaidi, Kaidi!' I shook her again. She seemed to be holding her breath, gripping her throat like she was starved of air.

I picked up a glass of water and threw it at her.

Her body went limp and she pulled in great gulps of air, looking at me, puzzled, exhausted from the effort of reliving whatever horror had visited her dreams.

'Kaidi, it's me. You were dreaming.'

I tried to hold her but she pushed me away, curling up into that tight little ball, her knees wedged under her chin, her face in her hands.

'It's OK, it's OK,' I said soothingly. 'You're safe now.'

I reached for the water bottle and refilled the glass. When I offered it to her she took it and gulped noisily, her back to me, strong like the stone walls of the medina. I took a towel and dried her skin.

'It's ok, sweetie. You don't have to talk about it.'

But I wanted to know.

I lay on the bed next to her. Waiting.

Hours passed. She had settled herself to face away from me, perched at the edge of the bed, her breathing low and deep, and I thought she had drifted off. A mosquito droned in my ear, but I dared not swat it for fear of waking her.

After a while, I tiptoed to adjust the AC and when I settled back beside her, she murmured, 'It is Foday.'

'Yes?' I said gently.

'I did not help that boy,' she said, whispering like she was at confession.

'Who is Foday?' I asked, guessing the answer, grateful that I had not had to ask the question and that she was giving me the information anyway. I strained to hear.

'He is the boy in the photo,' she said.

'The one at the airport … with the priest?'

'Yes.'

I waited. But she said nothing more.

'Where is he?' I asked gently.

'I don't know.'

There was a long silence and I waited, holding my breath. Eventually she said, 'He went in the car.'

'Yes?'

'They took him away.'

Her back was still towards me; it was hard to hear her voice.

'Where did you see this, Kaidi?'

'In Spain.'

'At the polytunnels?'

'At the plastic farms.'

'Ok.'

Her voice caught and her body heaved. 'I didn't help him,' she whimpered, a round sob filling her chest.

'How could you have helped him?'

Kaidi was full of desperate remorse for reasons known only to herself. She didn't know where Foday had been taken, but he left in the car with an angry-looking man, and he had forgotten his water bottle which she drank for herself on the way to the ferry. I stroked her skin until she finally slept.

I would need to call Eva about Foday.

TWENTY-FIVE
KAREN

'I've found the birth records for Kaidi Owuso.' Dorothy's voice was clear on the connection to Freetown. 'I will send to you.'

'Send them direct to Eva.' I gave Dorothy the address. 'CTM will get documents for her to travel as a trafficked person.'

'I will do it now,' she said.

'Do you know if anyone has reported her missing? She's spoken about her parents. She's their only child, they must be searching for her.'

'They are dead.'

Kaidi had spoken about her parents as though they were alive. That they were a popular couple, revered in their community.

I lowered my voice. 'Are you sure?'

'It was Ebola.' Dorothy said flatly. 'Her father contracted it from one of his patients. Then his wife was infected. They were among the last deaths before we got it under control.'

Dorothy's own father had succumbed to the disease two years earlier. She knew the pain of an Ebola death. My heart ached for Kaidi.

It was the end of our second day and I was sitting on the roof among the date palms, the sun dipping behind the city, the pulse of the first throbbing star now visible in the heavens, skeins of pink, lilac and tangerine drawn across the western horizon. The new moon had been sighted and the cannon from the port had fired seven times. Eid had taken over the city.

Kaidi was downstairs studying the galaxies on my laptop and could not hear the conversation I was having with Dorothy. She was safe. The external doors locked and bolted, her only means of escape was past me and across the hazardous rooftops, but by now I was convinced she had abandoned her own plans to escape.

'Has no one reported her missing?' My heart was heavy with the implications this might have for Kaidi.

'One,' Dorothy said. 'The teacher from her school contacted the authorities to say that she had missed lessons. The girl is a good pupil and her parents were educated.'

Top in maths and science.

'I'll try to get more information from her,' I said. 'But I can't push it. She's been through enough already.'

Dorothy went quiet; she would be unable to think of any good reason why I couldn't pump the child for information.

'She says she wants to talk to you,' I went on. 'I've told her you're a teacher at the mission school and she seems to like that idea, but please don't press her if she doesn't want to talk about her parents or her abduction. She's in denial about them, and I don't know what that means for her recovery.'

There was a long silence and I waited, imagining Dorothy's confused expression – empathy was something she did not understand – but, eventually, she agreed. Dorothy was from the same region of Sierra Leone as Kaidi and spoke the Temne language.

'Hang on,' I said, and descended to the first-floor salon with the phone.

'It's my friend, Dorothy. She's in Freetown,' I said to Kaidi. 'Would you like to talk to her?'

The girl grabbed the phone and proceeded with a conversation I could not understand. I watched her pretty face as she spoke – animated and hopeful. I wanted to show her the photo of Broekmann but an abundance of misgivings held me back. When I showed the same image to Maria, she had reacted badly. Panic stricken almost. There was no doubt she recognised him, but so far she had not told Eva that he was involved in her trafficking. She had only spoken of some random Albanians, who might or might not have been the same gang who had transferred Kaidi to Tangier. But these men were just foot soldiers. They didn't interest me as Broekmann did. Why hadn't Maria identified him? What terrible fear did he stir up in her?

After the nightmares of the previous evening, I didn't want to trigger more trauma for Kaidi by showing her Broekmann's photo. But I could not wait forever because who else was going to identify him as the 'Pied Piper' of Salone? He could at that very moment be selling more kids to the plantations. I had seen for myself his shopping list of children – G5, B2. And now there was Kaidi who I knew to have been trafficked to repay a debt to the Moroccan Mafia. Hand-picked from the villages of Salone to marry the head of organised crime in North Africa. My stomach turned at the prospect, that she had so nearly been enslaved to such a monster.

'How was your call with Dorothy?' I asked Kaidi, who was now back on the laptop.

'Ok,' she replied, head down.

I left her working and went to prepare food for our evening meal, but it wasn't long before she came to join me and I set her to picking over the rice, asking her to select her favourite spices from the rack.

Now aware that her parents were dead, I said tentatively, 'Are you looking forward to going home?'

Maybe the distraction of our chores would help the conversation; distractions of any kind often helped people to express what they really felt. Like me telling Graham I wanted to split up after the loss of our fourth pregnancy as we dug a trench to plant a beech hedge at Owl Cottage. That was years ago.

But there was only more silence from Kaidi, so I tried a different approach.

'How are you feeling now that you're free?'

She looked at me with those big black eyes as though I were mad, and continued picking. I wondered if she knew she was to be the bride of a Mafia boss. An unimaginable future.

So I ventured, 'Are you happy to be here with me, Kaidi … I mean, do you feel safe now?'

'Yes,' she said without hesitation. 'I am safe with you.' She slapped the wet rice from the sieve into the pan. 'You are a good person.'

A lump rose in my throat and I stuttered, 'Thank you. Yes. Good.' I was caught by feelings I didn't understand.

THE RICE WAS UNDERCOOKED but well spiced, and we sat with our bowls in our laps and ate together.

'Kaidi … it's such a nice name.'

She looked at me suspiciously.

'How are you feeling about maybe being able to go home soon?'

She kept shovelling in the rice like she had not heard the question but, from what she had said about her village, home was a place she loved.

'Your country's very beautiful,' I said. 'I've travelled through the forests and mountains, through the grasslands and green paddy swamps.'

Silence.

'And your beaches,' I continued. 'Such breathtaking beauty. They are famous across the world, did you know? That one … River Number 2.' My voice caught at the thought of it and I decided that I didn't want to continue with that line of conversation, but Kaidi was not listening anyway.

She stood to take our empty bowls into the kitchen and then returned to surf the net, typing into the search engine 'phases of the moon AND Eid'.

So she did know what was to happen to her at Eid.

'The food was good,' she said idly, scrolling the touchpad.

I went to sit beside her.

'Kaidi. I have something to ask you. It's important.'

She tipped her chin which I took to mean *I'm listening.*

'Can I show you a photo?' I shoved her elbow out of the way and slid the computer onto my knee. 'It's a photograph of someone you might recognise,' I said. 'I don't want to upset you, Kaidi, but it's very important that you take a look to see if you recognise the person.'

She nodded. Interested in this conversation.

'We think you were taken out of your country against your will,' I said carefully. I ran through the immense catalogue of photos now on the computer while her gaze remained steady on the screen.

'You don't have to look at the photo if you don't want to,' I said, 'but perhaps—'

'Show it to me.'

Quickly, I found the image of Broekmann who stared evilly back at us. A head and shoulders shot that Dorothy had captured from his passport when she had rifled through the safe at his hotel in Freetown. I prepared to comfort Kaidi, expecting her to show some sign of distress. This man could have abused her. God knows how he had treated the children on his 'shopping list' and his image might stir up memories of her abduction. Violence even.

'Do you recognise this man?' I whispered, studying her face for any signs of anguish.

She looked blankly at the screen and answered, 'No.'

But the girl was in denial. Didn't she believe her parents were still alive? Trauma of that kind could cleave an enormous welt in the psyche of a child.

'Look again,' I encouraged. 'He will have been wearing different clothes, maybe a sunhat or shades, or both. His hair is very distinctive.' That sculptured grey mass that resembled the modern roof of the Lungi Airport terminal, an undulating wave of grey steel.

She looked at me calmly. 'I do not recognise this man. Who is he?'

She wasn't giving me the right answers but I could not put the words in her mouth – even though I was beginning to learn that Kaidi Owuso was an unusually unimpressionable child. So I decided to give her the undisputed facts.

'His name is Hendrikus Broekmann. He is a Dutch national with property and business in Amsterdam. He regularly travels to West Africa, particularly to your own country. He is known by the Dutch police who suspect that he is involved in human trafficking.'

I left it there, waiting for her response, glad that the photo appeared not to have upset her and that she had not lapsed into silence again.

'You think that this man is the person who trafficked me?'

It was my turn to remain silent. Kaidi knew she had been trafficked, that was a start, but she shook her head, a resolute expression around her mouth.

'Our people are capable of trafficking themselves,' she said. 'They don't need help from outsiders like this Dutchman.' She stared at his photo again.

'Yes,' I said. 'But local traffickers work closely with others to move people into Europe. Like they did with you.'

She took the laptop and started scrolling through the

photos until she found the one she was looking for. The photo I had shown her when she first arrived.

'This is the man,' she said, pointing to the priest standing beside her in the queue. 'This is the man who took me away from my homeland, but he is not from the Netherlands.' She was shaking her head resolutely. 'Maybe Spanish, I don't know, but the men at the plastic farms, they sounded like him. This Dutchman … I do not recognise him.'

THE BURNER PHONE rang and it was Dorothy asking to speak to Kaidi. They engaged in a brief conversation then Kaidi rushed to the desk to find something to write on. They hung up.

I hovered, waiting to see if she would let me know what was going on, but she disappeared with the phone onto the roof. It was safer now that night had fallen; no one would notice her in the gloom among the date palms. I stood vigilant at the bottom of the steps listening to incomprehensible mumblings in Temne and her excited laughter.

A little time passed and Kaidi's happy babbling started to diminish, less laughter now. Eventually, the conversation ended but she did not return from the roof. I stood and waited on the second step, straining to see what she was doing, cautious not to interfere but keen to know who she had spoken to. After a while, she descended and I backed down the steps; I did not want to interrogate her. She moved past me, walking quickly to the bedroom but soon returning to the roof holding something in her hand. I went back to my position on the steps looking up, but I could not see what she was doing. After a few minutes I followed, sensing something was wrong.

The last glow of sun on the horizon had disappeared to total blackness, the stars blinking their lustrous light against the heavens. The call to prayer had started, the chanting of the muezzin blanketing the city like the dusk chorus of a million cicadas. I sat on the top step watching her silhouette, now leaning in against the wall, her head lifted, gazing up towards the velvet sky. She was looking through a monocular telescope at her beloved stars, oblivious to me, lost in her celestial world. Kaidi Owuso: a girl full of surprises.

I waited, maternally watchful, trying to think of a way to mend her shattered heart.

SHE LAY restless in the bed that night, curling up in a ball, drawn back into herself and as uncommunicative as when she first arrived at the riad.

As soon as she was asleep, I called Dorothy.

'What were the calls about?' I demanded.

'She asked me to find the contacts for her schoolfriend, Aminata.'

'Not her family?'

'Her family is dead.'

'I mean her extended family,' I said irritably. 'Aunts, uncles, grandparents. Anyone who may be concerned for her safety.'

'She doesn't want to speak about her family,' Dorothy said, dulled to my new intensity. 'But we found an aunt.'

'Yes?'

'She is a hysterical woman who claims a spell was put on the girl and that she wandered into the bush of her own free will.'

'She what?'

'Some of our people are uneducated and devious.'

But it sounded more sinister to me than that. There was a pause at the end of the line while Dorothy waited for me to ask the obvious question.

'Do you think the aunt sold her?'

'She is the sister of the girl's father. Now living in his house.'

For a moment we both fell silent, putting the pieces together. No wonder Kaidi didn't want to talk about her family.

'Do you know why Kaidi wanted to speak to her friend Aminata?' I asked.

'No.'

'Can you take a guess?'

'Friendships are important in our country. She may be looking for a new home.'

'Yes, but …' I couldn't quite formulate the question because it hadn't yet materialised in my head.

'Maybe she just wanted to tell her she was OK,' Dorothy went on. 'Most kids we never hear of again.'

But I knew the conversation with Aminata had not gone well for Kaidi.

We hung up, Dorothy promising to find out more about Kaidi's family, her father's house, who it actually belonged to, and the prospects of getting her home.

THE NEXT DAY all the arrangements were in place for Kaidi's return to Amsterdam. Eva had the documents and would meet us in the VIP lounge at Menara airport.

'A car will come for you,' she said.

'Who should I look for?'

'This is all I know,' she replied. 'The message has come from Mimi and there's little detail she can share.'

'OK. I understand.'

'Be prepared. The car will arrive at five thirty. I'll be waiting at the airport.'

'We'll be ready.'

'Don't worry,' she said. 'We will soon have you both safely back in Amsterdam.'

But I was worried. We had not left the safety of the riad for three days and I was frightened to bring Kaidi onto the streets of Marrakech. People would be searching down every alley trying to find the stolen bride. What chance these people would simply let her go? For sure, there would be a price to pay for the *big man*'s disappointment.

AT FIVE THIRTY precisely there was a thud on the door. We were ready, bags at our feet. It was a short journey that would take us through the medina and then west onto the busy highways towards the safety of the airport and Eva.

I inched open the door and peered through the gap, blinded by the light, so accustomed had I become to the shady corridors of the riad. When I managed to focus, standing in the heat was the same old man who had met me at the railway station and transported me to the riad on his ancient motorcycle. The red fez sat firmly on his head, its tassel dangling as he bent to reach the bags.

Instead of the motorcycle, this time behind him stood a small Renault motor car that he had reversed up the alley and wedged between the fan palms beside the door. He took our bags and swung them into the open boot then waved for us to climb in the back, slamming the doors behind us, then locking the riad himself, pocketing the keys in loose robes where he had carried them the day I first arrived. We edged down the alley and then meandered through the medina at walking pace, Kaidi hunched beside me, her natural curiosity tempered by the danger she knew was still close. She leant in, turning her face into my shoulder, her dark eyes alert to all around us.

The old man kept glancing in the mirror for a surreptitious glimpse of his strange passengers. Who was he working for? I wondered. Finn der Weese or Madame Toussaint? And was there even a distinction between the two? Pieces of the jigsaw were beginning to fall in place.

The Renault stopped to allow room for laden donkeys bearing bundles of mint and empty handcarts towed by weary men sweating in rough djellabas. Tourists stood around consulting maps. No one seemed interested in us.

Through the alleys we crawled, past canopied orange juice carts, streetside apothecaries, henna artists, and stalls piled high with boxes of cheap imitation trainers. But, when we emerged onto Avenue Jemaa el Fna, the way was blocked by an over-turned handcart, its load of souvenirs spilled out across the street. Miniature tagines, silver teapots, leatherwork, glass lanterns, goblet-shaped hand drums, ceramic tiles and coffee cups, all strewn across the ground, the traffic building up on either side. The vendor had righted his cart and had commenced the retrieval of his merchandise, stacking the items carefully while a cacophony of horns echoed around the square.

There was nothing to do but sit it out.

Across the vast expanse of Jemaa el Fna entertainers were setting up for the evening. A troupe of young acrobats were folding themselves backwards while standing on each other's heads. A crowd had gathered taking photos of the troupe in exchange for wads of dirham.

A group of Gnawa musicians had set up close to the bazaar and commenced a slow rhythmic beat on their hand drums. Their long satin djellabas shimmered in the sun's slanting rays, tassels quivering from their shell-encrusted caps, their metal castanets rattling in time with the drums. The deep tones of their lutes filled the square with rich swollen sound and I opened my window to listen.

Soon Kaidi went rigid beside me.

'What is it,' I asked, drawn back from my reverie.

Her eyes were transfixed upon a man in the square now moving in our direction, scanning the crowds, sauntering to investigate the ruckus that had been occasioned by the over-turned cart. He was dressed in a black suit, jacket pocket bulging, and his finger was jammed to an earpiece, its curly wire disappearing beneath his collar.

'Who is he, Kaidi?'

'A guard,' she whispered.

'From the palace?'

She nodded, her eyes fixed on him like she was lining him up for a shot.

I leant over the seat and said to the old man, 'Dépêche-toi. Allez! Vite!'

But there was nowhere to go.

He looked at me in the mirror and placed a finger over his lips. Calm, but watchful.

The man in the suit ambled through the crowd and down the line of waiting traffic, turning his head this way and that, speaking into his mouthpiece.

Kaidi pulled the hijab tight and covered her hands with her sleeves, clinging to me in a ball.

'It's ok, Kaidi. I'm here.'

The man in the suit moved down the line, his eyes on the crowds across the square, and stopped at our window, his back turned, the muscles of his buttocks straining against the tight jacket – single-vented and tailored in a synthetic black fabric. He spoke quickly in effeminate high-pitched tones, finger to his earpiece, an intense conversation in Arabic with whoever was on the line.

A flock of pigeons rose together from the square, rising high against the blue. The deep throb of the lute echoed on, the twang of the deep-timbred strings emitting round, deli-cious sounds, the rattle of the castanets and the eerie pulse of the hand drums. The crowd appeared mesmerised and motionless and time stood still as the odour of seared meat wafted through the window from a brazier somewhere close.

We clung together frigid, my eyes fixed on the handcart,

which was now fully loaded and moving to one side. Then the man at our window turned, his shirt stretched tight against a muscled torso. But the old man had slipped into gear, edging forward. A scooter flashed by on the pavement, bicycles weaving in front of us. We picked up a little speed and the guard fell back. Stealthily, we moved further away from him until he was no longer visible in the glass.

TWENTY-SIX

KAREN

'She won't talk to us. She is saying nothing at all about her abduction, or going home, or anything, actually.' Eva was on the phone from CTM's temporary shelter where Kaidi was staying. 'I think we need you here.'

I was back at the Absalom Guest House after returning to Amsterdam, happy that Kaidi was safe and being properly cared for under Eva's supervision. Now I had to concentrate on how I could trap Broekmann when I had no one to identify him. I was guessing that Finn der Weese could give evidence, but Eva had warned me off that idea. Then there was Foday, the boy who had travelled with Kaidi and disappeared from the polytunnels in Almería. We had lost his trail, but he was still a vulnerable child in need of rescue and, at the back of my mind, there was the tempting possibility that Foday could identify Broekmann.

When I imagined him getting away with his horrible crimes, all the vulnerable kids he might be trafficking right at that moment, anger fizzed in my veins. There must be something else I could do to catch him. An immense storm of violence was brewing inside me, unfamiliar thoughts and emotions at odds with everything I believed.

Every night Songola was there in my head waiting for me – her silent omnipresence a torturous reminder of how violently she had met her end. Dorothy's assurances had done nothing to quieten the demons still challenging me to atone. *What must I do to pacify Songola?*

It had been several days since we returned to the Netherlands and Kaidi had been interviewed by specialist teams at the Dutch police. She had identified the priest as her abductor, the one she met when she arrived in Freetown from her village, and the man who had been in charge of distributing the children held in captivity in the rundown house behind the barracks. The police had identified him as Pascual Ramos, a Spanish national, now in custody on charges of child trafficking. But his expensive lawyer had advised him not to talk.

I took the tram to the CTM hostel in Amsterdam Oost and found Kaidi alone in the day room sitting on a beanbag and reading Harry Potter.

'Hi, Kaidi,' I said, realising how much I had missed her the moment I saw her. She placed a bookmark to identify her spot.

'Would you like to go to the park?'

She scrambled to her feet straight away and we stepped out into the Amsterdam sunshine.

We walked along in the direction of the tram stop that would take us to Vondelpark, Kaidi close beside me, her head down, one hand clutching Harry Potter, the other hand brushing against mine. A tram clanked to a stop alongside the platform and a group of children alighted. We sat in silence all the way to the park's great iron gates where we disembarked by the bridge over the lake. It was a bright morning and a pleasant breeze was moving across the water, nudging the pastel green willows and disturbing the long grasses that yielded in undulating waves.

We headed in the direction of Blauwe Theehuis and chose a small iron table that looked over the lawns towards a gaggle of Egyptian geese gathered near the bandstand. We ordered strawberry ice cream and ate in silence, Kaidi avoiding my gaze. There was tension. So much still to say.

'What's the hostel like?' I asked, but she shrugged her shoulders, spooning the ice cream impatiently into her mouth. I ordered her another.

'Kaidi, sweetie, you're going to have to talk to me.' But she gave me that combative expression, the one I recognised as her default.

'Tell me what it is you want,' I said. 'Are you worried about going home?'

'I am not going home.' Her tone was emphatic, so I pushed a little harder.

'Don't you think people will be missing you?' But she looked at me like I had no notion of what I was saying.

'Your teachers, for example. Your friends.'

I hoped these would be good suggestions because she had not spoken again of her parents, and it was now time she gave me some indication that she knew they were dead.

But Kaidi was waiting for me to say something else. She expected better from me. So I tried, 'I don't think you can be forced to return if you don't want to.'

'I don't want to.' Pink ice cream was melting on her lips.

'Then what *do* you want? Tell me. How can I help you?'

She looked directly at me, her dark eyes like pools of oil reflecting the moonlight. Disappointment, resentment, impatience. What was it that I saw in her expression?

We had a connection, Kaidi and me. She didn't have to speak the words. She knew as well as I did what the answer was before I had asked the question. Unexpected feelings clawed at my chest.

'Let's go and see Eva,' I said. 'We can tell her how you feel and find out what options there might be. Will you talk to her if I am with you?'

'OK,' she said, standing up quickly and tipping over her

chair, a pink dribble sliding down her chin which she wiped away with the back of her hand.

I left twenty euros on the table and we set off round the lake in the direction of the tram stop.

A man in orange trainers and black running shorts was jogging towards us on the opposite path, the sweep of steel grey hair flopping over his sweaty face, bouncing back and forth with every step. The chill of recognition lifted the hairs on my neck.

He wore reflective shades, the white wires of earbuds trailing down his neck into a pocket on his T-shirt. He was tanned, a bright umber colour.

Grabbing Kaidi's arm I steered her in the opposite direction. Would he recognise her? Or me?

Kaidi had told me that she never met Broekmann and conceivably he may not know what she looked like. But if she had been payment in a deal with the Maroc Mafia, surely he must have seen her photo to approve such a high-risk exchange.

My gut churned with fear.

'What is it?' she asked as I marched her towards the park's main gates.

'Let's get on the tram.'

Hendrikus Broekmann was back in town and taking a morning run in Vondelpark – a pleasant green space situated close to his mansion on the Amstelkanaal. And no one seemed to have noticed.

'HE'S HERE, IN AMSTERDAM!'

'You've seen him?'

'I saw him running in Vondelpark.'

'And Kaidi didn't recognise him?'

Kaidi was sitting with a hot chocolate in CTM's reception as I delivered the alarming news to Eva in her office.

'How could she recognise him if she has never met him?' I apologised straight away for snapping. 'But Eva, I thought his house was being watched?'

'I'll check it out.' She looked sympathetic and a little embarrassed. 'I'll make sure they put a watch on his property now we know he's back in Amsterdam, but they should have known he was back, actually.' She seemed perplexed herself.

I fumed, pacing her office like a madwoman. The Dutch police weren't serious about Broekmann.

Eva asked, 'Is Kaidi talking to you yet?'

'Yes,' I said. 'She doesn't want to go home. She's very clear about that.'

'If there's no threat to her in her own country, it may be better for her to return. We need to know more about her situation. Have you heard from Dorothy?'

'It seems the aunt has temporary ownership of the property until Kaidi reaches eighteen and then the house and land transfers to her. The woman has every right to be there even though she may have thrown Kaidi out. Or even sold her.'

'Then we need Kaidi to say so to make it official that her aunt is a hostile person.'

'I want to take her back to the guest house with me,' I said. 'She doesn't like the accommodation you have for her. I don't think she feels safe.'

'I don't see a problem with that if it's what she wants. I'll need to talk to her if that's OK with you.'

'Sure. But if there's a good reason she can't go home, what then?'

'We will find foster care for her,' she said. 'A family situation if possible. It could be that in time she'll change her mind. She's an unaccompanied child as far as the authorities are concerned, and there's no one more vulnerable than that.'

I tried to imagine Kaidi in the home of foster carers, but I could not.

'Right,' I said, grasping for answers, seeking a way to

make Kaidi talk. First, to give me some indication she accepted her parents were dead, and second, to confirm her aunt was hostile. 'I'll take her to the museum.'

We boarded a tram to Central Station then walked the long footbridge over the deep waters of Oosterdok to the copper-green hulk of the Children's Science Museum, its sharp nose rising out of the water like a shark. A few hours of intense study later and we had ascended to the roof piazza, looking out across the panorama of Amsterdam where dark clouds assembled on the horizon, the breeze increasing in short strengthening bursts. We bought hamburgers and sat on a bench, our backs to the oncoming storm.

Carefully, I said, 'Eva says if there's no threat to your safety, it might be better for you to return to Salone. To be in your own culture, with your friends and among people who know and love you.' I was being deliberately provocative.

She lifted her head, chewing thoughtfully, staring out across the grey water of Oosterdok.

'The people who cared for me are dead,' she said.

At last.

'I'm sorry about your parents, Kaidi.' I put an arm around her shoulders but she didn't want me to.

'Ebola killed my father, then my mother,' she said, speaking in matter-of-fact tones like she was reading from an instruction booklet. 'The rest of my family … they hate me. They only want what my parents left me. Our bungalow, our savings, our land.'

'How do you know this, Kaidi?'

'My aunt is a hateful woman. Her children are spiteful. They were always jealous of us.'

Strong words for a child.

'I'm sorry your family are not kind to you after all you went through.'

'She sold me.'

Kaidi's eyes focused on the horizon. She wouldn't look at

me. But we were sitting shoulder to shoulder and I could feel her body warmth.

'Who sold you?'

'My aunt sold me for fifty dollars to a man she knew was trafficking people from our village.'

'Who was this man?'

'She pretended I was going *menpikin*,' Kaidi went on. 'But auntie knew where I was really headed.'

'Do you know this man … do you know his name?'

She paused for some time, brushing crumbs off her T-shirt and picking off the residue with scrupulous intent. Then she examined the polystyrene box that held her burger. Her feelings of shame were palpable.

'This is why I can't go back,' she said eventually.

'Thank you for telling me.' It was a struggle to keep the emotions out of my voice. 'Now I know what happened to you, Kaidi, I can help you.'

Her head stayed low but I sensed the tension that had been with us from the beginning starting to ebb – like the current dragging the cold flow of Oosterdok out to sea.

'Can you tell me anything about your friend, Aminata?' I asked. 'I think you called her when we were in Morocco.'

Another long silence, but I'd learnt to wait.

Then she said, 'She was my friend at school. We were the best mathematicians so we stuck together. We started school on the same day, when we were six years old. I thought she liked me.'

People on the piazza were beginning to move inside, and we held on to our polystyrene trash as the wind intensified, rushing across the water.

'I asked Aminata if I could live with her family if I came back to Salone,' Kaidi said. 'But her family are poor. They don't want me.'

It was time to make the call to Graham.

· · ·

'IS this going to be a temporary arrangement?' he asked.

'It's possible she'll have a change of heart if a good home can be found for her in Salone. Dorothy is working on it.'

'And if it can't be found?'

'Think about it carefully, Gray. Whatever happens, Kaidi will need a foster home until she's old enough to make her own decisions and look after herself. She's been through a lot.'

'Of course.'

'She thinks she will be sold again if she goes home.'

'Poor kid …'

I could imagine Graham's brain computing at speed. It was his habit to go quiet when he was trying to compartmentalise his emotions and decide what it was he was feeling. I imagined his pupils dilating in panic.

'The imperative is that we find her somewhere safe as soon as possible,' I continued. 'I'd like to get her out of Amsterdam now that Broekmann's back.'

Graham was quiet. Still thinking.

'She seems to have formed an attachment to me, Gray. I think I make her feel safe. That's important for her right now.'

'What does Eva say?' he asked. 'What is the process around fostering trafficked minors?' He seemed to hold great store by Eva Taal even though he had never met her. I bristled slightly.

'Well, I haven't broached it with Eva yet.'

'Why not?'

'Well, I thought it would be polite to consult you first, seeing as you will be the one opening your home to a complete stranger.'

'It is our home, Karen.'

'Yes, but … you know. It's a big commitment.'

'I'm good,' he said, 'if it's OK with Eva and Kaidi. The house is big enough. She can have her own quarters.'

Graham always had a practical solution. The last thing we

wanted was anyone destroying his routine, or complicating his space, or changing all the things that gave him comfort and allowed him to function in the chaotic world inside his head. I understood that as well as he did. We both knew what enormous change might do to his fragile psyche, but he seemed keen. And so was I.

'Think it over,' I said. 'You haven't met Kaidi yet. And we can't let her down once we've made the decision. And we'll have social services all over us, child protection, DBS and everything like that. I don't know how long it will take.'

'But she's good at maths,' he said flatly.

'Well,' I replied, 'I've no reason to believe she is lying.'

My spirit was lifting, beginning to sing an unfamiliar tune.

'Then we will get along just fine,' Graham said, a hint of excitement in his tone. 'I'm alright with this, Karen. Bring her home.'

TWENTY-SEVEN

KAREN

'He will make a mistake at some point. Trip himself over or become complacent. People like that often do.' Eva took a noisy slurp from her Sauvignon. She was in a philosophical mood. 'They can't help their hubris. They convince themselves they are invincible.'

We were sitting outside a small café on Keizersgracht, the sun slanting in, the light still bright at nine o'clock in the evening, the canal's green-black water passing smoothly under the willows' pale branches trailing in the flow.

I didn't agree with Eva. I believed Broekmann was the kind of criminal who got away with it, who remained invisible, no one able to connect him to his crimes, keeping a team of lower orderlies, managing them from afar. Corrupting police officers to protect himself.

But I kept my thoughts to myself because I had a favour to ask of Eva.

'He's under surveillance now,' she was saying. 'They have someone watching his house.'

'And the apartments?'

'Sure, sure.'

'And the club?'

'I think they will have some resources for that, also.'

A flight into Schiphol flew low over the city, its engines briefly drowning out our voices.

Eva just wanted me to go home and drop it. There were bigger operations underway for CTM – the police were getting closer to trapping the Serbian gang – and I knew there were no resources to monitor a man who left no trace of his crimes and was a small-scale operator in the massive problem of human trafficking in the Netherlands. Investigating Broek-mann was never going to be a priority and the only evidence I could offer the authorities was a hunch, and my suspicions; I had seen Broekmann with Pascual Ramos in Freetown, ergo the Dutchman was trafficking children. It was true that Maria recoiled from Broekmann's photo, but that was hardly evidence. She had not identified him formally and did not want to risk her new-found safety by making a positive ID. Who could blame her?

I stared into the waters of Keizersgracht struggling to shift the dark thoughts from my mind, trying to concentrate on Eva so she would not detect the change in me. Bicycles rattled past us on the cobbles and I felt the evening sun warm on my shoulders, a comforting glass of whisky in my hands. I swirled the amber liquid round and round.

A decision had been made about Kaidi's short-term future; she was to foster with Graham and me at our home in the UK. But the process of checks was going to be lengthy, so Graham had joined us in Amsterdam to spend time getting to know Kaidi. The two had hit it off straight away like I knew they would.

Meanwhile, I was filling my unsound mind with ideas of revenge against Broekmann, trying to keep the truth from Eva.

We sat together in companionable silence trying to find the answers in the slick slew of water that moved through the crumbling walls of the Keizersgracht channel where flowers grew in gaps between the stone, poppies and geraniums swaying gently, dipping their pretty heads – a soft choreography coaxed by the breeze.

Eva was a kind person and someone I had grown to think of as a friend, and it was obvious she did not want the incarceration of Broekmann to be the obsession of my life. Besides, it was too dangerous for an amateur like me to continue the investigation myself. These were Eva's thoughts. Rational, to be sure. But I knew the essence of Broekmann; I had tracked him all the way from the slums of Freetown and we had unfinished business that was deeply personal.

Eva leant over and gently tapped my hand, drawing my attention back to her.

'Karen, my friend, it's time for you to return to the UK to be with Graham and prepare for Kaidi. Your work here is done. Look at what you have achieved.' She smiled kindly, her elfin features arranged so prettily behind the huge glasses, her eyes wide and blue. I knew I couldn't have found Kaidi without Eva and I told her so.

'We are all working for the same outcome,' she said. 'To rescue people and give them hope. It is a noble ambition we share.'

I took her hand and squeezed it affectionately.

'What will it take for you to go home?' Her happy face was suddenly serious.

'I'll go home soon, but I still need answers to important questions.' She passed me a wary glance. 'I think Finn can help me, Eva. Could you arrange a meeting with him? Then I can go home.'

The cold calmness in my voice surprised me.

'I don't know.' Her expression looked hopeless. 'But I will speak to Mimi. Lives are at stake in Finn's operations. Including his own.'

Finn der Weese was back in Amsterdam and I wanted to meet with him. He would have answers to the many questions I couldn't fathom. And I had a message to give him from Kaidi. But my real reason for staying in Amsterdam was much more consequential than any of that.

IMAGES of the plantation had been coming to me in violent flashbacks. Boys worked like men, small bodies muscled beyond their years. Horrible injuries – and the death of a child. Kids rocking themselves to and fro, chanting in strange languages, torn from their families, kept as slaves. The missing boy, Foday. The beautiful waiter, Billy. And perfect Songola. Dead at the side of the road. Someone had to pay for it.

A plan was developing in my mind as I lay sweating on my bed at the Absalom Guest House, madness crawling beneath my skin, something sinister coiled around my heart, patient, squeezing gently in persistent pulses.

Cool air from the canal flowed through the open window, a light breeze rustling the plane trees, a bloated gibbous moon hanging in the heavens, bathing me in light like a loving mother's gaze.

I rose and went to the window to stare out at the canal; it looked lethargic after dark, the dim lamplights reflecting off the water. A huddle of young people walked past, drunk and high, laughing together. I had forgotten what it was like to lead a normal life like theirs.

THE NEXT DAY, I called Graham to see how Kaidi was doing. They had been taken to the UK by a representative from CTM so that Kaidi could see her new home and approve it. It was an opportunity for the pair to do some bonding.

'Hi, it's me,' I said, hoping he could not detect the tautness in my voice.

'You sound tired,' he said. 'Come home.'

Ignoring the question I asked how Kaidi was doing.

'She likes the house and veg patch. When are you coming home?'

'Eva has agreed to set up a meeting for me with Finn der Weese,' I said. 'Once I've got some answers about what happened in Morocco I'll be on the next flight home.'

I wondered if Graham believed me and felt the clench of guilt pulling at my chest, urging me to just go home.

'Where are you?' I asked breezily. 'I can hear voices in the background.'

'We've travelled down to Greenwich.' He sounded excited. 'Someone from the child protection authority is with us. She calls herself a supervising social worker.'

'Greenwich?'

'I've brought Kaidi to the observatory,' he said.

The tears pricked as I imagined them together, studying the telescopes and the planetarium and all the heavenly constellations. A special place that would fuel Kaidi's passion for astronomy. I knew Graham would care for her deeply. After all the years of disappointment, I had finally given him a daughter.

'That's wonderful,' I sputtered. 'I'm so happy that you're getting along.'

'She eats a lot of ice cream,' he said flatly.

'She eats a lot of everything.'

There was a long pause when I could hear him buying tickets from a staff member with a French accent.

'I want you home, Karen,' he said eventually. 'We're not a family without you.'

Regret surged and I felt light-headed, my stomach twisting in a tight ball.

But then a call flashed up from Mimi.

'I'll have to go, Gray. Mimi's calling and it will be about the meeting with Finn.'

· · ·

I TRAVELLED by tram to the furthest point of the network through a quiet part of the city and the eastern docklands, and then out towards the end of the line at KNSM Island where the blue and white ferries crossed on their shuttle to Amsterdam Noord. I alighted at the turning circle and made my way to the Amphitrite Fountain to wait. A child was playing in the water, his blond hair reflecting the brilliance of the midday sun, his pale skin luminescent as he dipped his hands, his mother close by, watching. The bronze statue of Amphitrite was sitting on a rearing hippocampus which stood in the shallow waters of the turquoise-tiled pool. Jets of water spurted from its nostrils. Beside it was Triton, Amphitrite's human–fish son, and a bronze dolphin which rose from the shallows like an afterthought.

It was too complicated a scene to comprehend so I moved to sit under a pagoda tree that had a bench built around its trunk.

The tram clanked to signal its return to Amsterdam Central and edged silently down the rails, leaving the area deserted. Not long after, a loaded tourist bus arrived and parked by the jetty. Then a different tram arrived and drew to a halt at the end of the line. The driver lifted his feet onto the dash, opened his sandwich and took a bite.

Out on the vast IJ the passenger ferry was edging its way across the water from Amsterdam Noord.

Then, out of nowhere, he appeared and sat down next to me. Not too close to suggest we were friends but close enough to have a conversation. He was dressed in black T-shirt, jeans and a leather waistcoat. Aviator shades obscured his eyes. His beard was recently clipped.

'Thanks for coming, Finn.'

'I don't have long. What is it you want to know?'

'Everything about Broekmann. Can you tell me what connection he has to the Maroc Mafia?'

'He had no connection until recently when he moved into

Mafia territory to do business for himself.' Finn looked past me, speaking directly to the child frolicking in Amphitrite's pool.

We both watched the boy.

'What more can you tell me?' I asked.

'I can say that Broekmann trafficked your child to order. He agreed to find a young African girl, educated, innocent, to join the man's portfolio of so-called 'wives'. This was as part payment, recompense if you like, for a deal Broekmann did that conflicted with the man's own business in Morocco.'

'When you say "the man", do you mean the one they refer to as the sultan?'

'Yes.'

'What sort of deal was Broekmann involved in?'

'Drugs, of course. This is why I know about him. Morocco is one of the most important producers of cannabis in the world. In fact it is the first in the world. Hashish is moved to Amsterdam mostly by Albanian gangs and the sultan heads this up. He's the biggest exporter of hashish into Europe. Which is why Europol is interested in dismantling his operations, and we also at the KM because there is a growing problem with the Maroc Mafia in our country.'

'And you're working undercover?'

He ignored the question. 'No one treads on the sultan's toes,' he continued. 'Broekmann was working with some cannabis growers in the Rif mountains but someone talked and the sultan got to know. Morocco has a drugs industry worth eight billion euros. There are big plantations in the northern Rif region. These things are well known.'

'If the Marechaussee know about Broekmann trafficking drugs and people, then why doesn't anybody arrest him in Amsterdam?'

'Because we are working on the bigger prize. As I said … he is a small deal in comparison and if we arrest him it will alert others.'

So Broekmann had trafficked the precious child, Kaidi Owuso, to pay off a drugs debt to the sultan.

'Can you tell me anything about a woman called Madame Toussaint?' I asked. 'She owns the Hamman Palmier in Tangier.'

Finn was thoughtful for a moment. The child in Amphitrite's pool was now flicking water towards his mother, sunlight catching the droplets as they arced in the air.

I pressed on. 'What is her connection to the riad in Marrakech? I found her photo. It's her house, isn't it?'

'I cannot say.'

'You know her, don't you? Why did she help me?'

'I believe she has a desire to protect children from the sexual advances of predatory men.'

He stared at the passenger ferry that was now docking at the quay. The travellers from the coach had alighted and were forming a queue to embark.

'But she runs a brothel in Tangier,' I said. 'Young African women were trafficked there with Kaidi.'

'That is her business.'

'But it doesn't fit.'

'Doesn't it? You don't know what choices she can and cannot make.'

I tried to understand what he was telling me and wondered about the scar across her neck. Who was controlling Madame Toussaint? Perhaps it was the sultan himself. Finn was not about to admit she was his agent in Morocco, but that was what I was reading between the lines. Finn and Madame were working together. In some way they were connected and on the same side.

'She's your asset or agent,' I said, more to myself than to Finn.

It all made sense. Her hammam and brothel were a perfect cover for an agent of the Dutch special forces, with all her knowledge of criminal activity in and out of the port at Tangier, her experience of trafficking activities on the route to Amsterdam through Spain. My admiration for her grew stronger.

Then something strange occurred to me. 'She must have known who I was when she first met me in the blue alley.' I looked at Finn for affirmation but his expression was impassive.

'I'll have to go now.' He was getting edgy. 'I congratulate you. It took guts to keep going and rescue the girl. If you hadn't done so she would now be part of a harem at the Red Palace … the property of one of the most vicious men in North Africa.'

Then I remembered the dirhams in my pocket.

'Finn …' I put a hand on his arm. 'I have a request from Kaidi. She has been anxious to find a way to return seven hundred dirhams to the gardener at the palace. His name is Abdullah. He befriended her and helped her escape but in the end she didn't need his money. Is there any way you could get it back to him … maybe let him know she's safe?'

Finn took the folded wad and pocketed it.

'I will see what I can do.' He rose and jogged towards the ferry, boarding it just as the ramp began to rise.

TWENTY-EIGHT
KAREN

I waited by the bins for Billy to emerge from the club. It was three thirty in the morning, around the same time I had seen him before. I didn't know if he was still working at Club VG, or whether it was his night off, but then I reminded myself there were no nights off for people like Billy. He surfaced as dawn was colouring the horizon, walking straight past me with laboured strides. I stepped in beside him as he crossed deserted Rembrandtplein.

'Did you find her?' he asked – the only acknowledgement that I was in his shadow.

'Yes.'

'Where is she?'

'She is safe. She is being looked after by an organisation called CTM until a foster home can be found for her.'

My heart was thumping at the audacity of my motives.

He nodded his approval, and we kept walking.

'I need your help again, Billy.'

We turned down Amstelstraat.

'No more help,' he said. 'I am glad you found the girl.'

He was picking up a little speed now, trying to shake me off.

'The man who trafficked her … he's going to get away with it, and I think he might be the same man who trafficked you.'

'No more help,' he repeated, his head low and shoulders hunched, wanting rid of me.

'You told me there are weapons at the club. Do you remember, you said that was why you were afraid. That you had seen weapons at the club.'

'Go away.' He was picking up speed now despite his exhaustion.

'Billy. I need a gun. I want you to get one for me.'

He stopped then and looked at me open mouthed. 'What you say?'

'I need it only for a few hours and then you can put it back like nothing happened.'

'You're crazy.' He looked horrified. 'Get away from me!'

He started walking again but I reached for his arm, urging him to stop.

'How many more Kaidis will he steal, Billy? How many more, just like you, will work as slaves paying off a debt that never gets any smaller? How many more humiliations?'

His face had become distorted with anger and I thought he was going to strike me.

'You know it's true, don't you, Billy?' I was goading him. I must have seemed half crazed.

'Billy is not my name!' Spittle flew from his mouth. 'I am Solomon Dumbuya from Yelendu chiefdom. In my country, women do not speak to me like that. Who you think you are?'

'You want him dead as much as I do, don't you?' The emotions were convulsing me. I was energised by a feeling I didn't understand, adrenalin rushing through my limbs.

'You're afraid to testify, but so is everybody. That's why he will get away with it. He's a frightening man, isn't he? This is the only way to stop him. Don't you want him to pay for what he did to you?'

This young man, hardly more than a boy, had experienced the horrors of trafficking first hand. How could his heart be less vengeful than mine? It was clear in his eyes and his chaotic expression.

'Don't be afraid,' I said. 'It's easy. Meet me here tomorrow night with the gun.'

I FOLLOWED him all the way from his mansion on the Amstelkanaal where he had jogged out of his manicured garden, down the avenue of elegant plane trees, across the canal and along the lanes into the leafy shade of magnificent Vondelpark.

I cycled at a discreet distance, cap pulled low, earphones plugged, the wire dangling to the phone in my pocket, which was switched off.

He was fit, overtaking younger runners on the many criss-crossing paths that cut through the gardens, but I kept him in my sights: over the bridge with the blue railings and past the bandstand where the Egyptian geese were still pecking at the gravel, then past the Blue Tearoom where I had sat with Kaidi and eaten ice cream. Over the bridge with the ornate iron-work and the swans gliding below and the willows trailing their branches in the water. It was a beautiful day in Vondel-park – a vivid blue sky with occasional wisps of cloud that moved in slow motion across the space.

Somewhere, a violin played the stirring notes of Pachel-bel's Canon in D Major. Calm and beautiful. Not a thing in the world to worry about.

Near the grand statue of Joost van del Vondel, he stopped to take a phone call, the thick hair flopping forward in his eyes, his T-shirt drenched with sweat, dark patches down his spine, a light paunch protruding over the waist of his shorts.

The area was busy with people enjoying the sunshine and he sauntered to take a seat on the low stone wall that surrounded the statue in a continuous circle. He sat and leant forward, elbows on knees, the phone to his ear, and it reminded me of all the times I had seen him, but he had never seen me. All the hours I had spent fathoming his crimes, all the risks I had taken trying to work him out, all the fear and loathing at the mention of his name. Yes, I had allowed this man to invade my head completely. Hendrikus Broekmann, you are a dead man.

But wishing it would not make it true.

I propped the bike against a tall lime and stood in the shade waiting, wondering when would be the best moment to approach. Eventually, I decided it would be better to just go and sit beside him and wait for his call to end. So I squeezed in beside a young couple nestled together drinking Coke and the man who had haunted me for months. Instinctively, he edged himself away. We were so close I could smell his sweat, mingling oppressively with his bergamot cologne, and we sat side by side in the sunshine, me knowing, him not knowing. At that moment, the power was all mine.

He ran his hand through his hair, sweeping it back off his face, listening to the voice at the end of the line, and I contemplated who he might be trafficking now. Who might be on his shopping list today: a child bride; more little boys to slave on the plantations; young women from everywhere sold to prostitution; young men like Billy.

The pedlar in misery sat calmly beside me, more vulnerable than he could know.

Abruptly, he stood up and turned to stare over my head at Vondel, the seventeenth-century poet immortalised in bronze on a high plinth behind us. The statue stared down at him judgementally. Fine grey hairs shimmered on his shins and thighs, his skin tone a rancid orange-brown and slick with sweat. Expensive running shoes laced from halfway – wide forefeet, maybe bunions. The shoes were neatly tied, the ends slipped below the cuff, white trainer socks below.

A group of girls sat chatting on the grass, the sickly odour of ganja floating in from their direction. Cyclists pedalled by, children chasing down the paths, a little dog cocking its leg against a bicycle that was leant at an angle against an elm. A moving picture show, temporarily frozen.

The sun was warm on my body, rising towards its zenith overhead. A cicada-type buzzing filled my ears, like a message trying to get through. All other sounds were muted. People in the park appeared a long way away, momentarily paralysed. Unhurriedly, I turned my gaze in his direction and he looked down at me, still nodding into his phone, a glimmer of recognition in the ice of his eyes. Yes, Broekmann. I have you now.

A plastic Coke bottle fell to the ground. The couple beside me were kissing now, a passionate embrace, oblivious to everything around them. They broke and tipped their heads together, looking out across the lawns of Vondelpark, hands locked, their fingers woven into each other. Inseparable.

TWENTY-NINE
KAREN

The house smiled its welcome. Warm Yorkshire stone bathed in soft light, the poplars casting long shadows across the lawn where blackbirds skittered, pausing to listen, their heads tilted down towards the earth. Over the arches at Owl Cottage the pale climbing rose was still flowering, the delicate cream heads dipping gently from their willowy stems. Graham had trained it against those old stone walls years ago, a fragrant arbour into the courtyard which led to the terraced gardens behind the house.

My steps were silent as I moved across the lawn.

They were kneeling in the vegetable patch, heads together, Graham's receding sandy pate and the new purple ribbons braided into Kaidi's dark cornrows. I stood at a distance and watched them – something entirely natural about the way they worked together, methodically sowing seeds in perfectly straight drills scooped out along the raised beds, lines of twine tied to short canes to delineate the exact distance between the drills.

My heart was full. This was a moment I would lock in time and I clung to the scene, letting it comfort my confused and tattered soul, recognising the vulnerability that had stalked me for months, that had distorted my judgement and altered my nature.

Light-headed, I stood in my garden with its gentle view of Milk Hill, observing my longed-for family. They looked up when they saw me, Graham rising quickly, Kaidi watchful, still studying the nature of our relationship and assessing the desirability of a new life with us.

Will she stay?

Graham pulled the rucksack from my shoulders and then his arms were around me, holding me in his unique, muted Graham-y style, head dug into my neck, unable to find the words. I stroked the back of his head, his fine curls damp with sweat.

'I won't go again,' I said, knowing it was true this time.

Over his shoulder, Kaidi was observing us, still kneeling in the soil, a packet of seeds in her hand.

'I brought you a daughter,' I whispered.

'She must stay,' he muttered, his body trembling uncharacteristically. 'I don't want this to be a temporary arrangement.' His tone was urgent like he couldn't wait any longer.

I kissed his face. 'I'm sorry for causing so much pain.'

He mumbled something I couldn't hear.

'How's she doing?'

'Good, yes … very well, I think.' He wouldn't cry but I knew he wanted to.

We wandered to where Kaidi knelt awkwardly, not knowing what to do.

'Hi, Kaidi,' I said lightly. 'What you planting?'

She looked at the packet in her hands, and then at me, but she thought better of her natural response.

Instead, she said, 'Carrots. And something you call chard. We cannot grow cassava here.'

'You're right,' I said. 'We don't grow cassava in England.'

It was touching how she wanted to have that connection in our garden.

'We're getting in a late carrot crop,' Graham chipped in. 'The soil is warm enough.'

Then Kaidi explained how she used to plant seeds in her mother's garden.

She demonstrated. 'You take this ruler – there must be an exact distance between each plant. It must be precise.'

I didn't doubt it.

'Then you measure the space between the rows like this …' She pointed to the distance between the heel of her hand and the tip of her middle finger and laid it on the earth.

'Great job, Kaidi,' I said. 'Your mother taught you well.'

She nodded in agreement.

Graham's phone rang and he moved away to take the call.

I squatted to help Kaidi draw the soil back over the rows and cover the seeds.

'Do you like England now that you're here?' I asked her.

'I think I will like the school,' she said, typically non-committal. 'And him.' She eyed Graham, who was pacing by the yew hedge.

We continued patting down the earth, sprinkling water from the can, and labelling each row judiciously.

'Nice work,' I said. 'Let's have some tea. I'm desperate for a cuppa.'

We rose together and Kaidi slipped her hand in mine. It was warm and gritty from the soil. I squeezed it gently to let her know it was OK and we stood together like mother and daughter, admiring our veg patch.

'Ma,' she said.

'Yes, Kaidi.'

'I wish to one day harvest these carrots for our table.'

THAT EVENING, Kaidi had gone to bed with Graham's omnibus of Harry Potter, a glass of hot chocolate and some coconut cookies – a recipe from her homeland. Before long, she would be returning to CTM's shelter in the Netherlands until all the approvals were in place for her official fostering in our home.

Graham slouched on the sofa with a heavy tome on astronomy – Aristotle's *On the Heavens* – swatting up for Kaidi's inexhaustible list of questions. He looked up with a vacant expression when I approached. 'Won't be a minute,' he said, eager to finish something.

'Sure,' I said, pouring us both a Scotch and wondering if he was going to tell me about the call from Eva Taal he had taken in the garden.

Eventually, he closed the book, grabbed his whisky and lifted his slippered feet onto a stool that was covered in the colourful Shweshwe cloth we had bought on our travels in South Africa. He patted my thighs affectionately and I raised my feet and draped my legs over his, pretending to relax.

'Gray, am I right in thinking I saw Eva Taal's name on your phone earlier? You took a call from her in the garden.'

'Hmmm?' He looked sheepish.

'You heard me.'

'Er, yes. It was Eva.'

'And?'

'Yes, it was her.'

I frowned at him.

'Well,' he continued, 'we've been working on something but I was waiting for the moment it bore fruit to discuss it with you.'

'Working on something?'

I felt irrationally jealous. Eva was my friend. Why didn't she tell me she was 'working on something' with Graham? I was used to his secretive style, but Eva had always seemed upfront.

'I see,' I managed politely.

'Yes,' he said.

'Spit it out before I get cross, Gray. What have you been working on and why have you not told me?'

'Because, well, because it's Lucas Bliek.'

'What!'

'The Dutch police …'

'Yes, yes, I know who he is. What are you talking about?'

My legs were down and I was facing him with intent.

'You suspected he was corrupt,' he said. 'Convinced about it. In fact, you were quite fixated on it.'

'Of course I was fixated on it! It was me working the streets of Amsterdam. It was me he had threatened.'

'It's ok. No need to get agitated.'

I narrowed my eyes, trying not to hit him.

'You assumed he was working with the trafficking gangs,' he said. 'And taking bribes from people like Broekmann as protection money.'

I flinched at the mention of that name.

'You even thought he might have followed you to Morocco,' Graham continued.

I folded my arms across my chest.

'Well, I thought I might try hacking into the system.' His voice was calm.

'You thought what?'

He looked pleased with himself.

'Do you mean the Dutch police?'

Of course Graham had the skills. He'd made his fortune out of them. But that had all been legal. Was it even possible to hack into such a heavily securitised and encrypted system?

'It was quite straightforward,' he said, reading my mind.

'And what did you find?' I asked, immediately forgetting any legal implications.

'I found his private email address stupidly copied into an official exchange. And that led to all kinds of other communication channels that he was using to contact the gangs.'

'The gangs? You mean Broekmann?' I asked, panicking.

'Not specifically. But the priest at the club. Pascual Ramos. The one in your photo.'

'But not Broekmann?'

'Not specifically. Not yet.'

'Why didn't you tell me this, Gray?'

'Because Bliek is a dangerous man and I didn't want to put you in any more danger than you had done yourself. Eva was worried, also.'

They had been conspiring behind my back – Eva and Graham. And they had learnt that Inspecteur Lucas Bliek had connections to the priest who trafficked Kaidi. It was the priest, Pascual Ramos, that Bliek had tipped off about the raid on the flats at Wittenburg. This all made sense because Ramos had been the one I had followed from Club VG to Lang Huis when I first arrived in Amsterdam.

Graham explained that Eva had confirmed the authorities now had video footage from Schiphol of Kaidi with Pascual Ramos, the evidence that Bliek had suppressed. And they had my own evidence of Kaidi's transit to Marrakech, and Kaidi's independent ID of the priest from the photograph. All this was plenty to connect Lucas Bliek himself to the crime of human trafficking. So, along with Pascual Ramos, he had also been charged. And now they were both in police custody awaiting trial in the Netherlands. It was found that Ramos's modus operandi was to mule children from West Africa with diamonds sewn into their clothing or backpacks. He had an established route from Freetown to Amsterdam with his own people at both ends to smooth the way. The sale of the gems through his contacts in the Netherlands funded Ramos's profitable trafficking route through Spain into Morocco.

Wasn't this exactly what I had hoped to achieve when I first left home for Amsterdam all those weeks ago? People in jail. The rescue of a child. There was no irrefutable evidence against Broekmann, yet. But there might be one day.

And we had found a daughter.

Wasn't this redemption? The absolution I'd been seeking.

I dared not think of Broekmann now. Of the insanity he had created in me, and the actions I would forever have regretted.

TWO MONTHS LATER, Kaidi was ready to start the second half of the autumn term at her new school in Yorkshire. The fostering arrangement had been approved and we were finally living as a family, unsupervised.

Kaidi was having trouble sleeping. The prospect of starting school had filled her with such anxiety and delight she did not understand how to deal with her emotions, and the night before she had made several visits to our room to check if it was time to get up. This would be her first day and she knew staff and pupils were ready to welcome her into a new home of learning. The excitement and tension absorbed us all.

'Get up, Pa,' she demanded.

She stood at the foot of the bed fully clothed in her uniform, her shirt a little big for her, gaping around the collar.

'Kaidi, it's only six o'clock,' I said.

But Graham leapt out of bed, understanding her anxiety.

We all hurried down for breakfast but she wouldn't eat the porridge I prepared for her, or the toast or sliced banana I put in front of her. She only sipped at a warm glass of milk, her rucksack on her back, ready for off.

Soon she wandered outside to stand by the car. We slipped on our coats and followed her out.

We stood at the school gates watching her move across the playground with a group of other pupils, through the front doors with no hesitation and no glancing back. She made us proud.

The adoption papers had been filed and soon Kaidi would officially be our daughter. When she was ready, I hoped that one day she would want to return and visit her homeland, and that maybe we would travel back as a family. I believed she should be reminded of her rich ancestral heritage, the friends she left behind, her unique African culture, and the country I loved so much. But that was something for the future.

We returned to the car and sat a while watching pupils arrive and parents disperse, trying to imagine our daughter's emotions, how she would cope with them, and the reactions of teachers and pupils who were yet to experience the phenomenon of Kaidi Owuso.

A car pulled up opposite and a familiar figure got out. Checking the traffic, she crossed to where we were parked.

I leapt out of the car to greet her. 'Eva!'

We embraced warmly, grinning like fools at the sight of each other.

'What are you doing here? It's so good to see you. Have they sentenced them already?' As always, I had so many questions.

'Karen, I have some good news for you.' Eva held my shoulders and nodded towards Graham who had joined us.

'What is it?' I asked impatiently.

'The boy, Foday. We have found him.'

My heart sang with joy.

'Where is he? What happened to him? How did you find him?'

'The gang driver – you know, he was arrested in the van at the port in Tarifa?'

'Yes, yes.'

'Well, he confessed to save his own neck. He told police that Foday had been taken from Almería to Barcelona by a gang based in Costa Blanca who had put him on the streets as part of a begging ring. They had put him to work, selling street drugs, begging, that sort of thing.'

'Do you have him safe?'

'Yes. He says he wants to return to his family in Sierra Leone.'

'This is the best news, Eva. I will tell Kaidi. Maybe now the nightmares will stop.'

'Actually, it's not the only good news I have for you, Karen.'

'What d'you mean?'

'Yesterday,' she said carefully, 'I can tell you that the coast-guard hauled the body of Hendrikus Broekmann from the Oosterdok.'

Just like that.

It took a moment to process. I gawped at her, and noticed that my breathing had stopped.

'He's dead, Karen,' she said, sensing I needed clarification.

'Dead?'

'Oosterdok is deep water. He had been weighted down.'

'Broekmann?' My body was shaking.

'Yes. It is him.'

'Are you sure?'

'I am sure.'

She squeezed my shoulders as I looked away in confusion, tears stinging my eyes.

'We've had the formal ID,' she said. 'I wanted to tell you myself, in person.'

I felt sick to my stomach at the memory of Vondelpark. At the thought of Billy and my request for the gun, and how his decision saved me.

'How did he die?' I asked.

'Bullet to the head, assassination style. They think he was dead before he went into the water. He was weighted but some vessel must have dragged him. The water churns up near the locks.'

I clutched my throat in disbelief. I had begun to accept that my nemesis was truly invincible.

'Broekmann. He's dead,' I whispered as a wash of relief, anger and guilt threatened to submerge me.

'They think it was the work of the Moroccan Mafia,' Eva went on helpfully. 'It seems your man trod on important toes. Most likely his competitors had enough of him.'

I blurted something as the breath poured out of me, but I didn't know what it was.

'In the US the gangs call it "exceptional clearance",' she explained. 'When they kill each other in revenge.'

I thought of Songola and the way she had been killed. Of all those small boys toiling on the plantations, ripped from their families and homes. Of the little one who had died there. Of the girls and women working in stinking North African brothels and seedy pits in De Wallen, of Billy, Maria, Foday and Kaidi, and all the others I would never know.

'One more out of the system,' Eva was saying to Graham in a voice that sounded far off. 'It seems Broekmann was moving women and girls from Eastern Europe into Amsterdam on a regular route,' she went on. 'Mostly headed for De Wallen. But also trafficking children all over West Africa – his speciality, it seems. Kaidi was an exception to this. Broekmann didn't have his own safe route for moving children out of Africa and had to depend on the priest's established network via Amsterdam and his regular trafficking trail through Spain into Morocco. The deal was done with the priest to get Kaidi to Marrakech as a one-off – to settle Broekmann's debt.'

My face was wet with tears and Graham's arm went around me.

'You OK?' Eva asked.

'Yes,' I said. 'OK now.' Because my soul was aching with the joy of work complete.

EPILOGUE

Testimony of Maria (Majlinda) Abrashi, nationality Albanian. Recorded by Eva Taal at the offices of CTM, Amsterdam, 14 July 2016

I had left my family and friends to start my studies at the Polytechnic University of Tirana. I was far from home and the world that I knew, and now I was in the company of strangers all around me. I took a part-time job waitressing at a bar.

At my college I met Kaltrina, who said she was a student. She was kind to me and supportive, and I trusted her. She befriended me. She said she had accommodation that I could share, a small room in an apartment close to the university, a cheap place for me to stay. Her kindness made me happy.

When I got to the flat I found she did not live there herself. It was occupied by one other girl who did not speak to me, and two men. The men were friendly at first, sharing food, having a laugh, but I never understood why they were staying at the flat or what they did.

I never saw Kaltrina again after the day she left me at the flat. Maybe she returned to the college to recruit others.

One day one of the men said I owed them money. This surprised me and I objected. That made him mad. He said I owed one thousand two hundred euros for unpaid rent and food, and that interest was accruing on the debt. I objected again. He hit me.

The man said he knew where my family lived, where my little sister went to school. Yes, he knew the name of the school and the name of my sister. He said he would threaten my family if I did not pay the debt.

I told him I did not have the money and that is when he said I must work to pay it off. I took more hours at the bar, but it was not enough. The debt was getting bigger all the time. I had to give up on my studies. My mother thought I was still at college but I was working twelve hours a day waitressing and cleaning and the new bar I worked in was dedicated to prostitution. There were lots of girls. I was too naive to understand what was in store for me. I worked from 9 a.m. when the bar opened to 9 p.m. when it closed.

Then the man said the interest on my debt was getting bigger and that I would have to go to Holland where I could earn more money to pay them back but also enough to keep for myself so I could return to college. They said it would only be for a few months. This time I had to tell my mother, but I did not tell her the truth. I said I was going with my friends during the college vacation to earn money and improve my skills. She wasn't sure, but she believed me.

That is when I took the photo. When I left in the van. To reassure her.

My debt was used to bond me to the men. On the journey to Amsterdam they raped me. Yes, both of them. It was their way to make me hate myself and accept what was to come.

They branded my skin with the name of the gang so everyone would know I was theirs. All the men that used me would see their mark and that would make them grateful to the gang. They took my papers and all my money. I could not go home. If I did, friends of the gang would be there to greet me. And when they caught me they would kill me as an example to others.

They threatened my family again. They said that if I ran, they would find my little sister to replace me. I disgusted myself. I didn't even recognise myself because of the things I was forced to do. I wanted to kill myself and abuse my body. So much anger and hatred and shame. My personality had altered. I was aggressive. I had no hopes. My ideas on life had changed.

The girls who worked for the gang all had nicknames. We never used our real names and we only ever spoke of what happened in the day. Nothing about the men and what they were forcing us to do. They drugged us, made us dependent.

Sometimes I found stickers from help organisations on the mirror of my booth, and once, hidden inside a lipstick container. I thought maybe they had been put there by the men who visited me. I don't know. Often they were messages of solidarity and support. Sometimes there was a contact number.

Then one day a woman came to my booth. She gave me the card for Campagne Tegen Menselhandel and she urged me to find Eva Taal.

GLOSSARY

- *Asr:* late afternoon prayer in the Islamic tradition
- *Babouches:* pointy-toed slippers
- *Barrie:* (West Africa) a village meeting place
- *Big Makit:* a historic market for artisans in Sierra Leone built in the eighteenth century
- *Bolilands:* seasonal swamps in Sierra Leone, fertile for growing rice crops during the floods
- *Chabola:* slums constructed of pallets, cardboard and plastic sheets
- *Dirham:* Moroccan unit of currency
- *Djellaba:* Moroccan kaftan with a baggy pointed hood
- *Fajr:* dawn prayer in Islam
- *Jemaa el Fna:* Marrakech's main square and symbolic centre of its medina
- *Iftar:* a meal to celebrate breaking of the fast by Muslims during Ramadan
- *IJ:* body of water in Amsterdam known as the waterfront
- *Menpikin:* a fostering system common in Sierra Leone, usually familial, primarily to support the

education of children but often linked to forced labour

- *Muslaiyah:* prayer mat
- *Nafar:* town crier (in Islam), predawn warning to commence the *suhoor* before the fasting
- *Oosterdock:* historic wet dock in Amsterdam constructed to form a deep port for shipping
- *Pastilla:* a savoury chicken pie made with filo pastry common in Moroccan cuisine
- *Pension:* hotel
- *Rokel:* Rokel River is the largest in Sierra Leone
- *Sabon Beldi:* Moroccan organic black soap made of volcanic ash
- *Salone:* local vernacular for Sierra Leone
- *Sande Society:* secret society in West Africa for the initiation of girls into womanhood
- *Sawm:* Arabic term used to describe the act of fasting.
- *Sheshia:* traditional reed hat of Morocco
- *Shweshwe:* traditional cotton cloth manufactured in South Africa
- *Sfenj:* doughnuts
- *Socco:* marketplace (Arabic)
- *Suhoor:* a pre-dawn meal taken by Muslims during Ramadan
- *Thabule:* traditional drum of Sierra Leone associated with the Temne tribe
- *Thobe:* an ankle-length long-sleeved robe
- *THB:* Trafficked Human Beings
- *Zellij:* a style of mosaic tile work made from coloured individually hand-chiselled tile pieces.

AFTERWORD

"Do we really need millions more victims to experience a true wake-up call. How many more 13 year old girls – your daughter, my sister, our children – need to be forced into prostitution before we wake up."

(Personal witness to the UN Council 2010 – Giving Voice to the Victims and Survivors of Human Trafficking)

ACKNOWLEDGMENTS

I would like to offer grateful thanks to early readers Rowena, Kathy and Elaine for their constructive feedback on first drafts of The Blue Alley; to my copyeditor, Lesley Jones of *Perfect the Word*, and proofreader, Noreen Lobo.

Special thanks to the magnanimous group of writers at our shared retreat in the Andalusian mountains whose generous responses and expert critique enhanced the final draft. Your friendship and heartening feedback have been a highlight on my writing journey. Thank you Corbin, Danielle, Elise, Freida, Jeannie, Joan, Teresa, Tim and, of course, Emjay.

Finally, warm thanks to my family and friends for their many words of encouragement and to my husband, David, for his unwavering support and belief in me.

ABOUT THE AUTHOR

P C Cubitt is the author of *Fly Catcher,* long-listed for the Bridport First Novel Prize 2023.

She has worked in the fields of business, education, and research, when she was contributor and editor to several academic journals. Her PhD research in Africa inspired the move to writing fiction. *The Blue Alley* is her second novel.

She lives with her husband in Yorkshire and is the proud mother of sons.

Note to the reader:

Thank you for reading The Blue Alley. Please consider leaving a review at your point of purchase or GoodReads.

Book group reading notes can be found on the website where you can also contact the author via the online form. She would be happy to hear from you.

pccubitt.com

ALSO BY P C CUBITT

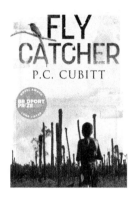

What readers have said about *Fly Catcher:*

"What a page turner! Unputdownable."

"You can almost feel the African heat, the dust and the press of the people as you turn the pages."

"A thriller where you feel like you are there in the middle of the action."

"An absolutely thrilling debut … I was going though every twist and turn as if I was in Africa myself."

"I've been totally captivated by this book … I could visualise in my mind what the places and people were like."

"An engrossing book. It reflects the author's years of experience and knowledge of Africa."

.

Printed in Great Britain
by Amazon